For my editor, Hanna Elizabeth. Well, here we are again at the end of another series of books. I honestly couldn't do any of this without you.

CHAPTER ONE

THE CHARITY FUNDRAISER banquet in the Christ Church refectory hall was in full swing. All the great and the good of Oxford were sitting at the long tables where the students normally sat. Candlelight danced along silverware and polished glasses, casting a soft glow over the silks and tuxedos of the guests wearing their finery for this very select event.

Member of Parliament for Oxford West and Abingdon, Martin Chambers, sat with the other VIPs at the top table on the raised stage. He knew more than anyone gathered in the room just how important that night's meal was for the future of his party, his country, and also himself.

A former lecturer with deep roots in Oxford's academic world, Martin had used quiet persuasion—and the efforts of his growing circle of supporters—to secure an invitation for himself and his wife to this pivotal event. It was the sort of evening where careers could be launched towards the stratosphere, thanks to the figures of real influence in attendance. Win them over, and the Prime Minister's Office might no longer seem out of reach.

Martin was determined to make the most of his moment at

the lectern. His record on education reform and green initiatives would strike a chord with the academics in the room, and he hoped they'd forgive the audacity of turning philanthropy into politics for a short while. Tonight was about proving he could lead his party to victory.

Once dismissed as a rebel and consigned to the back benches, Martin had seen his fortunes change as the Prime Minister's star waned. Colleagues who once avoided him now sought him out, hinting at the need for fresh leadership—and their glances lingered a fraction too long. The whispers already held tonight with wealthy backers had carried on along the same lines. If the rumours of an imminent resignation were true, Martin wouldn't just be a contender, he could be the frontrunner. But he also knew the ground was treacherous. One misstep could see it all slip away.

Thankfully, Martin was no stranger to the spotlight, having always been drawn to it. Even as a professor, the instinct to command attention seemed hardwired into him. That hunger had nudged him towards politics, but the deeper pull came from his father, a local councillor who treated his public service as a calling. His father had spent a lifetime trying, in small ways, to make the world better. But Martin had long recognised the limits of such work. A councillor could cause ripples, but a politician, armed with the machinery of government behind him, might set whole tides in motion. And tonight, Martin was in no doubt that the charity auction was his stage, and he was meant to shine.

At the high table, he sat beside Sir Reginald Harrington, the evening's patron. The hedge-fund magnate carried an air of authority, a kingmaker even. Martin was keenly aware that winning this man's approval could count for as much as any speech. He nodded and smiled, letting the man's words wash over him while chewing on his steak with its sharp peppercorn sauce.

But his mind was elsewhere, and his gaze kept straying to the lectern, waiting under the flood of candlelight. That was where he would be really tested, and where he intended to make the speech of his life. This night might have been framed as a charity event, but he was under no illusion that the grandees of the party were here, weighing him up, watching to see if he had the steel to lead. And Sir Harrington's shadow loomed larger than most.

The camera pointing back towards the lectern was evidence that the college had also arranged for the speeches to be live-streamed. For Martin, that single lens counted for everything. His speech would not only reach the great and the good gathered beneath the ancient beams of Christ Church, but it also had the potential to ripple out far beyond these walls into millions of homes. If he struck the right note, this night could be the spark to ignite a journey all the way to Number Ten.

Martin raised his glass of Bollinger, letting the crisp champagne linger on his tongue, when his eye caught Ragnar Higginson. Martin had made sure of his presence tonight with a personal invitation. Ragnar sat a few tables below the high table in the refectory seats normally reserved for students, but now was filled with dinner jackets and glittering gowns. Beside him was a striking young blonde woman, who was somewhere in her twenties, leaning close, speaking to the dean with an intensity that Martin recognised at once. She had to be one of his students, and one passionate about her studies, too.

Ragnar and he went back a long way. They'd been Oxford students together, who'd shared more than a few wild nights and half-formed dreams. Ragnar, an Icelander who'd now made England his home, stayed in academia and rose to become dean of the Blavatnik School of Government. Martin had taken a different path. A stint as a Balliol professor of political philosophy before stepping into the rougher waters of politics. How far they'd both travelled from those wide-eyed lads who arrived from opposite corners of the world to the very different lives they both led today.

'So, Joanne, you have to tell me, are the rumours true?' Sir Reginald Harrington asked, drawing Martin's attention back to the high table. 'Have you already picked out the wallpaper for Number Ten?'

Martin turned to his wife. Joanne was smiling warmly at the man on her left, the wealthy billionaire whose influence unlocked doors Martin desperately needed to get through, if he was ever to be taken seriously as a contender for the top job.

'Well, it's no secret I have every confidence in my husband,' Joanne said. 'With the right backing from the party, I've no doubt he could win, and win by a landslide.'

Sir Harrington's chin wobbled as he chuckled. 'That's what I like to see, real belief in your husband and in the party.' Then his brow furrowed. 'But tell me, Martin, what are your thoughts on the latest polls?'

'Yes, the surge behind the One Nation party is hard to miss. Impressive, maybe, but they're just the latest shiny thing. Like they always do, the public will see through them soon enough. Mark my words, One Nation is still a long way from winning a general election, however much their message seems to be striking a chord right now.'

'It's a seductive pitch, though, isn't it?' Sir Harrington pressed. 'A party that claims to rise above the old divisions, to listen even to its opponents. It's hardly surprising people are drawn to that message. Voters are sick of the mud-slinging and the circus that Parliament's become between the main parties.'

Martin let out a dry laugh. 'Even their slogan is a marketing dream. One truth, one voice, one people. And I'd be the first to admit it, there's a lot to learn from their freshness. And bloody hell, they're all so relentlessly nice and maddeningly photogenic, with it.'

Harrington's eyebrows pinched together. 'Careful, Martin. You're starting to sound like a fan.'

Martin held thumb and forefinger a fraction apart. 'Maybe, just a little bit. But we both know, when it comes to the real fight, they're unelectable.'

'I agree, but we'd be fools to dismiss them outright,' Sir Harrington said. 'One of their flagship policies is strengthening national security. Everything from cyber-attacks to terrorism. The press can't get enough of that because of the challenging times we live in, and the public's lapping it up as well.'

Martin leaned in, lowering his voice. 'Which is precisely why I'll be touching on those very same issues in my speech tonight. Our party must commit to increased spending across the departments that matter most.'

'Steal their thunder, in other words?'

Martin sat back with a sweep of his hand. 'Why not?'

Sir Harrington chuckled and nodded approvingly. 'Well played, sir.'

A waitress appeared at Martin's elbow, so quietly he almost didn't notice her. She leaned in with a deferential smile and placed a fresh serviette by his glass.

'For you, sir,' she murmured, then slipped back into the crowd without waiting for a reply.

Martin glanced down. The linen was neatly folded, pressed stiff with starch. But in one corner, faintly marked in pencil, was a curious design. It looked like a diagonal line with a second zigzagging line intersecting the first with smaller circles above and below it. The lines were so fine they might have gone unnoticed if the candlelight hadn't caught the graphite they'd been drawn with.

He frowned, absently rubbing the mark with his thumb, half-expecting it to smudge away, but it didn't. Probably some bored student with a pencil who'd been doodling, and the wash hadn't managed to eradicate the mark. With a small shake of his head, he folded the serviette over and shifted his glass on top. He had bigger things to focus on than some absent-minded scribbles.

A movement caught Martin's eye, and he glanced down to see Ragnar approaching the high table, with the young blonde woman beside him. His old friend's hand was already outstretched as he headed along the stage towards him.

'It's been far too long,' Ragnar said warmly.

'Indeed, it has,' Martin replied, gripping his old friend's hand with genuine affection. Then his gaze slid to the woman standing just behind him. 'And you are?'

'Ellie Stone,' she said. 'I was hoping I might steal a few moments of your time after your speech.'

'A reporter?' Martin asked, reassessing his initial impression.

Ragnar shook his head quickly. 'As though I'd unleash one of those wolves on you here. No, Ellie's one of our brightest final-year students. She's writing her thesis and needs to pick your brains. That's why I've brought her over.'

'And the subject of your thesis is?' Martin asked, curiosity pricked.

'Government—specifically policing policy,' Ellie replied. 'I'm looking at how community policing could be improved with some practical steps.'

'Not exactly my area of expertise,' Martin admitted, 'but I'm happy to listen, and perhaps point you in the right direction.'

'Anything you could do to help, I'd be really grateful,' Ellie said.

'She's got some excellent ideas you really should listen to,' Ragnar added. 'Given your background in education, I think you'll be especially interested in her proposal for a police mentorship scheme, pairing officers with at-risk youths to steer them away from crime.'

Martin leaned back, intrigued despite himself. 'All right then, I'll hear you out afterwards. But on one condition—if I hear something I really like, I'll pass it to the Home Secretary. Who knows, it might even make its way into the manifesto by the next election.'

Ellie smiled. 'You can steal whatever you like.'

Martin chuckled, but the moment was interrupted by his assistant, appearing at the high table.

'Just to give you a five-minute warning,' she said.

Martin glanced from her to his smartwatch—a gift from Joanne, who insisted he wear it as part of her health campaign after a recent worrying heart test. At least she'd granted him a reprieve tonight, letting him enjoy steak for once. He rubbed at his eyes and gave his wife a rueful smile. 'Strange thing, I feel half ready to nod off, and I have only had two glasses of champagne.'

His assistant leaned closer. 'You've been running on fumes all week, Martin. Anyone would be tired by now.'

'Or perhaps it's just nerves?' Sir Harrington said, watching him carefully as though he was weighing up the man before him.

'Nerves, after all these years?' Martin chuckled softly, though there was a flicker of discomfort behind his eyes. Then, turning back to his assistant, he asked, 'I thought my speech was scheduled for the end of the meal.'

She shook her head. 'Timings have slipped. If you want to hit the nine o'clock sweet spot for social media, you'll need to go on sooner. After that, engagement drops off a cliff.'

'So in other words, my speech will be served before the

pudding,' Martin replied. 'You realise that may cause a riot among our guests.' He winked at the others at the high table.

'Hopefully not,' his assistant replied. Without another word, she turned, snapping her fingers at a stagehand, who hurried to her side.

Martin watched her go, shaking his head. 'Far too serious for her own good.' He turned back to Ragnar and Ellie. 'Now, I am afraid you will have to excuse me. Time to get my head in the game. But I promise you, Ellie, we'll have that meeting after-wards. And Ragnar, you and I are long overdue for a proper catch-up.'

'Then I look forward to it,' Ragnar said. He and Ellie smiled and bade their farewells before slipping back into the crowd.

Martin reached into his dinner jacket and drew out a folded sheet of notes.

Sir Harrington arched an eyebrow. 'Notes, Martin? I thought you were famous for never needing them.'

'Only because I rehearse them until the words are burned into my skull,' Martin replied. 'These are just bullet points, something to keep me on track.'

Joanne reached across and squeezed his hand. 'Not that you ever need them. With your memory, you could have been an actor.'

'One way or another, aren't all politicians actors?' Martin replied with a smile.

'Not you, dearest. You've always spoken from the heart.'

His smile edged into a grin. 'And look at the trouble that's landed me in.'

Laughter rippled along the table.

Martin chuckled with them, then leaned closer to Joanne. 'Strange, I'm feeling more than a little drowsy,' he murmured.

'Maybe it was all the rich food,' she teased gently. 'I shouldn't have let you have that steak after all.'

He smiled as he lowered his gaze to his notes, forcing himself to focus despite the sluggishness creeping at the edge of his mind. One last glance over the key points, then the spotlight would be his. And if all went as planned, his words would echo far beyond these ancient walls, carried by cameras and headlines into homes across the country. Enough, perhaps, to draw the undecided in his party to his side. Enough to prove he was ready, not just to make a speech, but to take his first real step toward leading the party. And he intended to pass this test with flying colours.

Martin gazed out over the audience, fighting to steady himself. That feeling of heaviness had been coming on steadily; the same drowsiness he'd mentioned to Joanne only minutes earlier was deepening by the second. It was absurd because he'd hardly touched the champagne, but his head felt clouded. The minister forced his mind to focus. Whatever this was, fatigue or nerves, he wouldn't allow it to show.

The unblinking camera stared at him, ready to livestream his every word. If this was going to land well with the public, it had to feel natural.

'Good evening, friends,' he began. 'It's an honour to stand before you tonight in this magnificent Grand Hall of Christ Church College, among people who share a passion for our community and our future.'

Every face turned toward him. If nothing else, he had their attention.

'We've all endured challenging times recently. Within my own party, these last months have tested faith. But politics has never drawn its strength from personalities, it's drawn it from principles. Not from headlines, but from hard work. And now, with every fibre of my being, I believe we have the chance to turn a page, to begin a new chapter.'

Martin's words rolled out smoothly, but something began fluttering more strongly in his chest. He drew a steady breath through his nose and pushed on.

'We have an opportunity to restore Britain's standing in the world. To do so, we need fresh eyes, renewed energy, a clear vision for the future...'

Cold sweat prickled on his brow. He glanced toward Joanne, catching her encouraging nod, but any reassurance faltered as his awareness fixed on the camera—and beyond it, to the thousands watching from their homes.

A flicker of nausea twisted through him.

He took a sip of water, forcing the words to keep flowing. 'This is not a moment to retreat, but to press forward. To show our country that stability and integrity can go hand in hand. Leadership is not about ego, it's about service...'

A spotlight's glare swam before his eyes, haloed in a sickly yellow-green. His smartwatch buzzed against his wrist, insistent, but the minister ignored it.

'The only poll that matters,' he pressed on, his voice catching, 'is the one on election day—'

The sentence died in his throat, cut short by a strangled gasp escaping from his throat. A savage bolt of pain ripped through his chest, so fierce it felt as though his ribs were splintering. His breath snagged in his chest as his left arm sagged into dead weight, numb and useless. Fear and a sense of utter dread crashed into his mind as his vision blurred and he vomited. Then Martin's knees buckled beneath him, and the hall pitched violently sideways in his vision. He hit the floor hard, bitter vomit spilling from his mouth. But there was no respite, and the agony roared on, as a blazing coal burned deep in his chest. He was dimly aware of a chorus of shouts erupting around him as he tried to draw in a breath.

In the growing commotion, Joanne's face swam into view above him, her eyes wide, lips moving, but he couldn't hear her words.

Another face replaced hers, the young woman he'd met only minutes ago—Ellie. Her hand pressed firmly against his throat, searching for a pulse. His assistant was talking rapidly on her phone as she stared at him with wide eyes.

Then Ellie's palms were on his chest, pressing hard, rhythmically, as his eyes traced the ornate ceiling overhead, as the room dimmed around him, and sound slipped away. He barely registered Ellie's lips sealing over his, her breath forcing life into him.

One last thought surfaced, bitter and clear: *I'm bloody dying.* Then, Martin Chambers drew a final shuddering breath, before his eyes rolled back, and the darkness claimed him.

CHAPTER TWO

THE WARMTH of what had been an unusually sunny May day in Oxford lingered into the evening as the sun dipped lower, gilding the water in copper light. Joseph breathed it all in, a rare sense of peace settled over him as he stood at the barbecue on the deck of *Tús Nua,* his narrowboat moored in the heart of Oxford.

Maybe that was partly thanks to the fact that Dylan had left him with nothing more taxing than grilling peaches on his barbecue. They were going to accompany the homemade vanilla ice cream that the professor insisted on preparing for their little gathering. But even so, it wasn't a task the DI treated lightly. Small though his contribution might be to tonight's feast, he'd taken his culinary duties very seriously, especially in the matter of choosing the fruit. He knew Dylan would turn his nose up at any pale, tasteless supermarket offerings. That was why he'd made a point of swinging by the vegetable market in Gloucester Green on Wednesday, where he'd picked out the juiciest, most fragrant peaches he could find.

Kate wandered over from Dylan's boat, *Avalon,* a half-finished glass of the Bayou Moon in hand, Dylan's latest gin-based cocktail invention. Since she'd moved in, she was a big part of the reason Joseph felt so at ease with the world. Behind her, on *Avalon's* deck, Iris, Megan, and Chris could be heard laughing over something the professor had said.

'So how are things going over here?' Kate asked, eyeing the peaches with a smile.

'All grand. Even with my level of barbecue expertise, I can manage to cook a bit of fruit.'

She rubbed his arm. 'I just wish Ellie and John could have joined us tonight.'

Joseph nodded. 'Sadly, John's on duty, and our darling daughter is otherwise occupied, rubbing shoulders with all those bigwigs at the charity auction at Christ Church.'

Kate sipped her drink. 'Even so, she'll be kicking herself for missing this. I doubt the food there will be half as good as Dylan's. He's outdone himself yet again.'

'Aye, that he has,' Joseph said, with a smile. 'That New Orleans-style chicken from his smoker was something else, and absolutely mouth-watering.'

'Well, if you want another helping, you'll need to get your skates on. Megan's already eyeing up a fourth portion, and there's only one left.'

'Then I'd better save her from herself,' Joseph replied, sliding the grill shelf up a notch so the peaches wouldn't burn.

Kate leaned in slightly, lowering her voice. 'Speaking of Megan, do you think there's something going on between her and Chris?'

Joseph arranged his expression into a neutral one. 'Why, what have you noticed?'

'Just that there's an obvious spark between them.'

'Ah, that...'

Her gaze narrowed. 'Go on, tell me, because you clearly know something.'

He shrugged. 'Even if Chris does have feelings for her, he can't act on them. He's her boss and all that. Rules are rules.' But he also knew, and this was something he couldn't tell her, that it wouldn't be an obstacle forever.

Chris was actually an NCA, National Crime Agency, agent embedded in Thames Valley Police to investigate the Night Watchmen and their possible hooks into the force. Unfortunately, that wasn't something Joseph could share. But once the operation ended, and Chris stepped away from his DCI role, things would be different. Until then, any attraction between Chris and Megan had nowhere to go.

'That's a shame,' Kate said, unaware of this. 'I could really see those two together.'

Joseph only shrugged. 'It's just how it has to be.'

'Still, it's a shame.'

'Aye...' He slipped his arm through hers, and steered her back towards *Avalon*, where the towpath party was in full swing.

Joseph couldn't help but grin at the sight of his friend's boat. Iris Evans—now firmly the professor's partner—had all but launched a light-bombing campaign on the vessel, one that Ellie had fully approved of. Fairy lights criss-crossed the cabin roof and spilled into the overhanging branches, turning the canal into something between Oxford and A Midsummer Night's Dream. Passing tourists, stumbling upon the hidden gem, kept stopping to take photographs.

'So, tell me again about the rub you used on that chicken,' Chris was saying as Joseph and Kate joined the party.

Dylan peered over the rim of his glasses. 'The backbone is sweet and smoked paprika, cayenne, thyme, cumin, and celery salt. Plus a few secrets of my own. I'll write it down for you if you like.'

'Please,' Chris said with a smile. 'Although, you do realise this means I'll have to buy myself a smoker.'

'Then I can highly recommend a Big Green Egg like this,' Dylan replied, gesturing at the gleaming dark green dome by his side. 'A modern barbecue classic, if ever there was one.'

'I'll have to make room for one in my garden after tasting how good the food out of it is.'

'Does that mean we're all invited over for the inaugural feast?' Megan chimed in, setting down a bone she'd stripped so thoroughly it looked as if a flock of vultures had swooped on it.

'Dylan's food will be a hard act to follow, but I'll give it my best shot,' Chris said.

Iris patted Dylan's arm. 'I'm sure he'd be happy to give you a few pointers.'

Joseph nodded. 'You'll get them whether you want them or not. Trust me, Dylan won't be able to help himself.' He winked at his old friend, who was already chuckling.

'Guilty as charged,' the professor replied, holding up his palms. 'Anyway, can anyone manage that last chicken thigh? It would be a shame to let it go to waste.'

Before Megan could spring into action, Joseph was already there with a plate held out. 'Don't mind if I do.'

His colleague scowled at him before raising her empty glass. 'In that case, do you mind if I help myself to some more of that cocktail you conjured up, Dylan? It's the best thing I've had to drink in a long time.'

'Ah, my Bayou Moon, something of a homage to New Orleans. It's not bad, is it?'

'More like sensational,' Megan said. ' But what's in it?'

'Well, the choice of gin is critical as always. For this one, I used *Copper in the Clouds* Hertfordshire Spiced Gin. Its earthy taste is perfect for this cocktail. Added to that is a bit of absinthe, some lemon juice, and ginger syrup, homemade of course. Then finish that off with a dash of bitters, a pinch of smoked sea salt, and a sliver of red chilli, and you're all done.'

Megan pulled a face. 'Considering all I have in my drinks cabinet is a bottle of vodka, maybe I'll just have to keep coming back here.'

'And you'd be welcome, anytime,' Dylan replied, handing the pitcher with the cocktail in it over to the DC.

'Oh, don't encourage her, or before you know it, she'll be taking up permanent residence on your boat,' Joseph said.

'All I can say is, Iris, you have snagged yourself a keeper,' Megan replied.

'Don't I know it,' Iris said. 'He rather swept me off my feet with his cooking and hasn't stopped since.'

Joseph couldn't help notice the glance Chris gave Megan. He helped himself to the pitcher of Dylan's Bayou Moon, no doubt wondering if food really was the way to win her heart as well. But knowing Megan, all Chris needed to do was offer the DC her body weight in Maccy D's, and she would be putty in his hands.

Joseph's phone rang. When he saw Ellie's name, he took the call.

'Don't tell me that charity dinner is over already, and you're on your way to join us after all?'

'It is, but not for the reason you're thinking,' Ellie said.

Chris's phone started ringing, and he took the call.

'Why, what's happened?' Joseph asked, hearing the tension in her voice.

'You know our local MP, Martin Chambers, was giving a speech at tonight's charity dinner?'

'Yes, you were there to try and grab some of his time, to pick his brains for your thesis on community policing.'

'Exactly. I didn't manage to ask him anything because he literally died in my arms.' He heard her take an audible breath at the other end of the line. 'He had a massive heart attack, Dad. I tried, I really tried.'

Joseph's mind whirled as he tried to absorb the information. 'You tried to resuscitate him?' he asked, catching the worried look Kate shot his way.

'I did—' Ellie's voice broke with a strangled sob.

Joseph's heart twisted. 'It's alright, love. Take a breath, then tell me exactly what happened.' He put his mobile on speaker-phone as Kate moved closer to listen in.

'Martin Chambers had only just begun his speech when he collapsed, clutching his chest,' Ellie said. 'I was the first one to him. Thankfully, everything I learned on that Red Cross training day course at college kicked in, and I knew exactly what to do. When he stopped breathing, I started CPR, but...' They heard her take another long, shuddering breath.

'You did what you could, and that's what matters,' Kate said softly, trading a stunned look with Joseph.

'But it wasn't enough,' Ellie whispered. 'Even one of the professors managed to get hold of a defibrillator, but that didn't work either. The paramedics took over when they arrived, but after ten minutes, they gave up as well.'

'It sounds like there was nothing anyone could have done,' Joseph said, as across the deck, Dylan, Megan, and Iris fell silent, their eyes fixed on him.

'I know... but I'm watching his wife sobbing in the corner of the Great Hall right now—' Ellie's voice cracked.

'We'll come and get you,' Kate said.

'Sorry, Mum, Dad, you can't right now. I have to go. Amy's here with her team, and they're asking for our phones.'

Joseph felt a cold ripple pass through him. 'What do you mean?'

'I'll explain later. Please don't worry.' The line went dead.

Kate stared at the mobile in disbelief. 'What the hell is going on?'

Chris ended his call and crossed to them, his face grim. 'I think I can answer that. Ellie, and everyone else at that charity dinner, are being temporarily held back in the Christ Church quad.'

Kate's brow furrowed. 'Held back? Sorry, what exactly are you saying?'

But Joseph understood. 'In the event of an unexpected death—particularly when it involves someone as important as a Member of Parliament—the police have to lock down the scene. No one leaves until it's clear what happened. Right now, the Great Hall is a potential crime scene.'

Dylan straightened in his folding chair. 'You can't be serious. They don't really think someone at a charity dinner actually murdered Martin Chambers?'

'No one's assuming anything at the moment,' Chris replied evenly. 'Yes, it could be a straightforward heart attack. But until an autopsy rules otherwise, foul play can't be ruled out. And this is a rapidly developing situation, so you'll understand I can't share details yet.'

Kate narrowed her eyes. 'Presumably, because I'm a reporter. And since my daughter's caught up in this, you think you need to watch what you say around me?'

'It's nothing like that,' Chris said. 'But the sooner I get over there, the sooner Ellie and the rest of the other people can be released.'

Joseph squeezed Kate's shoulder. 'He's just doing his job. I would be doing exactly the same in his shoes.'

Kate exhaled sharply, her cheeks puffing out slightly. 'Sorry, Chris, that wasn't aimed at you, more at the universe in general.'

'I know,' the DCI said with a small smile. 'But there is one small complication, Joseph.'

The DI had already guessed. 'You're worried I have a conflict of interest.'

Chris grimaced. 'Sorry, you're right. But no one is seriously suggesting Ellie's involved. But you understand, I have to run this by the book. Mind you, Derrick's already suggested a work-around. Another officer will handle Ellie's interview, and you can still be part of the wider investigation.'

'I'd certainly appreciate that as I already feel invested in this case,' Joseph said. 'So yes, I'd like to be involved in one way or another.' But part of him was also taken aback by Derrick sticking up for him. That really wasn't what he'd expected. Also, the last time Ellie had stumbled into the middle of an investigation, Derrick had made it clear he thought Joseph's judgment was compromised. So why the change now? Could the DSU really still be labouring under the misapprehension that they were actually allies, even though Joseph knew better after seeing the compromising footage of Derrick being caught taking a bribe?

Chris turned to Megan. 'We all need to head in.'

'Of course,' the DC said, putting down the rest of her drink.

Chris raised his hand to Dylan and Iris. 'Thank you for your incredible hospitality. I haven't enjoyed myself this much in a long time.'

'Then we'll have to do it again,' Dylan said.

'Yes, and next time at mine,' Chris replied. 'And with Ellie and John too, hopefully.' The DCI glanced at Kate. 'And don't worry, I'll make sure Ellie's statement is prioritised, so we can get her out of there as quickly as possible.'

'I'd certainly appreciate that,' Kate said.

Joseph caught Kate's hand, squeezing it gently. 'Don't worry about Ellie. She was just in the wrong place at the wrong time.'

Kate's mouth tightened. 'If she'd saved him, people would be singing her praises right now, rather than this.' Her gaze suddenly flicked past him. 'Joseph, the peaches!'

He spun to see a column of black smoke curling from the barbecue back on *Tús Nua*. 'Oh, shite!'

'Don't worry, leave those to me,' Dylan said, rising from his seat.

'Thanks,' Joseph said, giving Kate a quick hug. 'I'll call as soon as I know more about Ellie, okay?'

She nodded, squeezing his hand before letting him go.

With a wave to Dylan and Iris, Joseph fell in alongside Chris and Megan, the three of them striding briskly down the towpath towards the heart of Oxford, and the St Aldates police station.

CHAPTER THREE

When Joseph followed Chris and Megan into the incident room at St Aldates, he was surprised to find it already heaving with detectives, with even more reinforcements filing in behind them. What stopped him short was Derrick in conversation with none other than Chief Superintendent Amanda Kennan.

'Looks like they've wheeled in the big guns for this,' Megan observed, dipping her chin towards Kennan.

'Not to mention, dragging in most of our detectives,' Joseph said, half-distractedly as he wondered what the two senior officers might be scheming together.

Chris nodded. 'That tells me the pressure is already on from Westminster. They'll want everything done to resolve this case as quickly as possible.'

Derrick spotted Chris and beckoned him over to join them at the front.

'It seems I'm wanted,' the DCI said, raising his eyebrows a fraction at Joseph, before heading off.

The DI had been in the room less than a minute, but he was already feeling uncomfortable about breathing the same air as Kennan. That had everything to do with him knowing the woman was heavily involved with the Night Watchmen. If there was any doubt in his mind just how corrupt she was, that had been swept away when Chris had shown him an NCA surveillance video monitoring a rival drug gang. Kennan had been there to offer them a working partnership with the Night Watchmen. But when the gang leader had refused to cooperate, she'd had them gunned down.

Yes, Kennan was as bent a copper as they came.

As for DSU Derrick Walker, thanks to the NCA's intelligence Chris had shared discreetly with Joseph, he knew the man had crossed the line when he'd accepted a significant bribe from Kennan, paid for with drug money. But the timing hadn't been lost on the DI either. It couldn't have been a coincidence that their DSU had finally cracked when he'd discovered that Kate and Joseph were back together. But taking the next step into full-blown corruption was something that appalled Joseph to the depths of his soul.

And there you are right now, big man, with the fecking queen of the nest of fecking vipers, and looking very much at home with it, the DI thought.

Joseph's gaze drifted to the large screen mounted on the wall. A muted BBC News feed was playing. The caption described how a man had been dragged from a river by his dog.

Megan's eyes flicked to the screen as well. 'So far, no mention of Martin Chambers then, which has to be front-page news. Looks like his death hasn't broken yet.'

'Sorry, what was that?' DC Ian McDowell's head popped up over the partition, his eyes darting between them. 'Is that why this place is packed out? I passed half our uniformed division gathering outside Christ Church on the way in.'

Joseph nodded. 'Sounds like you haven't been briefed then?'

'Not a word. Just told to get here urgently,' said DC Sue Evans, appearing with a steaming cup in each hand. She passed

Ian his battered Batman mug before setting her own tea down. 'So are we talking about Martin Chambers, our local MP here?'

Before Joseph could answer, Derrick clapped his hands for silence.

'All right, everyone, listen up. Chief Superintendent Kennan will brief you on why you've all been dragged in late on a Saturday night.' He gave her a nod.

Kennan stepped forward, her hard blue gaze raking over the incident room. A hush fell, the shuffle of chairs and the hum of conversation stopping dead.

'We'll keep this short,' she said, her voice cool and clipped. 'You'll have seen the activity at Christ Church College. Some of you may have heard fragments from the uniforms already on scene. But for the rest of you, I'll be blunt. Approximately an hour ago, Martin Chambers, the sitting MP for Oxford West and Abingdon, collapsed and died during a charity dinner. The cause of death is believed to be a heart attack.'

A ripple of surprise spread through the room.

Kennan continued, her expression giving nothing away. 'At present, there's a temporary media embargo—but that will be lifted in the next five minutes. After that, this will be national news. However, we've already learnt from his wife that Chambers was recently diagnosed with a very high cholesterol level, which could have led to his heart attack. But even though it appears he died from natural causes, we can't rule out foul play until the autopsy findings are complete.'

She gestured towards Chris. 'DCI Faulkner will be assigned as SIO for this investigation. However, because of the potential magnitude of this case, DSU Walker and I will also be closely monitoring this investigation, as well as liaising with Westminster. A spotlight will be shining on us for the duration, especially because of the potential national security implications of this case. I expect the very best from each and every one of you. So let's make sure we all do our jobs properly and to the highest professional standards.'

I'll give you the highest professional fecking standards, Joseph thought to himself.

'Now, I'll hand it over to your SIO on this case, DCI Chris Faulkner,' Kennan continued.

Chris stepped forward. 'Right now, Amy Fischer and her SOC team are next door at Christ Church College's Great Hall, gathering any potential evidence. Until we know otherwise, we have to approach this as a crime scene, and anyone who attended the charity dinner is a potential suspect.'

Megan shot Joseph a tight look as Derrick's gaze zeroed in on him.

'Yes, and I'm afraid that does include your daughter, Ellie, Joseph,' Derrick said. But then he quickly held up his hands a murmur spread through the room. 'But so the rest of you are absolutely clear on this, that's only because Ellie was there when Chambers died, and she did try to save him.'

A lot of eyes in the room turned towards Joseph with sympathy, some probably imagining their own daughters caught up in like this, through no fault of their own.

' Since that will be a routine interview, as long as someone else handles it, I don't see a conflict of interest with you remaining on the case,' the DSU said. He motioned for Chris to continue.

Joseph gave Derrick a short nod. *Almost reasonable for the big man,* he thought. A far cry from the ball-ache he'd put him through when Ellie had been dragged into the Midwinter Butcher case.

Chris's gaze swept across the room. 'If you're wondering why so many of you have been pulled in, it's because we're staring at a logistical nightmare. Over two hundred people attended that dinner, not including catering and waiting staff. They've all been held back until they can be interviewed. That's why we're going to have to triage this. You'll work in pairs and process as many as possible. Christ Church has offered up every spare room it has for us to use, as there's no way St Aldates could handle that volume of people. Meanwhile, Amy Fischer's SOC team will be combing through every attendee's mobile phones for anything useful.'

He paused, letting the scale of the task ahead of them settle in. 'Make no mistake here, the pressure's already on. Westminster will want answers, and fast. That's why I expect a written statement from every interview on my desk by tomorrow morning. It's going to be a long night, I'm afraid, ladies and gentlemen.'

Normally, Joseph would have expected a collective groan from the team at the prospect of an all-nighter. But not this time. He could put it down to Kennan's icy presence at the front of the room, but he suspected the real reason was simpler—everyone here knew what was at stake. If foul play really had been involved, every scrap of information needed to be gathered quickly, high-profile case or not. Reputations, perhaps even careers, would be on the line if the police were to miss something at this stage. And if it turned out Chambers had simply died of natural causes, at least they'd be able to point to the thoroughness of the police's response.

'I'll finish by saying this,' Chris said. 'The initial autopsy findings will be key. Dr Rob Jacobs will be joined by Professor Charles Whitaker, President of the Royal College of Pathologists, who is personally overseeing Chambers's postmortem. With luck, and before the night is out, we'll have confirmation it was natural causes. If and when that happens, we can all stand down.'

At the back of the room, a detective raised a hand and

nodded towards the wall-mounted TV. 'Sorry to interrupt, but it looks like the news embargo has just been lifted.'

Derrick picked up the remote and unmuted the TV.

'We're just receiving the shocking news that Martin Chambers, MP for Oxford West and Abingdon, died earlier tonight after suffering a massive heart attack,' the presenter announced. 'An update from Downing Street confirms Mr Chambers passed away while attending a private charity fundraising event at Christ Church College in Oxford. Early reports suggest he collapsed during a speech. A member of the public attempted resuscitation, but after transfer to the John Radcliffe Hospital, the minister was pronounced dead on arrival. At present, officials are treating the death as the result of natural causes.'

The screen shifted to a photo of Chambers cutting a red ribbon at the opening of a drug rehabilitation centre, scissors in hand, his smile broad for the camera.

'Tributes are already pouring in from across the political spectrum,' the announcer continued. 'Prime Minister Sarah Flint is expected to make a statement shortly.'

Derrick muted the sound again. 'If the news reporters are already hounding the leaders of the other parties, you can guarantee Oxford will be crawling with news teams. So watch what you say out there. "No comment" is the order of the day.'

Kennan gave a nod. 'Your work will be coming under intense scrutiny. Make sure you don't let yourself or your colleagues down.'

Once again, the irony wasn't lost on Joseph. Here was the woman preaching about keeping high standards when her own were so low she might as well be limboing under them.

Chris stepped forward. 'Let's get those interviews moving. And be prepared, as Derrick said, Christ Church will likely already be surrounded by press. The embargo may only have just lifted, but you can bet news crews are already in place to hound anyone entering or leaving Christ Church.'

Joseph arched his brows at Megan. 'Oh, sweet fecking joy,' he muttered under his breath.

As the room began to break up, Chris crossed to them. 'Joseph, Megan, you're with me.'

The two detectives nodded and followed the SIO out. But as the hum of voices from the incident room faded behind them, Joseph's thoughts were already on the chaos that almost certainly awaited them at Christ Church College, and his distraught daughter caught right in the middle of it.

CHAPTER FOUR

CHRIS'S PREDICTION about the press being ready for them at Christ Church College turned out to be bang on the money. The moment they headed towards the closed gates, the three detectives were met with a wall of flashing lights and cameras. Every news outlet Joseph could name, and plenty he couldn't, had vans parked nose to tail along the road, news logos emblazoned on the sides.

'Bloody hell,' Megan muttered, shaking her head at the gathered spectacle.

Uniformed officers lined the gate, doing their best to hold back the crush of journalists. Joseph had long ago learnt that when a pack of reporters gathered, they developed a kind of sixth sense for a potential story. Tonight was no different.

It took only seconds for a sharp-eyed journalist to clock the lanyards around his and his colleagues' necks. Then the pack surged towards them. Cameras raised, microphones thrust forward, voices barking over one another with shouted questions.

'Do you have any information about Martin Chambers's death?' a young woman demanded, jamming her mic so close to

Chris's mouth, Joseph was half-surprised the man didn't swat it aside.

But somehow their SIO managed to keep his composure. 'I've no comment to make at this time.'

Predictably, it did nothing to slow the journalists down; the SIO's reply only sparking a fresh round of shouted questions.

The detectives ignored the verbal barrage as they pushed their way through the scrum towards the gate. An officer swung it open just long enough to let them through before snapping it shut behind them again with a clang.

Moments later, the three detectives were heading towards the main entrance of Christ Church College, its great Tom Tower looming overhead in the darkness, and bearing witness to their passage.

Joseph had attended more crime scenes than he cared to count, but this was the first time he'd seen one guarded by armed officers from the Tactical Unit, who'd gathered outside the college. Among them stood an old friend, Sergeant Erol Kentli.

'I wasn't expecting to see you and your lads here,' Joseph said.

'Standard protocol for something like this,' Erol replied.

'Aye, I suppose it is as we're talking about an elected member of parliament,' Joseph replied, as Erol held the main door open for them.

Inside, the college quad was teeming with men in dress jackets and women in gowns, all milling around under the harsh glow of floodlights. Many clutched the inevitable British cure for shock, namely a steaming cup of tea. A few drew nervously on cigars or vapes, their smoke drifting together up into the night air. Unfortunately, more than a few were locked in heated arguments with uniformed officers, gesturing furiously towards the entrance the detectives had just come through.

Joseph wasn't surprised to hear the inevitable line barked out by one of the obviously well-to-do men, 'Do you know who I bloody am?'

Rather you than me, Joseph thought to himself, watching a knot of uniformed officers do their best to placate the man and the others like him.

A police sergeant and a college porter in a bowler hat spotted the detectives and made straight for them.

'Looks like you've got your hands full here,' Chris said as they reached them.

'Like you wouldn't believe,' the sergeant replied. 'Half of the people here are threatening to sue if we don't let them out immediately.'

'At least the good news is we've got six rooms ready for you to start interviews, with more being opened up,' the porter added.

'Good, then let's get this show on the road and calm things down a bit,' Chris said, just as a line of detectives from St Aldates began filing in behind them. 'We'll split the intervie-wees into groups of ten and work through them. At least one group will be taken back to St Aldates to begin processing there...'

Joseph barely heard the rest, because his attention had snagged on a familiar figure across the quad. Ellie sat there hunched in a blanket, both hands locked around a mug. A paramedic crouched beside her, checking her pulse. And John, though he should technically have kept his distance until after her interview, for the same reason Joseph was meant to, was squatting close to her side, his hand rubbing her arm.

The DI gestured towards his daughter. 'Chris, I need to check in with Ellie to see how she's doing.'

The SIO rubbed the back of his neck, then gave a short nod.

'All right. Once you're done, head over to the Great Hall and link up with Amy and her team. I'll join you in a bit.'

'And my conflict of interest? What if I'm seen as interfering with a crime scene?' Joseph asked.

Chris raised one eyebrow, a small smile tugging at his mouth. 'That's why Megan will be with you, to keep you out of mischief.'

Megan raised her eyebrows at him. 'If only I could.'

'Thank you,' Joseph replied, nodding to Megan before the two of them crossed the quad together.

Ellie looked up as they approached, already raising her hands. 'Before you ask, honestly, I'm fine.'

If anything, that only wound Joseph's concern tighter. 'So why are you in a blanket, being checked over by a paramedic then?'

'Because she fainted as we were leading people out into the quad,' John said, rubbing the back of her hand with his thumb.

'Look, I just passed out, that's all,' Ellie said quickly. 'It must have been all the stress after what happened.'

Joseph studied her closely. 'That doesn't sound like you.'

'Not normally, maybe, but this wasn't anything like normal, Dad. When Martin Chambers collapsed on stage and I was the second person to reach him. I knew how serious it was because his smartwatch was literally warbling a warning about an irregular heartbeat. And like I told you, that poor man literally died as I was trying to resuscitate him—' Her nostrils flared.

Perverting the course of justice or not, Joseph pulled his daughter into a hug. Megan stood close by, also reaching out and squeezing her shoulder.

'Please don't worry,' the paramedic said. 'Ellie's fine now, and all her stats are looking okay, although her heart rate is a bit elevated. But most people would be suffering from that after the stressful situation she had to deal with.'

Ellie nodded as she looked into her father's eyes. 'See, nothing to worry about.'

'But you're sure you're feeling okay now?' John asked.

'Apart from some tingling in my lips, and feeling a bit shaken, I'm fine,' Ellie replied.

'Tingling?' Joseph asked, frowning.

'Once again, that's probably down to stress and adrenaline,' the paramedic said.

'And the sensation's already fading,' Ellie added. 'This tea's helping too...' Her words trailed off as two St Aldates detectives strode across the quad towards them.

'Ellie Stone, we'll need to take you back to St Aldates straight away for your interview,' one of them said.

'Only if she's ready, you fecking will,' Joseph shot back.

Ellie scowled at him. 'I told you, Dad, I'm fine.'

'Aye, she did,' he said, forcing a smile at the detective. 'Sorry. Overprotective father and all that.'

'No problem,' one of the detectives said. 'If you'd like to follow us, Ellie.'

She stood, passing her mug to John, giving his hand a quick squeeze before heading off with the two officers.

Joseph and John stood side by side, watching her go. The young officer shook his head. 'I can't believe Ellie's caught up in the middle of this.'

'You and me both,' Joseph replied quietly.

Megan looked between them. 'Will you two stop looking so worried? You both know this is routine.'

'Aye, I do, but still...' Joseph traded a frown with John. 'Come on, Megan. We'd better get over to Amy, see how she's getting on.'

A short while later, now suited up in forensic gear, the two detectives stepped into the vaulted expanse of the Great Hall. The house lights blazed from above, supplemented by the SOC team's harsh arc lamps to illuminate every shadowed corner of the hall, making sure that if a clue was here, there was nowhere for it to hide. The long oak tables were still dressed with candle-sticks, crystal glasses, and plates of food abandoned mid-course when the guests had been hurried out.

'Do you really think Martin Chambers was murdered?' Megan asked Joseph as they headed into the room.

'I sincerely hope not, for all our sakes,' Joseph replied.

His gaze was drawn to the far end of the hall, where yellow evidence markers stood beside a plate of food and a half-drunk glass at the centre of the high table. On the raised stage area, one of the SOCOs, Alison Rogers, dusted carefully for prints.

Near the lectern, Amy straightened up from where she'd been crouched and glanced their way. She gave Joseph the barest nod. Once, that look might have been affectionate. But that was before the DI had uncovered the truth that she'd been playing him, and trying to draw him under the Night Watch-men's influence. The betrayal had ended whatever lay between them, leaving any contact now strictly professional and confined to work. Also, since word had spread about Joseph being back with Kate, even Amy's thin veil of civility had frozen over. And Joseph was content to keep it that way. The memory of how close the woman had come to ensnaring him still weighed on him like a stone on his shoulders.

'So how's it going?' Megan asked, unaware of the undercurrent between her two colleagues as they headed up onto the raised stage to join Amy.

'We're taking it slowly, checking for any hint of evidence, however unlikely,' Amy replied, her attention fixed on the DC. 'I've already taken swabs from the catering staff in case some kind of poison triggered his heart attack.'

'And the food and drink he consumed, in case there is a question of poisoning hanging over this?' Joseph asked.

Amy finally met his gaze fully. 'The main course had already been cleared away. So we'll be combing through the bins to see if any scraps were contaminated with toxins.'

'I bet that won't be pleasant,' Megan said.

'Actually, rooting through bins is SOC's bread and butter.'

'Pun intended?' Joseph asked.

A faint smile tugged at Amy's mouth. 'Maybe. There was also a champagne flute the minister had been drinking from. That's already gone off for analysis. And once the post-mortem's complete, it should show if anything suspicious made it into his system.'

Joseph's eyes drifted to the lectern and the carafe of water resting there. He gestured toward it. 'I'm guessing you've checked that as well?'

'Already done,' Amy turned back to Megan. 'The lab will be working through the night on this one because of its importance. With luck, we'll have preliminary results by tomorrow morning.'

'Hopefully, that will confirm there's nothing suspicious and all we're dealing with is a heart attack,' Joseph said.

'That would make life easier all round,' Amy replied, meeting his gaze again.

'Except for his family,' Megan said. 'Either way, they've still lost him.'

'That may be true, but natural causes will still be easier for them to cope with, rather than foul play.'

Megan grimaced. 'I suppose so.'

Joseph glanced at the evidence markers. 'So, is there anything else of interest you and your team have found here, Amy?'

'Nothing yet, although it's still early days. But Chambers's collapse was caught on the college's livestream from the event, so the Digital Forensic Unit will be going over that footage. If there is anything suspicious, they'll find it.'

The irony wasn't lost on Joseph. Amy might dig for the truth here, but on previous occasions, if the Night Watchmen had a hand in the crime she was investigating, her loyalty would lie with them.

As Amy headed away, Joseph let his gaze wander along the high table. That was when he noticed it, half-hidden beneath Martin Chambers's abandoned side plate, a serviette folded carelessly with something on the corner of it. At first, he thought it was just a stain. But his subconscious must have picked up on something more because it was already drawing his eyes back to it for a second look. Then he saw it. A faint pencil mark on one corner in a strange pattern, too deliberate to be random. His eyes widened as he took in the design, a diagonal line with a second zigzagging one intersecting the first. Small circles were also carved into the peaks and troughs of it.

The echo from his past instantly raised the hair on his arms.

'Fecking hell,' he muttered. Then he beckoned Amy and Megan over. 'Take a look at this.' He angled the serviette with a pen so they could see the faint mark drawn into the linen.

Megan's eyes widened. 'That's the symbol for Azrael from the Midwinter Butcher case.'

'Oh, I know, and both Aaron Fearnley and Helen Edwards, who were responsible for those murders, are dead.'

Amy examined it, her face unreadable, before she nodded. 'Yes, very strange indeed.'

'Exactly, we already know the symbol for Azrael doesn't just turn up at a crime scene by chance,' Joseph said. 'Which might mean that all of this somehow might be connected.' He looked up as Chris appeared in the doorway.

'We need to head over to the autopsy lab now to see how they are getting on,' the SIO called over.

'No problem, but there's been a development you need to

see.' Joseph snapped a photo of the serviette before he and Megan headed over to join the boss.

Chris bent for a closer look at Joseph's phone screen, and his eyes widened. 'That's the symbol from the Midwinter Butcher case.'

'Exactly, and it has to be significant. It might even suggest some sort of occult connection to Chambers's death.'

The SIO's mouth thinned. 'That's all we bloody need.'

Joseph nodded as they followed him out. But as he glanced back, he caught the faintest flicker of frustration in Amy's expression. What was that about? Just more of the same between them. Or something else? That thought lingered as they headed away to whatever Rob had discovered about their victim's death in the pathology lab.

CHAPTER FIVE

THE FIRST THING the three detectives heard as they entered the autopsy observation room was raised voices.

Through the wide glass panel, Doctor Rob Jacobs, Oxfordshire's chief coroner, stood squared off against a taller man. Between them, Doctor Clare Reece, the assistant pathologist, hovered anxiously, her arms half-raised as though she was seriously worried a fistfight would break out between her more senior colleagues.

But Joseph's gaze was drawn to the slab behind them. Chambers's body lay on it, the stark surgical lights perfectly illuminating his prised wide-open chest cavity to reveal bloodied ribs. Several organs had already been removed and laid out in stainless steel trays. The heart had been removed and sat glistening in the stark light.

Joseph's stomach tightened, and he pulled his gaze away, fumbling for a Silvermint, his go-to solution for exactly these sorts of moments. He popped it in his mouth and let the sharp hit of menthol drive back the sour bile that had risen in the back of his throat.

'That's Professor Charles Whitaker,' Chris said, nodding

towards the taller man on the other side of the glass. 'He's here from London, overseeing the autopsy on behalf of the Royal College of Pathologists.'

'Aye, and Rob doesn't look best pleased about it. He's wearing his chewing-wasps face,' Joseph muttered, fixing his attention firmly back on the men.

'So let's hear what they're debating so hotly in there,' Megan said, flicking a switch on the wall.

A speaker crackled into life.

'I strongly disagree,' Rob's voice snapped, as he pointed a latex-gloved finger towards Whittaker. 'We need to remove the liver and take samples for toxicology, and vitreous humour from the eyes, as soon as possible. We both know that fluid can preserve fast-fading poisons. The sooner we test for them, the sooner we'll know what we're dealing with here. If we wait, we'll have no idea if some short-lived toxin was in his system.'

Professor Charles Whitaker folded his arms, his eyebrow twitching. 'Doctor Jacobs, with respect, you're forgetting I'm here to ensure this examination meets the highest standards. There are protocols, and we need to follow them.'

Rob's jaw tightened beneath his surgical mask. 'I don't need a lecture on protocols, Professor. I've been doing this job for twenty years without someone from London breathing down my neck. Unbelievably, I've managed remarkably well.'

Joseph pulled a face, exchanging a glance with Megan and Chris.

'Yes, but the priority is to also take heart tissue, along with his blood work, to confirm cardiac causes,' Charles said.

'As though that isn't already perfectly obvious as his cause of death,' Rob replied on the other side of the glass. 'We've already seen heavy cholesterol plaque build-up in the arteries. The real question is whether the victim's heart attack was actually brought on by natural causes rather than by a poison of some sort.'

Joseph turned to the others. 'Okay, that sounds to me like we're not the only ones keeping our minds open to foul play being a real possibility,' he whispered, but still loud enough to be picked up by the microphone in the observation room they were standing in.

Clare looked around at once and, spotting the detectives, cast them a beseeching look, quickly beckoning for them to enter.

To underline her concern, Rob all but jabbed his finger into the taller man's chest. 'Time is of the essence here, man.'

'We'd better get in there before actual blows are exchanged,' Chris muttered under his breath.

'Oh, great,' Joseph replied with zero enthusiasm, while Megan, as usual, lit up as though she'd just been handed a free Maccy D's Happy Meal.

A short while later, suitably robed and masked, the detectives entered the autopsy room, where the two silverback pathologists were still trading professional insults.

'You've always been far too quick to make up your mind during the autopsy,' Rob was saying.

Charles's face had turned a livid shade of red, but whatever retort he was about to unleash died on his lips as he spotted the detectives.

Do not look at the corpse again, do look at the corpse again, Joseph repeated in a silent mantra to himself. He never did well with that sort of thing.

Megan, the mind reader she was when it came to him in these situations, cast the DI a brief look. He raised a hand in a, *No, honestly, I'm fine,* non-verbal reply.

'Sorry to interrupt your debate, but I was wondering if you'd had any chance to draw an initial conclusion yet?' Chris asked.

Rob gestured to the professor. 'As you're the senior man for this autopsy, I'd better leave that to you to answer.'

'Nice of you to acknowledge that at last,' Charles replied.

Rob made a huffing sound in the back of his throat.

Clare, standing just behind them, practically rolled her eyes.

Joseph had never thought of Rob as the type to get into a pissing contest with anyone, but here they were anyway.

Charles fixed his gaze on the detectives. 'Our preliminary examination shows the heart is notably enlarged, which is consistent with chronic hypertensive changes. The left ventricle is thickened, suggesting long-term pressure overload. There is also moderate coronary artery atherosclerosis, and one of the major vessels shows narrowing that may have been enough to compromise blood flow under stress. The lungs are also congested, which would align with acute left-sided heart failure. Apart from that, the liver, kidneys, and spleen look unremarkable for a man of his age.'

Behind him, Rob performed a slow, silent handclap.

Joseph just managed not to laugh, as Megan bit the inside of her cheek to do the same. Chris just raised his eyebrows a fraction at the men.

'So are you saying this was a natural heart attack?' Megan asked, as though these two grown men weren't acting like kids on a playground.

'At this stage, my impression is the heart tells a very clear story,' Charles replied. 'His medical records back that up. High cholesterol was recently flagged in routine GP tests, and although his blood pressure readings were normal at the time, we've seen narrowing in the left anterior descending artery, a common site for fatal blockages. I am afraid this man was a walking heart attack waiting to happen.'

'That's one interpretation, but there is no visible rupture, or clear intracardiac thrombosis,' Rob immediately countered.

'Until we examine the tissue under a microscope and confirm myocardial infarction, we're not there yet. And here you are already inferring cause from risk factors, not evidence. We cannot declare natural causes without corroboration, not in a high-profile case like this. Poisons like digoxin and cyanide can mimic heart failure really effectively. And they don't always leave a trace, as you well know.'

'Hang on, isn't digoxin derived from foxglove flowers?' Megan asked.

Both of the medical men and Clare shot her an impressed look.

Charles nodded. 'I see someone has been doing her homework.'

'I swear Megan spends her time studying books on how to kill people,' Joseph said, trying to lighten the tension in the room.

'Or at least burying my head in a good crime novel,' Megan added.

Rob managed a small smile at his favourite potential recruit into the world of pathology.

'Digoxin could certainly be a candidate,' Clare said. 'It affects the electrical performance of the heart. Its presence is relatively short-lived, but only detectable in blood tests for twenty-four to forty-eight hours after death.'

A triumphant look crossed Rob's face. 'Exactly. Which is why we need tests that go beyond alcohol, recreational drugs, and prescriptions. We need a full toxicology panel to rule out deliberate poisoning.'

'I'm not saying we won't run those tests, only that it is very probable we already have the answer—a natural heart attack,' Charles replied.

'And evidence of foul play not being obvious doesn't mean it isn't there,' Rob shot back. 'Especially when we haven't looked for it. You, of all people, know that. Until toxicology is complete, the cause of death remains undetermined. And for the record,' he looked directly at the detectives, 'I recommend treating this as suspicious until we have conclusive evidence to say otherwise.'

Charles gave a curt nod. 'Even though you think I don't, I do actually agree. I'm just not sure I'd waste too many resources on an investigation unless the tests suggest otherwise.'

Chris gave the man a straight look. 'For now, we need to keep all our options open; we're certainly not in a position to write anything off. Which leads me to my next question. How long will a full toxicology report take?'

'If we fast-track the basics, about twenty-four hours,' Clare replied. 'But expanded testing for digoxin and other rare poisons could take five to ten days.'

'I would appreciate it being closer to the lower number of that range,' Chris said. 'But even a five-day delay will cause a serious headache for our investigation.'

'Which is why I think you will be safe to say the initial findings appeared to indicate the victim died from a heart attack, although further tests are still being carried out,' Charles said.

Rob pulled a face. 'I think you run a risk there. If we say it's natural causes now and next week, the toxicology screen says otherwise, that will call our professional judgement into question.'

'Then maybe we should tell the press we're waiting on the full results from the autopsy,' Joseph said. 'That's accurate and probably the safest play here.'

Clare was already nodding, grateful there was somebody sensible in the room.

Chris nodded as well. 'I'll lay out all the options to Derrick and Chief Kennan and let them make the call, but it will be your suggestion, Joseph, that I'll be recommending.'

Rob shot a triumphant look across at Charles, but, thankfully, didn't go full schoolboy and thumb his nose at his rival, although to Joseph it looked like the man was sorely tempted.

If Charles noticed, he was at least professional enough to pretend he hadn't.

'We will let you know the moment we have anything back on the toxicology report,' Clare said.

'I'd certainly appreciate that.'

'Oh, one last thing that may help you, my daughter was actually there,' Joseph said. 'She was the one who first tried to resuscitate the victim, and mentioned something about his smartwatch flagging an irregular heart rate. Presumably, any data on there might be of use.'

The three pathologists exchanged a surprised look.

'What smartwatch?' Clare said. 'He wasn't wearing one when he arrived here.'

'Maybe one of the medical team removed it before he got here,' Megan suggested.

Charles shook his head. 'That's unlikely precisely for the reason Joseph suggested. The data it contains could be really valuable, especially when we're missing pieces of the puzzle to make a full diagnosis.'

'Perhaps he lost it after he collapsed,' Megan suggested. 'If that's the case, Amy and her team are likely to have found it by now.'

Chris glanced briefly over at Joseph, and the DI knew exactly what the boss was thinking. Yes, Amy was excellent at turning up clues at a crime scene, but only when it didn't involve the Night Watchmen.

'Wherever that smartwatch is, we'll make it a priority to find it and get it to you,' Chris said.

'It certainly might be useful,' Rob replied.

'In that case, I think we're done here. We'll leave you to get on with it,' Chris said.

Rob nodded before turning to his senior colleague. 'Okay, we still need to remove the liver, Charles,' he said, almost conversationally.

Megan glanced casually into the open body cavity and barely batted an eyelid, like she was examining a butcher's counter at the supermarket.

Joseph, mantra forgotten, followed her gaze. The sight of wet, glistening internal tissue under the harsh lights evoked a wave of fresh nausea.

For feck's sake, he thought, wrenching his eyes away and sucking furiously on his Silvermint.

CHAPTER SIX

As JOSEPH and Megan followed Chris into the incident room, every computer station was occupied by a detective tapping away at a keyboard. Considering the lateness of the hour, heading towards one a.m., Joseph wasn't surprised that there wasn't any sign of either Chief Kennan or Derrick anywhere. Overseeing an investigation obviously only stretched so far, and wasn't allowed to get in the way of their beauty sleep.

The BBC's twenty-four-hour news cycle was still playing on the large screen, muted with subtitles running across the bottom. Outside Christ Church College, a reporter was talking to a woman wrapped in a pink silk shawl. Her face was pale, her body trembling.

'You were there in the Great Hall when it happened?' the subtitles read.

'Yes, I was only a few tables away,' the woman replied, visibly pale and shaking. *'One moment Martin Chambers was speaking, and the next—'* She swallowed as she took a moment. *'It felt like the air had been sucked out of the room when he collapsed.'*

'I'm going to check in with the team and get up to speed on

the interviews,' Chris said, pulling Joseph's attention away from the screen.

'Aye, but if you wouldn't mind, could you see how Ellie got on in her interview?' Joseph asked.

Chris gave him a small smile. 'Don't worry, I was already planning to make that a priority. Meanwhile, could you get an update from Amy and see if that smartwatch has turned up at the scene?'

'I'm already on that,' Megan said, powering up a screen.

With a dip of his chin, Chris headed away.

Sue stopped typing and spun her chair around as Joseph dropped into the desk chair beside Megan. 'So how did you guys get on at the autopsy?'

'Nothing conclusive yet, although the preliminary signs do suggest a heart attack,' Joseph said, as Megan picked up the phone and started dialling. 'Whether it was natural or foul play, we won't know until the tox screen comes back, and that could be at least five days.'

'That's not good. It'll only fuel speculation in the press, and they'll hurry to fill in the gaps,' Sue said, gesturing towards the TV feed. 'Mind you, they're already saying he had high cholesterol, and it was a fatal heart attack.'

Joseph shook his head. 'Sometimes I think we should let the journalists investigate for us. At least then we might get an early night sometimes.'

Ian appeared, clutching a half-eaten Mars bar. 'No such luck,' he said through a mouthful. 'We've still got at least fifty people to interview, and then a mountain of paperwork. If this turns out to be nothing but a heart attack, it's already been a monumental waste of manpower.'

Joseph shot the man a frown. 'A normal heart attack, is it? Try saying that to Martin Chambers's widow.' He hesitated, then added, 'And that's before we even factor in the symbol I found on the serviette.'

Sue frowned. 'Symbol?'

'Azrael's sigil, the angel of death,' Joseph said. 'The same symbol we saw carved in the goats and Zoe Bryce in the Midwinter Butcher case.'

Sue stared at him. 'Are you thinking it might be related to this case somehow?'

'I don't know, but it's one hell of a coincidence if not,' Joseph replied. 'Either way, an occult connection or not, someone gave that marked serviette to Martin Chambers. There has to be a significance behind that, which leaves me questioning this whole natural causes angle.'

Ian bit down on his Mars bar and shook his head. 'Bloody hell, that's not the sort of thing I wanted to hear at this time of night. That will complicate this investigation tenfold. So what are we talking about here, a possible copycat murderer?'

'All I know is if Azrael's symbol has cropped up again, we can't afford to overlook it.'

'In that case, I'd better do a tea run to the kitchen because this night could get even longer. Can I make anyone a cuppa?'

Joseph shook his head. 'No, I'm grand.' Of course, Ian's tea-making was infamous across St Aldates; dishwater, only less pleasant, was the man's usual standard.

Ian's gaze swept over Sue and Megan. 'What about you two?'

Megan, still on the phone, held up her palm.

Sue pointed to her Red Bull. 'All good here.'

As Ian headed away, Joseph's mind was already back on the symbol. *So could this all be linked somehow to the Midwinter Butcher case, and if so, how?* he wondered.

Then his attention was caught again by the TV. On it, a

man he vaguely recognised was emerging from what looked like a theatre, speaking to a reporter.

Sue followed his line of sight to the TV. 'That was recorded earlier with Marcus Blackwood, head of that One Nation party everyone's been talking about in the press recently.'

'Oh, the one who's been banging on about how politicians need to grow up, stop being so partisan, and actually work together for a change?' Joseph asked.

'That's him, and I have to say, Blackwood makes a refreshing change. He's all about straight talking, and no mudslinging, and cross-party support. He certainly doesn't seem to be into any of the spin and the half-truths the rest of them seem to thrive on.'

'Good luck pulling that off with that lot in the Commons.'

'Well, he certainly has the other major parties rattled,' Megan said, cupping her hand over the receiver. 'His message is apparently going down too well with the members of the public, especially his stance on domestic terrorism. Some pollsters are even saying that if things stay as they are for the upcoming election, it could be a hung parliament with One Nation holding the balance of power.'

'Not bad for a newly formed party,' Joseph said, before turning his attention back to the screen as Marcus Blackwood continued to speak.

'Like so many others, I was shocked to hear the tragic news about Martin Chambers.'

Marcus took a moment, visibly moved as he composed himself before continuing. 'Martin and I didn't always see eye to eye, but that's politics for you. However, he was a passionate advocate for the people he represented. He was certainly someone who believed in service to their country and never lost sight of the human cost behind the headlines. That's a rare commodity, and something I will always admire him for.'

The political party leader glanced at the ground, then lifted his gaze back to the reporter. *'My thoughts are with his family, and if there's anything I or my team can do to support them, we will.'*

Then his expression tightened. *'I understand the police are treating this with the utmost seriousness, and rightly so. But for now, maybe we can all just pause and remember the man, not just the circumstances of his passing.'*

Joseph couldn't help but feel impressed by the leader's obvious integrity, no point-scoring in sight. To him, that seemed an increasingly rare commodity among politicians.

Megan put down the phone and turned to Joseph. 'Okay, no sign of the smartwatch from Amy's side. If it disappeared, maybe it happened before his body was moved from the Great Hall.'

'Then it might be worth checking with the paramedics in case it was left in the ambulance to the John Radcliffe Hospital,' Joseph suggested.

'Sorry for earwigging, but Martin Chambers was wearing a smartwatch?' Sue asked. 'I'm guessing you're after it for any useful heart data?'

Megan nodded. 'Yes, and now it's gone missing.'

'You could check its data online, when it last synced to the cloud.'

Megan gave her a sharp nod. 'Of course we could, and we could even use the built-in tracking system and ask the Digital Forensics Unit to locate it.'

'Now you're talking,' Joseph said. 'Check with Chris, but I think this should be made a priority.'

'If you want to work out when it went missing, there's one other thing you should look at, and that's the live-streamed footage that captured Chambers's death,' Sue said. 'Thankfully, the college pulled it before social media got its greasy hands on it.'

'Thank God for small mercies. Can you imagine how upsetting that would have been for Chambers's family if that had ended up all over the internet? Have you got access to this video?'

'Yes, the college sent it straight over to us. Do you want to see it?'

Joseph nodded, and a short while later, Sue had pulled up a file on her screen. Megan rolled her seat closer as she pressed play.

Martin Chambers stood in front of the high table in the Grand Hall of Christ Church College, hands clasped on either side of a lectern as he looked out at the audience.

'Good evening, friends,' the politician said. 'It's an absolute honour to stand before you tonight in this magnificent hall, surrounded by individuals who share a passion for our community and our future...'

Sue pointed at his right wrist. 'Okay, so he's still wearing his watch at this point.'

'That's in line with what Ellie told me when I saw her briefly over at Christ Church College,' Joseph said. 'Could we fast forward to the moment when he collapsed?'

'Of course...' Sue scrolled through the timeline until the politician lay on his back on the floor.

Even knowing Ellie had rushed to the man's aid, it was still a shock for Joseph to see his daughter bent over the prone man. Her hands were locked together as she worked his chest compressions, trying to force the man's heart to beat again. Even though she hadn't ultimately succeeded in saving the man, the DI couldn't help but feel pride at her quick thinking as she moved on to mouth-to-mouth.

An older man in a dinner jacket rushed onto the stage with a defibrillator. He joined Ellie after she moved aside, her head bowed, shoulders sagging as she stared at the floor. As the man worked quickly to place electrodes on Chambers's chest, the detectives could see that the watch was still on the minister's wrist, a warning message clearly flashing across its screen about his heart rate.

In the incident room, Ian came over and joined them as the video continued: the desperate attempts to shock the man's heart back into life, Chambers's wife standing to one side, tears streaming down her face as she watched the paramedics arrive and take over the fight to save her husband's life.

All the while, Joseph kept his eyes glued to the watch like this was a variation of a shell game. When the paramedics finally moved Martin onto a stretcher as the first police officers arrived on the scene, John among them, a group of people crossed the stage and briefly blocked the camera's view. When Martin Chambers reappeared on screen, there was no sign of his watch.

'For feck's sake,' Joseph muttered.

'Okay, this is obviously the moment his watch went missing,' Ian said, stating the bleeding obvious.

Megan was already pointing at members of the audience, some of them clearly filming everything on their phones. 'But as always, there were people there with a lack of empathy and who had no problem recording something this tragic for their social media feeds. In which case, we need to trawl through those phones for anything useful.'

'What's this?' Chris asked, appearing behind them.

'It looks like Martin Chambers's smartwatch was taken during the event,' Joseph said. 'The problem is we can't tell by whom because the camera was obscured at the critical moment. We need to check the phones of people in the audience to see if they caught anything.'

Chris nodded. 'As Amy was already pulling material from them, I'll ask her and her team to look for the watch specifically in the footage and see if we can work out who took it. The next question is, why would anyone want it?'

Joseph nodded. 'Good question. It's certainly suspicious...' His words faltered as he spotted Ellie rubbing her lips on the still-running video footage. A moment later, she staggered and began to collapse as Ragnar Higginson, the dean of the Blavatnik School of Government, rushed to help her.

'Oh, fecking hell,' the DI said.

'It looks like Ellie fainted,' Sue said. 'Not surprising with everything she just went through.'

Even though that's what Joseph had first thought when he'd heard, seeing the incident for himself had set his mind racing. 'Please back it up a few seconds and play it again.'

Sue did as the DI asked.

There Ellie was, rubbing her lips again.

Joseph leaned forward, forehead ridging as a heartbeat later, she staggered and her legs started to fold. He reached over and hit pause.

'Did you all see that?' he asked the others.

'You're obviously not talking about her collapsing, are you?' Ian asked.

Joseph managed not to glower at the man. He rewound the video and froze the image on Ellie's hand pressed against her mouth.

'Look at what she's doing. Does that mean anything to any of you, given the timing?'

Megan's eyes widened. 'She'd just given Martin Chambers mouth-to-mouth, and then a few minutes later she collapsed. And if he'd just ingested a poison...'

Joseph nodded. 'Exactly. This could be the first confirmation we're dealing with foul play here—' His face drained of colour and he whirled on Chris. 'Where's Ellie right now?'

'That was what I came to tell you,' he said. 'She's just

finished her interview and has been cleared of any involvement. John's taking her home to their flat. But you might catch them if you hurry.'

Joseph didn't even answer as he bolted from the room, almost colliding with a detective coming through the door in the opposite direction. He tore through the station and out into the rear car park, where he spotted John helping Ellie towards her battered Ford Fiesta.

'Ellie, hold up a second,' Joseph shouted, sprinting across to them.

His daughter turned, startled, as he reached her and gripped her shoulders. 'Are you feeling okay?' he asked.

'Yes, fine, apart from being utterly exhausted after hours of questioning.'

'At least Ellie's been cleared of any involvement now,' John added.

'I don't mean that,' he replied, his pulse hammering. 'We were just watching the footage of Martin Chambers's heart attack. It also caught you fainting. Ellie. Do you remember rubbing your lips just before you passed out?'

'Yes. They went numb and tingly, probably all part of the shock, like everyone said.'

Joseph's gut turned to ice. 'Okay, we need to get you to hospital right now. I think you may have ingested a poison.'

John stared at him, then at Ellie. 'Oh shit.'

'But Dad, I honestly feel fine now,' his daughter protested.

'We can't assume that, so no arguments.'

Ellie started to speak, but John cut her off with a shake of his head. 'No, I'm with Joseph here. I'm not prepared to take any chances with your life.'

'Then that makes two of us,' Joseph said.

'Do I get a say in this?' Ellie asked.

Both men shook their heads as Megan appeared in the car

park at that moment, clutching a set of keys. 'I thought you might need a driver,' she called, heading towards the unmarked Volvo V90.

Joseph didn't hesitate. 'Right, but you know all the usual things I say about slowing down?'

'What about them?' Megan asked as she unlocked the car.

'Ignore them and go as fast as you fecking can, blue lights all the way.'

Any other time, Megan would have grinned, but not now. She only nodded, slid into the driver's seat, and fired up the engine. Joseph, Ellie, and John piled into the back seat. With a squeal of tyres, the Volvo tore out of the car park and roared through the arch and out onto the main street with a blare of the siren.

CHAPTER SEVEN

As the heart rate monitor Ellie was hooked up to quietly blipped in the background, Joseph felt a sense of helplessness settle in his stomach like a stone. He sat with Kate and John in the Ambulatory Emergency Care Unit at the John Radcliffe Hospital, where Ellie was being assessed. Now, deep into the small hours, Megan had headed off in search of decent coffee to keep them going.

'Look, I don't know how many times I need to tell you this, but I honestly feel fine,' Ellie said.

'Maybe you do now, but you're also the one who passed out earlier after giving Martin Chambers mouth-to-mouth,' John said.

Joseph nodded, appreciating the young officer's directness. 'You might think we're overreacting here, but I'm not prepared to take the risk that you've been exposed to some sort of toxin.'

'And for the record, I totally agree,' Kate added. 'I don't think I could live with the consequences if you've been inadvertently poisoned, and we didn't do anything.'

John reached over and squeezed Ellie's hand. 'Besides, what's not to love about hospital food?'

Despite herself, a smile tugged at Ellie's mouth. 'Oh, yum.'

'Actually, as someone who's spent more time here than I'd like, the food isn't half bad,' Joseph said.

'I remember that from the last time I was here, when I got knocked out after running into Aaron Fearnley at City Farm,' Ellie added.

'Yes. And just a request here, could you stop making a habit of getting caught up in cases I'm investigating? It's really starting to get old.'

Ellie shrugged. 'If only. It seems I've a talent for being in the wrong place at the wrong time.'

'At least there was one silver lining to that Midwinter Butcher case,' John said. 'If it hadn't been for that, I might never have met Ellie when I was posted to guard her home.'

Joseph resisted pointing out that John had also managed to get himself knocked out during that duty, which had allowed Ellie to be abducted. But who was he to rip the rose-tinted glasses off the lad's eyes?

Kate gave Joseph a thoughtful look. 'Could we have an off-the-record chat?' she asked.

'You mean you'll keep your journalist's notebook in your bag?' he replied.

'You know that's never been an issue in the past, and I'm not about to start now. But if we are talking about Martin Chambers being poisoned, have you stopped to consider the reason why?'

John shot Kate a look. 'You know Joseph can't talk about an ongoing case with you.'

'And you've been part of this family long enough to know that's exactly what we do,' Kate replied. 'Not once has anything said to me in confidence appeared in print until Joseph has given me the thumbs-up to go ahead.'

Ellie nodded. 'We all need someone we can confide in. Just like you do with me about work, John.'

The PC actually blushed and jerked his head in Joseph's direction, as if to say, '*Not in front of the DI.*'

But Joseph was smiling at him. 'Don't worry. Nearly every serving officer at one time or another needs to share this sort of thing with their partner. Okay, maybe we're not technically meant to, but we all occasionally need someone we know we can trust and confide in. I honestly think I would have lost the plot long before now if I hadn't been able to talk things through with Kate. And obviously this also applies to Dylan as well as Iris now, who, as you know, have been instrumental in helping us to solve many a case.'

John rubbed the back of his neck as he nodded. 'Sorry, don't mind me, and I didn't mean any slight by it, Kate.'

'None taken, and believe it or not, Joseph was just like you when he was a young officer on the beat. On a bad day, he just needed someone to talk to. That's all.'

Joseph shot her an affectionate look. 'You've always been there for me.'

'And I always will, just as you've been for me.'

Ellie looked between her parents and smiled. 'Okay, before you get all soppy, back to Martin Chambers. As a journalist with your ear to the ground, any idea why someone might want to hurt him, Mum?'

Joseph considered for a moment jumping in and telling them about the sigil he'd found at the scene, the mark of Azrael, but he pushed the thought aside. The symbol's possible connection was too murky at this point. It was also a painful memory for his family, especially for Ellie, who'd lost her best friend, Zoe, at the hands of Aaron Fearnley and Helen Edwards. They'd used that sigil when they'd murdered her at the Hawk Stone. Bringing it up now would only worry Kate and Ellie. And the last thing he wanted was to dig up old shadows that still haunted his family. So he kept silent as the conversation went on.

'There are a lot of unstable people out there, and he wouldn't be the first MP to be attacked,' John said.

'Yes, but maybe not so likely with poison,' Joseph replied. 'If that's really what we're dealing with here. That doesn't strike me as a spur-of-the-moment thing, but something that took serious planning.'

'Actually, I can think of a very clear reason for a political rival wanting Martin dead,' Kate said.

Joseph sat straighter. 'Go on.'

'You're probably not aware of this, but the whisper on the grapevine is, or I should say *was*, that Chambers was destined for great things.'

'In other words, one of your political contacts who loves to leak things to you?' Joseph asked.

Kate shrugged. 'I'm neither going to confirm nor deny that. But let's just suppose it was. And that same contact in the inner circle also told me the current PM was seriously considering resigning in the run-up to the next election, in order to give his party their best chance to be re-elected. And let's also suppose Chambers's name was being tipped to take over from him.'

Joseph's eyes widened. 'Fecking hell, you're not seriously suggesting that a politician decided to take their potential rival out with poison to clear the way so they could take a run at the top job?'

Kate held up her hands. 'I'm not suggesting anything of the sort. But doesn't it strike you as something of a coincidence that a man right on the edge of great things dies before he takes over as leader of the party currently in power? After all, we all know how cutthroat politics can be.'

'But surely figuratively, not literally,' Ellie said.

'Not normally, but it's also not beyond the realm of possibility either,' Kate replied. 'Politics has become increasingly partisan. Maybe somebody in Martin's party decided to take matters into their own hands.'

Joseph peered at Kate. 'So you're suggesting we should seriously look at anyone else who might have their hat in the ring for the PM role?'

'Yes, and I can give you a list of those candidates. But if I were you, I wouldn't stop there.'

'What do you mean?' John asked.

'I mean, if you want to really throw open your suspect list, I'd also be looking at rival political parties as well. Apparently, the other parties already knew about Martin's likely candidacy for PM. His fresh, no-nonsense attitude might have been his party's best chance to win the next election, and it certainly had them all rattled.'

'But I thought his party had been doing really badly in the polls?' Ellie asked.

'Which is why the current PM is thinking of standing down,' Kate replied. 'Until yesterday, before his untimely death, Chambers might have been on the outside of the current cabinet. But as the blame game played out about the party's sliding performance in the polls, behind closed doors the grandees apparently thought Chambers's distance from the incumbent would be viewed as a positive by the public.'

'So, in other words, Martin was seen as a fresh broom?' Ellie said.

'Exactly.'

John pulled a sceptical face. 'You're not seriously suggesting that rival political parties are starting to bump each other off now, are you?'

Kate shrugged. 'All I'm doing is throwing ideas out here. Just because something's improbable, doesn't mean it's impossible.'

Joseph turned the thought over in his head and nodded.

'Aye, I suppose we shouldn't be too quick to write it off as a theory. Of course, we may just be getting ahead of ourselves. After all, there could still be a perfectly innocent explanation for Martin Chambers's death.'

'Exactly,' Ellie replied. 'Personally, I can't help but feel this is all a storm in a teacup, and everyone is overreacting about me passing out, too.'

At that moment, the door opened with a soft click, putting a stop to their conversation. A dark-haired doctor wearing tailored trousers and shirt stepped inside. Joseph recognised her at once, and a glance at her badge hanging from her lanyard refreshed his memory—Doctor Kelley Stanbridge. The last time he'd run into her had been in the John Radcliffe Hospital, the JR, on a previous case.

'I've got the initial results back, and they make for some very interesting reading,' the doctor said.

Joseph felt his stomach do a slow flip as Kate cast him a pale look. John gripped Ellie's hand harder.

Even his daughter cast the doctor a worried look. 'When you say *interesting*?'

'I mean, in light of the fact you passed out, what we haven't found is significant. Your initial full-panel blood tests all looked fine. We checked your blood sugar levels, electrolyte balance, and haemoglobin levels, and can rule out anaemia. The ECG they took when you were first admitted also indicates your heart health is perfectly fine, as are the readings we've continued to take in here. However, you did initially have an elevated heart rate. The paramedics who checked you at the scene also picked up on that. But that wasn't seen as surprising in the circum-stances. The main thing is that it's settled back down to normal now.'

'So in other words, I'm fine and can go home?' Ellie asked.

The doctor quickly held up her hand. 'We'll get to that in a moment. Anyway, we didn't find anything physical, which is obviously a good sign, so we're probably dealing with vasovagal syncope.'

Joseph felt the air being sucked out of the room. 'What the feck is that?'

The doctor turned towards him, and her eyes widened a fraction. 'Have we met before?'

'Yes, you helped me when one of our officers was bashed over the head by one of your patients that he was guarding in the JR. DC Anderson and I were there when you gave our man a bit of a talking to.'

'Ah, yes. I had to read him the riot act to persuade him to be kept in overnight for observation after being knocked out.'

'That's the one,' Joseph replied. 'And he was less than cooperative, but you handled him brilliantly.'

Joseph inclined his head in thanks, but before he could add more, Ellie spoke up.

'Anyway, getting back to this vasovagal syncope?' His daughter raised her eyebrows a fraction at her dad.

'All that means is that it's a faint caused by emotional shock,' Doctor Stanbridge said. 'Another possibility is hyperventilation brought on by the stress of giving CPR. That could explain your tingling lips as well.'

Ellie shot the others a triumphant look. 'There you go then. I told you that you were all overreacting. Happy now?'

'So poison might not have played any part in Ellie's collapse?' Kate asked.

'I'm afraid we can't rule that out just yet. If there was a toxin involved, it will take time for the lab to pin down what exactly, if it's even detectable now. Some poisons are very short-lived. As you know, Ellie, a swab was taken from your lips and mouth after you were first admitted. But I'm not confident it'll show anything, given you've had plenty of time to lick your lips.'

Ellie frowned. 'Not to mention all the cups of tea I drank before getting here.'

'Quite. But even if you did ingest a small amount of poison, after several hours of observation, I'm happy to let you go home. If there were going to be any issues, they would have presented by now.'

'So you're saying I'm free to go?'

'Yes, as long as there's somebody who can stay with you in case you take a turn for the worse,' Doctor Stanbridge replied.

'Don't worry, I'll be watching her like a hawk,' John said.

Ellie sighed. 'So that means lots of pampering as well, doesn't it?'

Doctor Stanbridge chuckled. 'That can never hurt.'

'You heard her, John. After all this excitement, I'm definitely in the mood for a fresh blueberry juice from that smoothie place we both love.'

Joseph shot the young officer an amused look. 'It sounds like our daughter is getting ready to give you the runaround. So we'd better get you signed off with a day's compassionate leave.'

'That might be an idea; I suspect I'm going to have my hands full.'

'And you're going to love every moment,' Ellie said, grinning at him.

John chuckled. 'Probably,' he replied just as Megan walked in, carrying a tray of coffee.

'Sorry it's taken me so long, but the only coffee I could find was from a dodgy vending machine at the other end of the hospital,' she said.

Doctor Stanbridge grimaced at the cups. 'I wouldn't touch that stuff with a bargepole, unless you like coffee that tastes like the bottom of a kitchen compost bucket.'

'Great, now you tell me,' Megan said. 'So how are things going here?'

'I'll get you up to speed in the car,' Joseph said. 'But the headline is, the doctor here has given Ellie permission to go home. I don't know about anyone else, but I could seriously do with my bed.'

Kate stifled a yawn and nodded. 'God, yes.'

'So poisoning has been ruled out?' Megan asked, putting the tray down.

Doctor Stanbridge shook her head. 'Not entirely. But even if it was involved, I'm confident Ellie is going to be okay.'

Megan turned to Ellie. 'Which is great news.' Then she glanced back at Joseph. 'But it also sounds like we're no nearer the truth of what happened last night?'

'Maybe not,' Joseph admitted. 'But thanks to Kate, we do have some potential political leads I'd like to look at first thing tomorrow. I'll give Chris a quick call tonight. They might be significant.'

'Sounds promising,' Megan said, as she absentmindedly took a sip of one of the coffees and shuddered. 'Bloody hell, you weren't exaggerating,' she said to the doctor. 'That's truly awful.'

'I did try to warn you,' Doctor Stanbridge replied. She looked at Ellie. 'Okay, I'll let a nurse know you can be discharged now. But if there are any changes in symptoms, you are to come straight back to the hospital at once.'

'Don't worry, she will,' John replied.

Ellie frowned at him. 'Am I not allowed to answer for myself?'

John grinned at her. 'Not on this occasion.'

Joseph chuckled. 'Brave man,' he said, winking at the PC as Ellie scowled at them both.

CHAPTER EIGHT

Joseph's alarm cut through his dreams in a warbling shriek, dragging him from the depths of sleep back into the world. The clock's glowing digits showed seven a.m. as sunlight spilled through the small porthole.

How am I expected to be grand on just three hours of fecking sleep? he thought. Out loud, he said, 'Kate, I'll put some strong coffee on to help us both wake up.'

When there was no response, he edged his foot across the bed to give her a gentle nudge and quickly discovered the distinct absence of anyone sleeping next to him. Sitting up, his gaze was caught by a note resting against his thermal mug next to the bed.

'I've headed off to work early, so I can draw up a list of those rivals for the PM role to get to you sooner rather than later. I've also filled your mug with some Brazil Yellow Bourbon coffee. Kate xxx.'

'Now that's true love,' Joseph said to himself.

Tux responded with a miaow as he appeared in the doorway, his tail half wrapped around the frame.

'Oh, I know you and your catty ways,' Joseph said. 'There's

no way on Earth you'd have let Kate leave for work without feeding you first.'

Tux blinked slowly at him.

Joseph sighed. 'Fecking hell, I really am putty in your paws. Fine, second breakfast it is.'

Grabbing his dressing gown and, more importantly, his coffee, Joseph soon had Tux purring away as the cat crunched through his expensive dental-friendly kibble, apparently very good for his teeth and gums. With that task done and thermal mug in hand, the DI stepped out onto the deck of *Tús Nua* to breathe in the scent of the new day. The river was still, a mirror broken only by the faint wake of a passing moorhen.

The DI settled into a seat at the stern and took a sip of his coffee. Notes of caramel and honey, with a nutty undertone—comfort in a cup right there. His brain gave a long, contented sigh.

That, Kate, is one damned fine cup of coffee, he thought.

'I hear you had something of a late night,' Dylan's voice called from the towpath.

Joseph looked around to see his friend returning from a walk with White Fang and Max. Spotting their neighbour awake, both dogs yipped greetings and bounded across the gangplank, nails clicking on the deck before they both ended up sitting expectantly at Joseph's feet.

'A second breakfast for you as well now, is it?' Joseph asked.

Max barked. White Fang offered a paw, which Joseph shook gravely before reaching for the treat tin tucked by the rail on the cabin roof. Each dog snatched up a biscuit in the blink of an eye.

'They've got you so well trained,' Dylan said as he caught up.

'You better believe it. Them and Tux, both.'

'Very true,' the professor replied with a smile. 'Anyway, Kate told me the good news this morning about Ellie getting the all clear, before she headed into work.'

'Aye, and that is a massive relief. Of course, Ellie thinks we all overreacted.'

'Naturally, but you didn't. You can't muck about when you suspect a poison is involved. Time is obviously of the essence.'

'Even if our daughter can't quite see it that way yet.'

'I'm sure she does deep down, even if she won't admit it to herself. That aside, Kate also mentioned this political rival theory about Martin Chambers's death. Do you think it has legs?'

'It might explain why the man specifically was targeted if he really was in line for the PM's job. But before we get too carried away, the doctor did say that Ellie's tingling lips could simply have been down to emotional shock.'

Dylan's expression grew thoughtful. He scratched his chin. 'Maybe, maybe not… give me a second.'

He hurried onto his own boat and returned moments later with a heavy, black leather-bound book stamped in gold. Morning sun glanced off the gilt lettering, making the title gleam strangely out of place against the homely narrowboat setting.

Joseph raised his brows as he read the spine. *The Codex of Forgotten Toxins.*

'Sorry, but why do you have a book about poisons on board your boat? You're not planning to bump anyone off, are you? One too many heated arguments with Iris?'

His friend scowled at him. 'Of course not. It was actually Iris's suggestion that I add it to my collection, just in case it ever came in useful for one of your cases.'

'Well, I appreciate the support, but I don't expect you two to become full-blown criminologists. We do have experts on our own payroll, you know.'

'You may indeed, but we're enjoying ourselves regardless. Put it this way, and as I've told you before, it's more fun than doing crosswords and helps to keep our minds active.'

'Fair enough. So, is there something in there you think might be relevant?'

'Actually, I do. That mention of tingling lips reminded me of something...' Dylan flipped through the book, then tapped a page. 'Here it is. Monkshood, also known as Wolfsbane, is apparently the Queen of Poisons.' The professor cleared his throat and started to read. 'Favoured by poisoners of the old courts and whispered of in Druidic circles, Monkshood is said to still the tongue before the heart.'

'Okay. And the symptoms are?' Joseph asked.

Dylan scanned further. 'This is what I remembered.' He read aloud again. 'Tingling and numbness in the lips and tongue are the earliest and most recognisable signs.'

But his triumphant look faded as his eyes moved down the page, before he looked up again. 'I'm sorry. I really thought I was onto something here.'

'Why? What else does it say?'

'That the initial poisoning is followed by a burning sensation in the mouth and throat over the next sixty minutes.'

'Which, as far as I know, Chambers didn't report to anyone,' Joseph said.

'That's what I thought, based on the press coverage. I doubt he'd have just sat there suffering in silence if he were going through something like that. Do you happen to know if he vomited at all?'

'Yes, just before he collapsed with the heart attack.'

Dylan nodded. 'At least that fits. There's also a slow or irregular heartbeat leading to death. You can see why, especially when combined with Ellie's tingling lips, I thought of this poison.'

'Aye, I can. Unfortunately, this poison of yours doesn't fit all his symptoms. Take that with Ellie's clean bill of health when she was discharged, it points us to one obvious conclusion.'

'That this is exactly what it first seemed, a natural heart attack?'

'Exactly.'

Dylan slowly nodded. 'Perhaps I've been helping you investigate one too many cases, and I'm starting to see conspiracies where there aren't any.'

'That's also the danger of being a policeman. We all have a tendency to overthink things, even when there's a perfectly innocent explanation. But on this occasion...' Joseph reached into his pocket and took out his phone. 'There's something else I need you to look at. I need you to promise to keep it between us for now. I don't want to freak out Kate and Ellie until we know more.'

Dylan's brows knitted. 'Of course.'

Joseph showed him the photo of the symbol. 'This was scrawled on the serviette Martin Chambers used moments before he died. Remind you of anything?'

The professor stared at it, his gaze widening. 'Bloody Nora, that's almost identical to the Azrael mark you discovered in the Midwinter Butcher case.'

'Exactly, which begs the question, what the actual feck?'

His friend nodded. 'I'll need to do more research before I stick my neck out, but in this context, I'd say it was meant as a curse mark. Don't forget Azrael was also the Angel of Death.'

Joseph let out a slow breath. 'But Aaron Fearnley and Helen Edwards, who used it in the Midwinter Butcher case, are both long dead.'

'Indeed...' The professor's gaze tightened as he pondered the idea. 'That might suggest that one or both of them were part of a wider conspiracy.'

'Oh, I know, and if true, there could be a lot to unravel here.'

'In that case, with Iris's support, I'll dig further into the archives at the Bodleian Library. There may be other references to the use of this symbol in there somewhere. But on the face of it, someone wanted to give Chambers a death sigil.'

'Marked for murder, you mean?' Joseph muttered.

'In a word, yes, and it suggests, if the minister was murdered, they have a strong belief in the occult at the very least. Also, like the Midwinter Butcher case, maybe this was some sort of sacrifice as well.'

Joseph's gaze widened. 'That's all we need, some lunatic sacrificing politicians to some ancient deity.'

Dylan nodded. 'But regarding Kate and Ellie, as this might be linked somehow to the Midwinter Butcher case, my advice is to tell them when the moment is right. I know you mean well by not wanting to worry them, but they do have a right to know, Joseph.'

'Aye, I hear you, and you're right, of course. And I will. I just want to get a better idea of what we might be dealing with here.'

'Then let Iris and me see what we can dig up to help you with that.'

'Good man. As always, it's appreciated. I'll also pass on your comments about Wolfsbane to Rob and the other pathologist who's working with him to see if the two of them might have some thoughts. But the sooner the full toxicology screen comes back, the happier we'll all be.'

Dylan nodded, then cast a sideways look at his friend as he closed the Codex. 'Investigations aside, can I have your advice about something?'

'Anytime; what is it?'

'Iris has been bending my ear about getting something called a Well Man Check done.'

'Oh, you mean where they give you the once-over for any health issues?'

'Yes, basically it's an MOT for humans. But the thing is, I've never been a fan of going to the GP.'

'Which is every reason to go,' Joseph said, levelling a look at him, 'especially if you've been avoiding regular check-ups.'

'That's exactly what Iris keeps saying. She also keeps pointing out all the rich food I eat, saying it can't be good for me.'

'She might have a point there. You've never been one to cut back when it comes to cooking, or eating, or drinking for that matter.'

Dylan pulled a face. 'It's who I am, not to mention one of my great pleasures in life. So if a doctor's about to turn round and put me on a diet of lettuce and water, I think I'd rather jump off Magdalen Bridge and be done with it.'

'Hey, less of the drama there, my friend. There's nothing else going on I should know about, is there? You do feel okay?'

'Never better. But Iris keeps reminding me, not all conditions show symptoms until it's too late.'

A narrowboat chugged past on the far side of the canal, its diesel engine thrumming as Joseph took another sip of his coffee. 'She's not wrong. Don't forget, the only reason she wants you checked over is because she cares about you.'

'Or perhaps she's weighing up whether to take out a life insurance policy on me.'

A smile curled Joseph's mouth. 'That's a possibility too. I know you're nervous about what you might hear, but it's human nature to catastrophize a bit. The thing is, getting tested will almost certainly lift the weight off your shoulders when you get the all clear. Worst case, they find something, but then at least you'll know and can deal with it.'

'That's the problem. A big part of me would rather not. Ignorance is bliss and all that.'

'You know I'll never agree with that sort of philosophy. All I can tell you is I'm very grateful for my regular police medical assessments, and so is my family.'

'You're saying I should use you as a role model and do something about it?'

'I'm not sure I've ever been anyone's role model before.'

Dylan smiled. 'I wouldn't be so sure. You're a far greater inspiration than you realise, especially to young Megan.'

'I'll take your word for it.'

'You should. That aside, I suppose I'd better ring the GP's surgery and get myself checked in.'

'Good man.' Joseph raised his mug in a toast. 'Trust me, you'll feel better for it.'

'I certainly hope so.'

Joseph drained the last of his coffee. 'Anyway, I need to get my skates on and brief Chris about this whole political angle that's emerged.'

'Then don't let me stop you.' Dylan whistled softly for his dogs, who rose, tails wagging. With his dogs padding at his heels, he walked back to his boat, shoulders slightly bowed as though the weight of the world had settled there.

Shaking his head, Joseph headed inside *Tús Nua* to get ready for work, his mind on the case, and how Chris would react when he heard the news that Martin Chambers might have been his party's next leader. That cast the whole investigation in a very different light and now one with possible occult connections, as well.

CHAPTER NINE

THERE WERE a lot of tired-looking detectives in the incident room in St Aldates. On his arrival, the DI had quickly learnt he hadn't been the only officer up for most of the night. Because of the sheer number of people involved in the interviews, it had taken a Herculean effort from the investigating team to process them all. It was because of that, Chris, who'd had as little sleep as the rest of them, had ordered decent coffee for everyone from The Roasted Bean. He'd also bought every baked good they had, clearing them out, but in the process, making himself popular with the team. Detectives appreciated gestures like that when the pressure was really on.

Thanks to his boss's efforts, Joseph now munched on a rather good chocolate brownie as he scanned the evidence board, which remained noticeably blank considering the number of people interviewed. Hopefully, that would change once Chris surfaced from the meeting he was in and updated it with the information Joseph had briefed him about regarding a possible political motive for Chambers's murder.

After that, the DI had been busy getting himself up to speed with the others.

'So let me get this right; basically nothing useful came out of two hundred-plus witness statements?' Joseph said.

'Nobody noticed anything suspicious, if that's what you mean,' Ian replied. 'But Amy still has DFU going through all the phones, at least the ones handed over without a fuss. The hope is, one of them caught something useful in the background.'

'Such as someone helping themselves to Martin Chambers's smartwatch?' Megan asked, already moving in for a third brownie.

'Exactly.'

Megan gave them a thoughtful look. 'What still doesn't make sense is why take it at all, when the data is stored on the cloud?'

'Aye, I grant you that's odd,' Joseph said. 'Of course, it might just have been an opportunist thief picking up the watch after it fell off Chambers's wrist, rather than anything more suspicious.'

Sue looked over from her screen. 'That could be one explanation, apart from one small fact that I've literally just heard from DFU. Whoever took it powered it straight off, so they haven't been able to track it. Thanks to it being powered down, the cloud data for the period Chambers collapsed on stage wasn't synced.'

'But that's also what anyone with half a modicum of sense would have done, especially if they planned to wipe and sell it on,' Megan said.

'Just one. Once it would have been nice if our lives had been made a bit easier on an investigation,' Joseph muttered.

'We can but dream,' Ian said.

That elicited a smile from Joseph. 'Okay, so what about the person who served Martin Chambers his food? If he was poisoned, someone would have to make sure the toxin was slipped into his food or drink. A member of the waiting staff, maybe?'

'Actually, that's where the first hint something's off has come up,' Sue said. 'Not one of the waiting staff claims to have delivered Chambers his food. But there's still a kitchen docket for a steak with peppercorn sauce, and the head chef swears it was collected by a blonde waitress. Chambers's wife also vaguely remembers a blonde waitress with bobbed hair serving him.'

Joseph sat up. 'Now that sounds suspicious.'

'And it also narrows it down possibly to one of the waiting staff,' Megan said.

'You'd think so,' Sue said. 'But when we showed his wife photos of the two blonde waitresses on the team, she said neither of them looked like the woman she saw. Then she backtracked, saying she hadn't really been concentrating and might have misremembered. The thing is, the kitchen staff said the same thing.'

'And what about anyone else at the high table? Did they notice this mystery waitress?' Joseph asked.

'Nothing; probably too much champagne,' Ian said, then his eyes narrowed. 'Of course, it could have been his wife. She could have slipped something into his meal, then given us a red herring about the waitress. Or maybe the poison wasn't in the food at all. A poisoned umbrella tip, anyone?'

Sue shook her head at him. 'Seriously? You've maybe been watching one too many spy thrillers.'

'But we shouldn't rule anything out...' The man's words trailed away as Amy, Chris, and Derrick entered the room. The SIO clapped his hands, his face lined with tiredness.

'First off, I know it's been a long night for everyone, and I appreciate the effort you've all put in. But I'm pleased to announce Amy's team has unearthed something significant. Please take a look at the main screen, everyone.'

All eyes turned to the SOCO as she tapped the keyboard. A set of cropped, pixelated images filled the screen. Every shot showed the same woman, a blonde waitress with bobbed hair, her heavy makeup making her almost unrecognisable.

'As you can see, we now have confirmation the waitress who Joanna Chambers and others mentioned was indeed present at the dinner,' Amy said. Then she tapped again, bringing up a single photo of a couple posing with champagne.

'And they are?' someone asked.

'Just other guests, but look behind them.' Amy zoomed in on the photo. Over the man's shoulder, Martin Chambers could be seen at the high table, a grainy image of the blonde waitress in question now filled the screen. She was handing the minister a fresh serviette.

Surprised looks rippled across the room. Joseph's mind raced. 'So she also gave Chambers the death sigil.'

'That's certainly what it looks like.'

'So, what happened to her?' Megan asked.

'The Digital Forensics Unit, DFU, has been combing through CCTV in the surrounding area and came up with this,' Amy said. She tapped a keyboard, and the paused video filled the screen. 'This frame shows our waitress at eight-thirty p.m., just outside Christ Church College. But now, as you can see, she's changed into gym gear and is jogging away. Just another person exercising in Oxford. Unfortunately, this is the last footage we've had of the woman before she was lost from view heading down Poplar Walk towards the River Isis. I'm afraid all the cameras in the surrounding area have come up blank so far.'

'That might be explained if she had a boat waiting for her,' Joseph said.

'That's certainly a possibility,' Derrick said. 'We're going to put up notice boards on both embankments asking witnesses to come forward. Even without the confirmed poison in Chambers's system, this latest information seems to suggest some sort of foul play.'

'Any idea who this woman is?' Sue asked.

Amy shook her head. 'No matches on the databases. But the woman's heavy makeup was clearly designed to make using facial recognition more difficult in identifying her. The good news is, DFU worked through the night and digitally stripped it away using AI. They even generated hair colour variants in case she was wearing a wig.' She clicked the mouse.

A new image appeared on the screen. This time, the woman's face was pin-sharp, her distinctive dark eyes unmistakable without the war paint of heavy eye makeup. Amy clicked to another version, their waitress now with brunette hair.

'That's absolutely bloody incredible,' Ian said, voicing what everyone was thinking.

'Thanks, and I'll pass that on to the team,' Amy said with a smile as he pinned the variations of the generated photo on the incident board.

Derrick gave her an impressed look. 'Excellent work, both to you and DFU. This could lead to an important breakthrough. We'll get this image out across the news outlets and across social media as fast as possible. Someone will recognise her. Then we'll know who we're dealing with. The next step is working out the woman's motive. Why would she want Martin Chambers dead? Also, why slip him the Azrael symbol?'

'Which, apparently, is some sort of death sigil according to some research I did,' Joseph said.

As heads turned towards him, Chris and Megan both gave him a knowing look. They both realised that his so-called *research* basically entailed the DI talking to his neighbour.

'Okay, that is an interesting angle,' Derrick replied, looking as though he was taking the suggestion seriously. 'So not only might this woman have slipped some poison into his food, but she also left a calling card with this serviette stunt of hers.'

'Which then begs the question, why do that at all if she was going to poison him?' Megan said. 'To make a point? Also, and I know we're all thinking it, could this murder, if that's what it is, somehow be linked to the Midwinter Butcher case?'

'That does seem like a natural conclusion, so let's hear people's thoughts,' Chris asked.

Joseph had become very focused on that after his conversation with Dylan and had some ideas. 'Aaron Fearnley and Helen Edwards are dead, but we know they met through a dark web forum. It may be a long shot, but what if one of them— Helen would be my guess—might have come up with that whole idea of the Azrael symbol, or found it on the forum they both hung out on? Maybe someone there suggested it could be used as a death sigil, and a victim could be sacrificed to him? Don't forget, before Fearnley met Edwards, he hadn't used the Azrael symbol before then, suggesting she was the one who set him on that path.'

'So you're suggesting our mystery waitress might be linked to that same forum as well?' Chris asked.

'I'm just throwing ideas out there, but it's certainly worth considering,' Joseph replied, noticing the slight flicker in Amy's expression like a mask that had slipped slightly. Immediately, his suspicions were raised. She'd had a similar reaction when he'd discovered the Azrael mark on the napkin, and his mind was already racing towards an obvious conclusion.

If he had read the SOCO's unconscious response correctly, did that mean she knew something about this? Maybe Amy was also being selective in what evidence she revealed to the team. And if so, that also suggested a link between Chambers's death and the Night Watchmen. But then why was she being so helpful in pinning everything on the waitress?

Derrick nodded towards Joseph, actually looking impressed. 'Okay, we should seriously look into the possible connection of the Azrael symbol to both the Midwinter Butcher killings and Chambers's death.'

As murmurs of agreement rippled through the room, Joseph was struck by the contrast between Amy's reaction and how the big man actually sounded like a copper, rather than someone taking backhanders from the Night Watchmen. If there was a connection here to the crime syndicate, it seemed it was one he hadn't been briefed about by Kennan.

'So let's return to motives. We may have one,' Chris said. 'I've followed through on the information that Joseph unearthed. All I can say is that it would have been useful had Martin Chambers's party let us know this sooner. Anyway, to cut to the chase, it turns out the minister was very much in the running to take over as PM.'

Surprised looks were traded among the officers in the room.

Derrick's gaze zeroed in on Joseph. 'I don't suppose there's any need to ask where you got that particular political tip-off from?'

'Yes, Kate was very helpful and pointed me in the right direction,' Joseph replied, doing his best to keep his expression neutral. He noticed the grimaces traded among his colleagues as they braced for their DSU to explode. It was no secret in St Aldates that Derrick's breakup with Kate had been followed by her rapid reconciliation with Joseph. But if the team expected the big man to use that as a pretext to lay into the DI, they were about to be sorely disappointed.

'Right,' Derrick said, and that was all he said. His gaze swept across the room, daring anyone to smirk. Nobody seemed to have a death wish as they all made a show of making it look as though they had no idea of what he was on about.

Chris seized the opportunity to steer them back on track. 'With the possible political motive of wanting Chambers out of the way, combined with our mystery waitress and even with some possible connection to the occult, I would still say the likelihood is this is still a politically motivated murder.'

'If that's true, then it sounds like it needed considerable planning to pull off,' a detective in the room said.

Amy nodded. 'The lack of CCTV footage certainly supports that theory. The waitress knew exactly where to go to drop off the radar and where there was any camera coverage. Whoever she is, she was certainly organised and had planned everything in detail.'

Chris wrote *Chief Suspect* next to the waitress's image on the board, with *An interest in the occult* written beneath that. Under motive, he wrote one word, *Political?*

'So we're basically saying one of the rivals in his party who wanted the PM's job, paid this witch woman to assassinate their competition with poison?' Ian asked.

'As far-fetched as it sounds, it's something we must seriously consider,' Chris replied. 'For that reason, we'll need a comprehensive list from Whitehall of everyone in the running for the PM's job.'

'I think before we all get too carried away with this, we should remember that Chambers still could have just died from a natural heart attack,' Sue suggested.

'Maybe, but until toxicology proves otherwise, we're going to treat this as a murder investigation,' Chris said.

Derrick nodded. 'Make no mistake here, our collective necks are on the line, people. The worst thing we could be accused of right now is being overzealous. That's far better than having an accusation of dereliction of duty levelled at us. And if that happens, heads will roll.'

The words were for the whole team, but Joseph felt the weight of Derrick's stare linger on him. *For feck's sake, here we go again*, he thought.

Doctor Jacobs hurried in and whispered urgently to Chris, who nodded as his expression became grim.

Chris turned back to the room. 'Doctor Jacobs has significant information to brief us on.'

Rob stepped forward, paper in hand. 'I wouldn't normally rush over like this, but this is important enough for me to deliver it in person. Incredibly, the toxicology report is already back.'

'That was fast. I thought you said it would take at least five days,' Chris said.

'You can thank Professor Whitaker for that. It seems being President of the Royal College of Pathologists has its advantages. He leaned on the lab to expedite their findings by pulling an all-nighter.'

'There seems to be a lot of that in the last twelve hours,' Joseph said, nodding towards Amy to keep up the pretence he wasn't onto her.

She almost smiled back at him. 'So, Rob, what did you find?' she asked.

'To start with, my worst fears have been confirmed. Martin Chambers was definitely poisoned.'

Knowing nods were exchanged around the room after everything they'd just heard.

'So what poison was it, Rob?' Megan asked.

The pathologist smiled at her. 'Yes, that was quite a challenge to identify. It turns out more than one substance was used and worked together in combination to kill Martin Chambers. The first of which was aconite.'

Joseph instantly remembered Dylan's words from earlier that morning. 'That's monkshood, isn't it?'

Rob looked seriously impressed. 'That's right. It's also known as wolfsbane. It's among the most lethal plants in Britain. Just a few milligrams can stop the heart by shutting down the nervous system. The symptoms are vomiting, paralysis, and then cardiac arrest, well within an hour of ingestion. But our poisoner was very clever here. If Chambers had been given aconite alone, he would have known something was wrong quite quickly. A burning sensation in the mouth, pins and needles, along with stomach cramps. It is not exactly a subtle poison.'

'But according to his wife, apart from vomiting and feeling tired beforehand, he didn't complain of those other symptoms before collapsing,' one of the detectives said.

'Exactly, and that's where the second substance came in. Clonidine, an old-school blood pressure drug. It lowered his heart rate and made him drowsy, which correlates with what his wife told us. The ingenious part is the poisoner knew exactly the right dose to suppress the early symptoms of aconite.'

The doctor looked out at the detectives. 'I need to be very clear here, this was a calculated murder, by someone who knew exactly what they were doing. When Martin Chambers started to experience the early symptoms of the poison, he would have had no idea it was the first sign he was dying. But from the moment Chambers ingested that lethal cocktail, he was on a one-way street, heading towards a cardiac arrest. The very clever part is that this combination was designed to mimic a natural heart attack. And neither aconite nor clonidine would show up in a standard toxicology screen. You have to go the extra mile looking for them, which is exactly what we did in this instance.'

Joseph's gaze shifted to the brunette version of the waitress's photo projected on the screen. *Who the hell are you?* he thought.

'So we're clearly dealing with an expert in poisons?' Chris asked.

'Without question,' Rob said. 'That level of precision doesn't come from the internet either. Whoever did this had clinical knowledge. A doctor, a pharmacist, perhaps even, dare I say it, a toxicologist.'

A chill ran through Joseph at the thought of that. And the murderer, presumably the waitress, also had some sort of interest in the occult. It was an unlikely combination, but then again, he knew plenty of scientists who were also people of faith. The only difference here was that this woman also subscribed to a much darker belief, one where sacrifices might be made to the Angel of Death.

'Okay, thank you, everyone. There's a lot to consider here, especially the possible connection to the Midwinter Butcher case,' Derrick said. 'Now I just need to brief you about the news conference we're going to be holding later today. I think, in light of the AI-generated images we have of our waitress, we need to enlist the help of the public in tracking her down as quickly as possible. But I think at this point we should keep any mention of the occult out of it. We don't want the press to jump to the conclusion that there might be a link to the Midwinter Butcher until we're ready to make that conclusion ourselves.'

Everyone nodded.

Derrick spoke for another five minutes, and the meeting broke soon after that, the detectives spilling out into the corridor in twos and threes, some heading for coffee, others for a smoke. Joseph waited until Chris headed out of the room and followed him into the corridor.

'Chris, there's something we need to talk about.'

'Go on,' the SIO said, turning to him.

Joseph dropped his voice to a whisper. 'Okay, this is just my instinct talking here, but I'm pretty sure that Amy would have preferred us not to find the Azrael sigil on that serviette at the crime scene. In fact, I'd go as far as to say, if I hadn't come across it, it might not have come to light at all.'

Chris swore under his breath. 'We both know what that means.'

'Aye, we do.'

For a moment, the SIO said nothing, just rubbed the back of his neck as though trying to work a knot loose. Finally, he gave a small nod. 'Okay, leave it with me. But this occult aspect does bring a whole different angle to this, Joseph. If the Night Watchmen are involved in something like that, this will be news to everyone involved in the NCA investigation.'

'No doubt. As for Derrick, my instinct is that this is all news to him as well.'

'I agree. Maybe you have to be part of the inner sanctum like Kennan to be privy to that sort of thing.'

Joseph nodded. 'That would make sense. Also, I'm having Dylan and Iris look deeper into this Azrael connection. If they come up with anything, I'll let you know.'

'Taking the initiative there again, I see.'

'You know me.' Joseph shrugged.

'Indeed, I do,' Chris replied with a smile.

'There's one last thing. It was Dylan who was looking through an ancient book of poisons, suggesting Chambers might have been drugged with monkshood before it was confirmed by Rob just now. He said the few symptoms listed fit that poison, although not completely. Then again, he didn't know about the second drug being used to suppress the symptoms of monkshood.'

'You think that choice of poison might be significant then?'

'I'm not sure yet, but it's not exactly a run-of-the-mill poison. Also, when combined with an ancient symbol for Azrael, it has to make you wonder.'

Chris slowly nodded. 'It does, doesn't it?'

Joseph gave him a grim look. He could already sense that whatever shadow from the Midwinter Butcher case stretched over this case, it was going to be a significant one. The question was what form that would take. He thought they'd long ago put the Midwinter Butcher case to bed.

CHAPTER TEN

THE BRIEFING ROOM was packed with journalists, the air heavy with heat that no amount of St Aldates' limited air-con could manage to cool down. Outside, Oxford sweltered in the grip of a sticky May afternoon, and the number of people crammed in the room only magnified the temperature. Jackets had been stripped off and sleeves rolled up, ties loosened, but sweat still shone on brows. Camera tripods sat at the back ready to capture the briefing, whilst at the front, Chief Kennan, Derrick, and Chris sat together with a large screen behind them displaying the Thames Valley Police logo.

To Joseph's ear, the restless murmur of voices around him sounded a lot like a hive about to swarm.

'This is one hell of a large turnout,' Megan said to him, as the two officers stood at the back of the room.

'Aye, but are you really surprised? The news conference about the death of a politician is always going to draw a crowd. The fact that Westminster hasn't already released a statement categorically confirming Martin Chambers died from natural causes will have set a lot of tongues wagging. Whatever else journalists are, they are very good at joining the dots up.'

'Do I hear you disparaging my profession?' Kate's voice came from behind the DI.

He turned to see her standing there with an eyebrow raised.

Megan grinned. 'You're so busted.'

'Hey, I was only saying you're very good at doing your collective jobs,' Joseph said to Kate. But then he saw none other than his least favourite tabloid reporter, Ricky Holt. The weasel-faced man had just walked in and, spotting them, headed straight over.

'This looks cosy,' Ricky said in his nasal voice. 'Trying to get an inside scoop from your ex-husband, Kate?'

She glowered at him. 'You know I never do that until things are made public by the police.'

Ricky sneered. 'Yeah, right. Thankfully, I've got my own sources for this case. How about it, DI Stone? Care to make a comment about the suspicious circumstances surrounding Chambers's death?'

Joseph narrowed his gaze at the festering armpit of a man. 'What suspicious circumstances?'

'Isn't it right that the minister was actually murdered?'

Megan and Joseph both stared at him, but it was Kate who spoke first.

'Ignore him. He's just fishing. Typical tactic from someone like you, Holt.'

He sneered again. 'I don't hear either of the detectives rushing to deny it.' The man gestured at the room of assembled reporters. 'This isn't exactly the setup for a natural death state-ment, is it? Tell me I'm wrong.'

'I'm afraid we can't comment on anything ahead of this press conference,' Megan said, her tone calm and professional.

That was in distinct contrast to how Joseph was feeling. He wanted nothing more than to tell this rodent of a human being to *feck right off*.

'So you're not going to confirm his death was allegedly the work of terrorists?' Holt pressed on.

Joseph's gaze sharpened. 'Where did you hear that?'

The tabloid journalist rubbed the side of his nose. 'Like I said, I have my sources.'

The DI resisted the urge to grab this apology of a man by the scruff of the neck. Instead, he tried to follow his colleague's lead and kept his voice measured. 'If you know something, you need to tell us.'

Ricky's smirk grew wider. 'If you scratch my back, I'll scratch yours.'

'Are you telling us you're deliberately withholding information that could help us with our enquiries?' Megan asked, her tone harder now.

Ricky held up his hands. 'Hey, don't get your knickers in a twist, darling. Like Kate said, I was just fishing.'

'Well, you can go and fish somewhere else,' Kate said, raising her eyebrows.

'You're really no fun,' he said, giving a backward wave as he slouched toward a seat at the back.

Kate shook her head. 'Don't mind him, we all know what he's like.'

But even as Joseph nodded, his instinct told him the journalist might really know something. But before he could give that any more thought, Derrick's voice, amplified by the speakers, filled the hot, restless room.

'Could everybody please take their seats for the briefing?'

Kate nodded to Joseph and Megan before grabbing a spare chair.

The two detectives remained standing at the back as Chief Kennan began speaking. 'As you're all aware, we've asked you here today in relation to the tragic death of our local minister, the Honourable Martin Chambers. He passed away while attending a charity dinner at Christ Church College at the weekend. It is normal procedure to launch an investigation under such circumstances. Now I'll hand it over to my colleague, Detective Superintendent Derrick Walker, and also the SIO for this case, DCI Chris Faulkner. They will brief you on the investigation's initial findings and also make an appeal for your help in this matter.'

The background chatter in the room grew louder with whispered conversations.

Derrick leaned toward the mic. 'When a public figure dies unexpectedly, foul play has to be ruled out. At first, everything pointed toward this being a case of a natural heart attack. However, the autopsy has revealed Martin Chambers was actually murdered.'

Shutters clicked and flashguns fired as cameras caught the moment. Joseph noticed Ricky's smug look, his photographer throwing him an, *I told you so* glance.

Hands shot up, and a barrage of questions was hurled at the DSU.

'We'll take questions at the end,' Derrick said firmly. 'SIO Faulkner will now brief you on what our investigation has discovered so far.'

Chris nodded, picking up the remote for the screen behind him. 'Initial lab tests have revealed the presence of a poison in Martin Chambers's system that he ingested at the charity dinner at Christ Church College. The substance in question is called aconite, otherwise known as monkshood or wolfsbane.' He glanced at his notes before continuing. 'This is a rare plant-based poison that affects the way the heart functions, causing it to beat irregularly until it shuts down. It was this substance that killed the minister.'

More flashes lit the room as one journalist's voice cut through the hubbub.

'How was he given this poison?' a woman called out.

'I'll take this one question, but please reserve the rest for the end of this briefing. The aconite appears to have been slipped into the food consumed by Chambers at the charity dinner. The autopsy found trace amounts in his stomach contents. Based on the analysis, this confirms it was delivered orally.'

'Do you know who did that to him?' Ricky Holt asked.

'As I just said, we'll be taking questions at the end,' Chris replied, batting the question away. 'We're still at a very early stage of our enquiries, but there is one person we are very keen to speak to in connection with this matter.' He clicked the remote, and the screen filled with one of the clearer photos of the waitress.

'The woman you're seeing on the screen was the one who served Chambers his food that night,' the SIO continued.

The air in the room seemed to thicken as every eye fastened on the blurred image on the screen.

'It turns out she was an impostor posing as a member of the waiting staff, who managed to slip her way into the charity dinner. At this moment, we do not know this woman's name, and we urgently need to speak to her.'

Once again, a dozen questions were fired at Chris. He ignored all of them and gestured for silence.

'This is where we need the public's help. As you can see from the photo, the woman was wearing heavy makeup, no doubt in an attempt to disguise her appearance beyond her being a Caucasian female. However, thanks to the efforts of our Digital Forensics Unit, they have created a digital image where her makeup has been removed. They have also created variations of her hairstyle and colour in case she was wearing a wig. This should make the identification of this individual far more straightforward.'

Chris clicked the button, and a series of photo-realistic

images filled the screen, one after another, the same slightly oval face but with different hair. Each was a portrait-like shot, the woman staring directly into the lens.

To Joseph, it almost felt as though she was looking out at all of them, a challenge in her dark eyes.

Catch me if you can, he thought.

Megan leaned closer and murmured, her voice hushed beneath the whir of cameras. 'The Digital Forensics team has really done an incredible job creating those images.'

'Aye, but the proof will be if anyone actually recognises her,' Joseph whispered back.

Chris pressed the remote again, and grainy footage flickered onto the screen of the waitress leaving Christ Church and heading down Poplar Walk towards the Isis, wearing gym gear. The evening light still had the last wisps of gold in it, soft tree shadows stretching long across the college lawns.

'This is the last footage we have of her leaving Christ Church around eight-thirty p.m., a good thirty minutes before Chambers died. She was not picked up again by any of the cameras we have access to. That suggests she may have changed her appearance, or possibly used a boat to escape on the River Isis. That is the first area where members of the public may be able to help us.'

His gaze locked on to one of the lenses of the TV cameras broadcasting this news conference live. 'Did you see this woman posing as a waitress at the charity dinner, or walking down Poplar Walk, or do you know where she went next? Or do you recognise this woman and can tell us who she is? Please do not approach her as she could be dangerous. We've set up a hotline, so please contact us with any information that may assist us with this critical investigation.'

The hotline number glowed across the screen, accompanied by a ripple of camera shutters.

Chief Kennan leaned in. 'Okay, we'll take questions now.'

Out of all the hands waving in the muggy air, Joseph was most surprised to see her nod toward Ricky Holt. The tabloid man shot a self-satisfied look around at his colleagues, preening in the glow of the unexpected opportunity. Chris and Derrick frowned, but the woman had no idea what a gobshite he was.

Looking like a cat with cream, Ricky raised his chin. 'Have you got any opinion whether this incident might be terrorist related?'

Joseph braced for the dismissive rebuttal that should have followed. Instead, Kennan solemnly nodded. 'With a death like this, we certainly cannot rule that out.'

'In that case, have you heard of Iron Dawn? You might want to start with them.'

Megan shot Joseph a confused look. 'Who?'

'Never heard of them,' Joseph replied. From the blank faces of the other journalists, he realised he wasn't alone.

'Do you have any information on this group?' Chief Kennan asked, almost like she was following a practiced script.

In answer, Ricky raised his phone high. 'This video was just posted to social media.' He tapped play and cranked the volume up.

Even without seeing the screen, Joseph heard the words clearly enough.

'We see you now,' a man's heavily synthesised voice intoned. 'Year after year, face after face, you have stood behind your podiums and told us everything was fine. That justice was working. That the economy was stable. That we the people were being served...'

The words rolled on, venomous and filling the hot room. Every reporter leaned forward, eyes fixed on their phones as they scrambled to find the same online manifesto.

Megan was already there, showing her screen to Joseph. 'Bloody hell, this looks legit. It was posted five minutes ago.'

'Jesus H. Christ on a bike,' Joseph muttered. He wasn't surprised to see that Chris, Derrick, and Kennan had their heads bent together, talking urgently.

Chris straightened up and addressed the room. 'We obviously need time to process this new information. On that note, we'll draw this news conference to a close.' He gestured at Ricky Holt. 'We would like a word with you.'

'Of course you would.' Holt smirked at the other journalists, revelling in the attention.

Chris nodded across the room to Joseph.

Already moving, the DI made his way through the press pack toward Holt. 'If you would like to follow me, we have a cosy interview room with your name on it.'

'As long as you're nice to me,' the journalist replied. 'And there better be tea and proper biscuits.'

Joseph was ready to tell him exactly where he could stick a biscuit, but Megan cut in smoothly. 'I have a packet of chocolate Bourbons in my desk, if that will do?'

'I suppose. But I prefer a chocolate Hobnob. Could you be a dear and pop across the road to that supermarket on the corner and grab me some?'

Megan tilted her head, eyes narrowing. 'In a word, *no*.'

Ricky grinned. 'Can't blame a man for trying.'

Joseph fought to keep his annoyance in check, although the urge to wipe the supercilious look off the gobshite's face was almost overwhelming. 'If you would like to follow me, Ricky.'

'Well, as you asked so nicely...' He held out his wrists in mock surrender.

Joseph was painfully aware that cameras were turned toward them, hunting for B-roll to spin into the breaking story. And among those who would eventually see the footage would be Martin's widow, Joanna Chambers. That thought kept him steady, even as his patience rapidly began to thin. Ignoring Holt's mock salute, he simply gestured to the door.

'Please follow us.'

'I'd be delighted to,' Ricky replied, waving theatrically to the room as he trailed the detectives out.

CHAPTER ELEVEN

KATE WAS NOWHERE to be seen when Joseph finally got back to *Tús Nua* later that evening. A quick check of his messages confirmed what he'd already suspected. She was still hard at work, writing up the breaking news story about Iron Dawn being connected to the minister's poisoning, and would be back late.

But with all the serious implications of the case, even though he had already spoken at length with Megan, it still circled in his head. If a terrorist group really had been behind Martin Chambers's death, the whole investigation inevitably was going to be taken to a whole other level. Chris had already indicated to Joseph that the National Crime Agency would be formally brought in to liaise with their investigation. He could not help but see the irony in that. Technically, they already had an agent assigned to the case, albeit one working undercover. Chris.

All this was still swirling in his thoughts as he finished the last of his falafel and salad takeaway from the excellent Chick Pea restaurant in Oxford. Tux looked up from the pillow he'd claimed as his own, ears pricking a moment before a knock came from the cabin door.

'Are you still up?' Dylan's voice called from outside.

'I am indeed.'

'Good. I need a friend's ear to bend. I also have some of that *Copper in the Clouds* gin left to help lubricate the tonsils.'

'Then feel free to bend away,' Joseph replied, popping the last falafel into his mouth and heading to the door to open it.

One look at his friend's drawn expression told him there was something amiss. Even his dogs, White Fang and Max, seemed subdued, perhaps picking up on their master's mood. For once, rather than bounding in, they padded into the cabin quietly. They barely exchanged a sniff with Tux, who gave them an expectant look for their usual boisterous greeting. Instead, both dogs settled beneath the table.

Joseph took this in, his gaze tightening on the professor. 'Jesus, just how bad is it?'

Dylan managed a faint smile. 'Oh, I've had better days. But putting that aside for the moment, I saw the news conference about your investigation. Flipping Nora, I didn't see that one coming.'

Realising Dylan would get to the real reason for his visit when he was good and ready, Joseph simply nodded. 'Aye, you're not wrong. So take the weight off and join me in a glass of the good stuff you have there.' He gestured at the gin bottle cradled in the professor's grip.

'Actually, I'd better stick to a herbal tea if you have any.'

Joseph's jaw did not quite hit the deck, but his mouth did drop open. Dylan refusing a glass of gin was unheard of.

'Okay, I have some of Kate's mint tea bags in the cupboard, if that will suit?'

Dylan didn't quite shudder, but it wasn't far off either. 'I suppose that will have to do.'

A short while later, both men were seated in the cabin, Dylan drinking his mint tea with as much enthusiasm as a man licking a nettle. Joseph, on the other hand, very much enjoyed the *Copper in the Clouds*, almost as much as he had the first time he'd tasted it.

'You must all have been blindsided by that revelation from the journalist about the terrorist group's involvement,' Dylan said, gazing at Tux as he fussed his head.

'That's one way of putting it. Of course, Ricky Holt, the scummiest of scumbags, waited until the press conference to show his hand, instead of talking to us beforehand.'

'He obviously wanted maximum publicity for himself as much as the story.'

'Aye, you're not wrong there. There's something else I should tell you. Off the record, of course.'

Dylan nodded. 'Fire away.'

'When we interviewed Holt, he refused to reveal the source who tipped him off about Iron Dawn's manifesto being released online.'

'That doesn't surprise me. You know how protective journalists can be.'

'Indeed, and including Kate at times. But in Ricky's case, when Megan and I interviewed him, I got the distinct impression he'd known about Iron Dawn's existence for longer than he was letting on. I honestly wouldn't be surprised if the man had known about that terrorist group for weeks.'

'In other words, long before Martin Chambers was murdered?'

'Exactly. And if I'm right, maybe our local minister would still be alive if that toerag had come forward sooner. Not that we can prove he was deliberately sitting on the story.'

'Even if he was, maybe he didn't think there was any credibility to it?' Dylan suggested.

Joseph scoffed. 'Then you don't know Ricky Holt. We're talking about a man who rarely lets the truth get in the way of a headline. He has the moral code of a street rat. Other people's pain and misery are what that bastard thrives on.'

'Then he obviously has no scruples.' Dylan shook his head. 'Anyway, in relation to that, I did a bit of digging, but haven't been able to find anything out about Iron Dawn. Whoever they are, they seem to be a newly formed group.'

'There's absolutely nothing about them on Holmes 2 either. Whoever these people are, they have managed to fly under everyone's radar, including the NCA's.'

'You don't think it's some group taking credit for something they didn't actually do?' Dylan asked.

'No, because they mentioned the poisoning angle before the press conference began. Remember, only the investigating team, and people like your good self, had any idea that a toxin might be involved in Martin Chambers's death.'

'Have you considered a leak then?'

'That's certainly a possibility. If the Night Watchmen could infiltrate our ranks, who knows how many of our officers have lost their moral compass. But for now, we have to assume this terrorist organisation is the real deal.'

'So where exactly does that leave your investigation?'

'Good question. The only lead we have is the waitress. Find her and we can start to piece together just how real this threat is to other ministers.'

Dylan took another sip of his tea, grimaced again, and set the mug down. 'I assume security is going to be stepped up around every member of Parliament?'

'I'm out of the loop about what's being discussed there, but I would imagine so. The problem is, you can only protect people from so much. After all, our very own local MP was poisoned.'

'And how can you guarantee anything a minister consumes has been fully vetted first?'

Joseph smiled. 'Maybe put them on a strict diet of Maccy

D's. But talking of poisons, you were on the money there. It turns out it was monkshood, after all.'

Dylan's brow furrowed. 'But why didn't he exhibit all the symptoms?'

'Because the poisoner used clonidine to suppress them. Doctor Jacobs believes whoever it was knew exactly what they were doing.'

The professor's frown deepened. 'That doesn't exactly sound like your average terrorist.'

'That's pretty much what Rob said as well. He believes our poisoner has to have some specialist medical training of some sort.'

Dylan slowly nodded. 'Someone who understood exactly how to mask symptoms until it was too late.' He took another sip of his tea and pulled another face.

'Right, let me empty that out for you and give you a glass of this excellent gin,' Joseph said.

The professor shook his head. 'I really better not.'

'Why, have you had one too many wee drops tonight?'

'I wish...' The professor dropped his gaze to Tux.

Joseph scowled at his friend. 'Okay, out with it. You've had a face like a wet day at Limerick ever since you stepped on board.'

Dylan raised his eyes. 'It's to do with my health.'

'Oh Jesus, tell me what it is already!'

'Okay... Whilst I was waiting for my Well Man check with my GP, Iris insisted I should try to get one of those instant cholesterol checks at the local chemist's in the meantime. Apparently, I have elevated levels.'

Joseph felt the tension building up around his shoulders let go. 'That doesn't sound too bad, does it? After all, I've heard that statins are very good for getting that sort of thing under control.'

'I'm not going to take any form of drug unless as a last resort. To be honest, I would have carried on as I was, regardless, high cholesterol or not. After all, life is meant to be lived. Food and drink, as you well know, are among my greatest pleasures in life. Take those away from me and I might as well end it all now.'

Joseph held up his hands. 'Whoa, I think you may be being a touch overdramatic here. After all, it just means cutting down on certain foods, doesn't it?'

'Yes, far less cheese to start with, but the list from the pharmacist went on and on. Cut back on all sorts of things, from not surprisingly things like butter, but all the way to white rice. I mean, how am I meant to make my famous mushroom risotto if I can't use that? Then, of course, there's cutting back on alcohol.' Dylan gave the bottle of gin a forlorn look.

'I thought I heard red wine was good for you?'

'Yes, it is, but in moderation. The pharmacist almost seemed to take great delight in telling me how too much can raise my triglyceride levels, which leads to fat building up in the bloodstream.'

'So in other words, you need to cut back a bit, and maybe swap out some ingredients. Worst case, if that doesn't work, you'll need to start taking statins. Is that about the sum of it?'

'Yes, but who knows what else they'll find when they run a full battery of tests on this old, and admittedly, slightly abused, body of mine.'

Suddenly, Joseph knew exactly where all this angst was coming from. 'Basically, you're telling me that you're starting to feel a bit mortal there, Dylan?'

'Exactly, my friend. Until now, I was happy to carry on as I was. Ignorance was bliss and all that. But now that I have Iris in my life, I need to actually start taking care of myself. I know I sound dramatic,' Dylan continued, his voice catching, 'but the truth is, I'm bloody scared.'

Joseph was surprised to see tears welling up in the corners of his friend's eyes. He reached over and patted the professor's arm. 'And she wouldn't be the only one who would be heart-broken if you checked out too soon, and that goes for me and my entire family.'

That was all that Dylan needed to tip him over the edge. The tears were in free fall now as he fished out a silk handker-chief from a pocket and wiped them away. The dogs gazed up at their master with worried eyes. Even Tux looked concerned.

'Sorry, I swear I get more emotional as I get older,' the professor said.

'Can you stop already with the use of that fecking word, *old*? If you don't want to age yourself mentally, you can start by dropping that from your flipping vocabulary.'

'It's a bit hard when I've seen written in black and white that I've a fifteen percent chance of a heart attack over the next ten years.'

'Okay, which is not zero, but is hardly an enormous number either.'

'You think I'm overreacting then?'

'Maybe just a little bit, but you wouldn't be the first one to go off the deep end over something like this. But if anyone can come up with a cholesterol-lowering diet, it's you, my friend. True, maybe you'll need to cut down on the gin a bit, but that's surely a price worth paying, isn't it?'

'It is.' Dylan took a long breath. 'Sorry for all this emotion.'

Joseph patted his arm. 'Don't you worry, we're all allowed to be human occasionally. Anyway, I'll have a word with Kate. Her dad has suffered from high cholesterol, and his wife is all over cholesterol-friendly food options. I'm sure she can pass on some tips to you.'

'That would be really helpful. I also intend to head to the library tomorrow and start my own research.'

'Good man, you'll be on top of this before you know it.'

'I hope so. Anyway, as regards the investigation, whilst at the library I'll also have a look into that poison combination to see if I can unearth anything useful because it does sound unusual.'

'Good luck with that. So far, we've not found it used before in recent times.'

'Which is intriguing itself. That aside, have you considered the psychological aspect to all this?'

'What do you mean?'

'I mean, doesn't it strike you as all a bit unnecessary? If the poisoner, assuming it was that waitress, came up with such a clever poison combination, why not give Martin Chambers something far more straightforward? That would have killed him just as effectively.'

'Maybe she was deliberately trying to mask the symptoms until Chambers had started to deliver his speech, which was being streamed online.'

'I suppose that could be one explanation, but there are slow-working poisons out there. This just seems almost like someone wanted to flaunt their skill with poisons,' Dylan replied.

Joseph's gaze widened. 'You're not wrong. One thing that's becoming clearer by the second is that the waitress is the key to everything.'

Dylan nodded. 'Then let us hope you find her as quickly as possible.'

Joseph looked past him, out through to the fading light of the day. 'Aye,' he murmured. 'For all our sakes.'

CHAPTER TWELVE

When Joseph arrived at work later that morning, the first thing he noticed was the number of faces he didn't recognise in the incident room.

'Who are the new bodies?' he asked as he sat at the desk next to Megan, and opposite Ian and Sue.

'The boys and girls from the NCA have come to join us, now that it looks like Martin Chambers's death is terrorist related,' Sue said.

Joseph couldn't help but cast a glance towards Chris. He was currently deep in conversation with a woman in front of the evidence board they were studying together.

'So they're taking over the investigation like they did with the Daryl Manning case?' he asked as he deposited his bag beneath the desk.

'Not this time round,' Megan replied. 'Apparently, it's all hands to the pump on this one, and they'll be working alongside us.'

'So who's in charge of this investigation now?'

'That's a good question,' Sue replied. 'I don't see the boss being happy to relinquish control of the case.'

'Then perhaps they'll just have to learn to play nicely together,' Ian said, grinning.

The SIO clapped his hands. 'Everyone, if I could have your attention for an update. First of all, I just wanted to introduce Emma Lawson from the NCA. She and I will be jointly running this investigation. Emma, you wanted to say a few words and brief them from your side.'

Her penetrating gaze swept over the team, seeming to linger a moment on Joseph, before moving on. The DI guessed she was roughly in her early forties, her dark blonde hair scraped back in a no-nonsense bun.

'Hi, everyone, you've probably already met some of my team, who will be working alongside you,' Emma said. 'I just want to make it clear we're here to assist you, rather than step on any toes.' She nodded to Chris, who smiled.

'Seems they won't be getting into a pissing contest then,' Ian whispered.

He was rewarded with an elbow to his arm from Sue, who scowled at him.

'But I wanted you to know that our main focus is on this new terrorist group who have claimed responsibility, Iron Dawn,' Emma continued. 'They may, of course, just be opportunists looking to extort maximum publicity for their own cause. There's a lot we can't tell you as the investigation is of a very sensitive nature at this stage. But what I can share, though, is that there is evidence to suggest that we're dealing with a very professional operation. My team has been trying to locate where their manifesto originated. You can probably guess what happened when we did that.'

'They were all bogus burner accounts?' Megan asked.

Emma gave the DC an impressed look. 'Exactly, although these weren't exactly run-of-the-mill. Someone put a lot of effort into setting them up.' She picked up the remote and clicked through a series of images.

Joseph took in the photos of the normal sort of thing he would expect to see on a real account. Men and women generally having a good time, the shots of pets, and the inevitable images of food. Nothing to raise any suspicion.

'Notice anything unusual about the posts?' Emma asked.

'Looks like a fairly typical feed to me,' Sue said.

'Exactly, and that's the whole point. At first, we assumed they'd just scraped the images from legitimate accounts, but it turns out that every single image you've just seen was AI-generated. Then, just to make sure they wasted as much of our time as possible chasing dead ends, they even spoofed the geolocation data everywhere from Oxford to Bristol, and we even located some in France.'

'That seems like a lot of trouble to go to for fake accounts, so why bother?' Joseph asked.

'Because we suspect we're just scratching the tip of a very significant iceberg here. These accounts were used to like extremist political posts, helping to amplify their message. Luckily for us, someone in Iron Dawn got sloppy, and there was cross-posting from another of these bot accounts. It seems that Iron Dawn is linked to a serious attempt to undermine democracy in this country. Their specific group could be the activist wing of a wider group, which is taking its mission to the next level.'

'So we're not just talking about a few random nutters here?' Ian asked.

'Our job would be much easier if we were,' Emma replied. 'But unfortunately, this seems to be a very slick and organised group who's decided to make their existence public with the murder of Martin Chambers. That's why we need to take their threat to carry out further assassinations very seriously indeed. That's where the focus of my team's efforts will be. However, the woman who posed as the waitress is, without a doubt, a key person of interest in all of this. If we can arrest her, we have a good chance to stop this plot in its tracks, hence our presence here. Anyway, please feel free to discuss this with me or any member of my team. We really are here to help in any way we can. Thank you, everyone.' Emma nodded to Chris.

'Okay, let's get back to digging through all those leads from the hotline, which is already heading past five hundred,' he said.

As everyone returned to looking at their screens, Joseph wasn't totally unsurprised to see the SIO heading in his direction.

'Joseph, can I just pick your brain for a moment about something?' Chris said.

'Of course.' He shrugged at Megan, who gave him a questioning look as he followed the boss out the door.

The DI was even less surprised to find Emma Lawson waiting for them in one of the meeting rooms. Chris closed the door behind them.

Emma extended her hand. 'Joseph, it's good to finally put a face to a name.'

'Hopefully, you've only been hearing about the good stuff,' he replied, shaking her hand.

'You wish,' Chris said, winking at him as they both sat. 'Anyway, it won't surprise you, Joseph, that Emma and I know each other from the agency.'

'I had sort of imagined that would be the case, not that I think anyone would have guessed.'

'That's good to hear,' Emma replied. 'The last thing I want to do is blow Chris's cover, especially when we're getting so close to a resolution with the Night Watchmen investigation.'

Joseph raised his eyebrows at Chris. 'You are?'

'Yes. We're finally realising just how ambitious their agenda is, and it may be directly related to this latest investigation.' Chris's gaze tightened on the DI.

Joseph stared back at him. 'Shite, you're not suggesting they really are behind the assassination of Chambers, are you?'

'We're not sure yet. Do you remember I mentioned that the NCA had uncovered links to a specific politician?'

'Of course, but you didn't say who it was.'

'If you watch this, it should become clearer.' Emma pressed play and handed Joseph her tablet. 'It's a statement from Marcus Blackwood about Chambers's death.'

'You're saying he's your man?'

'That's what our information suggests, although so far we still have no hard evidence. Anyway, you should watch his statement.'

'But I've already seen this,' Joseph said, as he took the tablet.

'Not this one, you haven't,' Chris said. 'It was only recorded this morning from outside his home near Chipping Norton.'

The DI found himself watching a news item on the BBC. Blackwood was standing outside an old red brick and timber manor-style house, with ivy curling up many of the leaded glass windows. The whole building exuded age.

'You all know that security has long been a key issue for me, both domestically and overseas,' Blackwood was saying. 'For too long now, we have sat back and not been proactive enough. The tragic death of Martin Chambers underlines why that has to change. We mustn't just root out these despicable people, but we must also have the courage to go after the ideology that breeds them. There can be no compromise with extremism. The British people are tired of excuses. It's time we stopped simply reacting to terror and started preventing it. This is going to be one of our key pledges in the upcoming general election.' He looked straight into the camera lens. 'You all deserve more, and I intend to be the one to give it to you.'

The video ended, and Joseph handed the tablet back to Emma, giving her and Chris a questioning look. 'Are you trying to tell me that Marcus Blackwood is linked to the Night Watchmen?'

'That's what we believe,' Emma replied. 'As is often the case, we followed the money trail. A large proportion of the syndicate's funds seemed to have found their way from an offshore bank account into a Swiss one.'

Joseph blew his cheeks out. 'I thought they were meant to be untraceable?'

In response, Emma just raised her eyebrows at him.

'But of course, you're the NCA,' he added.

'Let's just say, we have our ways,' Chris said.

Joseph nodded. 'Okay, but what was this business Marcus said about an upcoming election?'

'You really haven't been watching the news, have you?' Chris said.

'I've been a bit busy.'

'In that case, you probably missed the statement the PM made last night. She called a snap election for next month,' Emma said.

'But I thought she was going to step aside, and Martin Chambers was the frontrunner for her job? Before his untimely death, of course.'

'Exactly. With her successor out of the picture, it's created a power vacuum in their party, one the PM seems to have seized upon as an opportunity. They are already experiencing a temporary bounce in the polls, and to head off another leadership challenge, she's decided to use this to secure her position by going to the country with a general election.'

'So, in other words, making hay whilst the sun shines.'

Emma gave him a thin smile. 'Basically, yes.'

The DI nodded as he processed all this. 'I'm certainly

starting to see a motive here for why the PM might want Martin Chambers out of the picture.'

'Don't worry, we've already considered that, but thankfully, there's no evidence to support it. However, getting back to the Night Watchmen and the Marcus Blackwood connection. We've always known the crime syndicate has had serious ambitions, and maybe now, for the first time, we're realising just how high that goes if they are backing him. Make no mistake, Marcus Blackwood has a real chance of leading this country one day. Imagine what that would mean.'

Joseph gawped at them. 'Through him, they would have the keys to absolute power.'

Chris cupped his hands together. 'Exactly. Do you know anything about Marcus Blackwood's background?'

'Wasn't he a former captain in the army?' Joseph replied, remembering what had been in the briefing notes.

'He actually was in the SAS, working far behind enemy lines in Afghanistan. He was even taken prisoner, but managed to escape. After leaving the army, he took up a political role. Our intelligence indicates that some of the people he worked with in the armed forces have been compromised by the Night Watchmen.'

Joseph's mind whirled. He knew enough about the SAS to understand what that meant. Blackwood was not just another slick politician with a sharp suit and clever words. Now it turned out he was a man who'd survived the most brutal conditions imaginable, trained in deception, endurance, and tactics. A man like that, with political ambition and the Night Watchmen at his back, was not just dangerous. He was downright terrifying. For a moment, Joseph imagined Blackwood standing on a stage, every ounce of his soldier's discipline and charm turned towards convincing the public he was the saviour they needed.

'Okay, so if all this is true, why not have Blackwood arrested?'

'Because we lack any hard evidence,' Emma said. 'It's only supposition on our part at this stage, as that's where all our evidence seems to be pointing, even though they seem to have lots of people working hard to disguise any direct links. But make no mistake, if Blackwood is being backed by the Night Watchmen, and this Iron Dawn group is all part of their plan as well, our democracy really is under a very real and dangerous threat.'

'Then it sounds like the sooner you take that crime syndicate down, the sooner we can all sleep safer in our beds.'

'And we're about to,' Chris replied.

'So, if you don't mind me asking, why haven't you done it already?' Joseph asked.

'Because now that we're forming a clearer picture of just how far their corruption has reached, we need to tread extremely carefully here,' Emma said. 'If we are talking about locking up ministers, judges, senior police officers, and even key officers of our armed services, the fallout could be enormous. But ironically, if they really are behind the murder of Martin Chambers, they may have tripped up. As you've just seen, Marcus Blackwood is already making it a key political issue for the coming election. If we can arrest our mystery waitress, that may be the first clear piece of evidence linking the Night Watchmen to it, and also catching Marcus Blackwood in the same net. Do that, and even at this eleventh hour as we head rapidly towards a general election, we could still bring their carefully crafted plan tumbling down on their collective heads.'

Joseph nodded as a sharp knock rattled the door.

'Come in,' Chris said, exchanging a look with the others.

The door burst open, and Megan rushed in.

'Sorry to intrude, but we've just been informed that a restaurant owner has confirmed the identity of our waitress. She's called Sally Green. He sent a photo through, and it's pretty much an exact match to one of the AI photofit images. He also said Green missed her shift yesterday, which is apparently very unusual for her.'

'That sounds promising, so where is she based?' Chris asked.

A smile filled Megan's face. 'Oh, this is where it gets even better. She rents a room in a house on East Street.'

'Jesus H. Christ, that's right next to the River Isis, and less than a mile away from where she was last seen leaving Christ Church College,' Joseph said. 'I know that street well. It's full of lovely old terraced houses next to the river, including an architectural design-winning yoga studio. All very Oxford. It's also the last place anyone would think to look for a wanted criminal.'

'Then we'd better get a raid organised on her home, ASAP,' Emma said. 'Let's just hope she hasn't had time to fly the nest. We'll also need a tactical team deployed as we are potentially dealing with a very dangerous terrorist here.'

Chris nodded. 'Okay, let's get those wheels spinning. Joseph and Megan, you'll join me on the raid.'

'And I'll be coming with you with some of our agents,' Emma said. 'We can't take any risks in letting Green escape our net.'

'Apart from anything else, we have a real chance to get to the bottom of this fecking case,' Joseph said as he stood.

'Exactly,' Emma replied, grabbing her tablet as they rushed for the door.

CHAPTER THIRTEEN

SERGEANT EROL KENTLI spoke into his radio as sunlight glinted on the visors of the tactical unit gathered around him.

Joseph felt the usual stir of adrenaline deep in his gut in anticipation as he checked his stab vest. He stood with Megan, Chris, and Emma, along with three of her agents, at the corner of the street, a cordon already in place behind them. Traffic had also been stopped from passing over the nearby Osney Bridge for the duration of this operation. The bus operator companies weren't going to be happy.

A second cordon had also been set up at the opposite end of the street, where uniformed officers, including John, had sealed off all the approaches. There, the second tactical unit waited for the order to move in a pincer movement with the first team to box the suspect in from both sides.

Joseph studied the pretty line of well-kept homes with their painted doors and flowerpots. But the ordinariness of it all only sharpened his sense of growing unease.

'Does it strike anyone else as odd that for someone meant to be a terrorist, this feels a bit amateurish?' he said. 'If you really wanted to vanish, wouldn't you want to pick a safe house that wasn't practically on the doorstep of where you carried out your crime?'

Emma's eyes scanned the facades of the terrace houses. 'I don't know. Maybe that's the cleverest part. As you said yourself, especially in this well-to-do setting, it's basically the last place you would expect someone to hide out, especially so close to the crime scene.'

'Even so, the likelihood is she may already have bolted,' Megan said. 'That's certainly what I'd have done in her shoes, especially once her photofit came to light.'

Emma nodded as Erol headed over.

'All units are in position, including our officers positioned in the neighbours' gardens at the back,' he said. 'If Green makes a run for it, she won't get far.'

'Good, but I want you all to exercise extreme caution here,' Emma said. 'If she really is part of a terrorist cell, we cannot afford to underestimate her.'

'Don't worry, none of us will do that in a hurry,' Erol replied.

'Then move when you're ready,' Emma said, then caught herself with a faint grimace. 'Sorry, force of habit. Chris, your call.'

Joseph traded a look with Megan as the faintest look of irritation crossed their boss's face, but it was gone as quickly as it had appeared.

Chris dipped his chin towards Erol. 'As the lady said, you have my permission to proceed.'

Erol nodded and headed back to his team, who all lowered their visors. He raised his radio to his mouth. 'Move towards the target.'

With weapons poised, he and his team headed forward in formation, the well-oiled machine of the TU kicking into action.

Joseph's heart rate was already accelerating. This was always the most dangerous moment. Even the best-planned operation could quickly go sideways if a suspect turned out to be armed.

He threw out a silent prayer. *Please let this all go okay.*

Chris followed Erol's team with Joseph and Megan, and with Emma and her team close behind them.

The tranquil summer day almost made this raid feel surreal as, at the far end of the street, Joseph saw the second tactical team moving in on the pale blue maisonette. But life on the river carried on as if nothing were happening: the two swans shepherding their cygnets downstream, the water gleaming under the sun; sparrows chattering noisily from the trees as they darted between branches. All the while, the distant hum of Oxford traffic was a constant soundtrack as the two tactical teams converged on the blue-painted maisonette where Green was staying.

As an officer raised a battering ram, Joseph's gaze swept to the windows of the house, but he didn't spot any movement.

Then Erol clenched his fist. 'Go, go, go!' the TU sergeant bellowed.

The ram swung into place, and the door shuddered under the blow, giving way with a crash. The TU officers immediately surged inside, boots pounding over the threshold, challenges bellowed.

A startled cry rang out.

Then a minute later, Erol reappeared on the step. 'Property secure. There's an elderly woman inside, but no sign of Green.'

Emma swore under her breath, and Chris frowned.

But Joseph wasn't exactly surprised. It seemed Megan had been on the money.

'Right, let's head in and do an initial assessment before the SOC team gets here.'

Joseph spotted Chris trading a frown with Emma. He knew immediately what that meant. If the Night Watchmen really did have anything to do with this, thanks to Amy's involvement, any relevant evidence would vanish before anyone else saw it. No wonder Chris was keen for them to do an initial sweep.

The SIO led the way inside with Emma, followed by Joseph and Megan, just as neighbours' faces started to appear at their windows. The local Facebook group would be humming tonight.

From inside, a woman's furious voice, sharp and indignant, came from a front room. 'What the hell do you think you're doing?'

Erol raised his eyebrows at them. 'You should probably start in there with the owner. She says she's Sally Green's landlady.'

'Emma, you'd better come with me to deal with this,' Chris said. 'Joseph and Megan, please check out Green's room.'

'It's upstairs, first on the right,' Erol added.

Both detectives nodded. But as they headed up to the first floor, the landlady's voice carried up from below, rising to a shrill pitch. 'How dare you knock my door down like that! What will the neighbours think—?'

Chris closed the living room door behind him, muffling the woman's tirade.

'Rather them than us,' Megan said with a faint smile.

'Too right,' Joseph said, snapping on a pair of latex gloves as Megan did the same.

On the landing at the top of the stairs, they opened a door into a small bedroom. It was neat, lived-in, and utterly ordinary.

Joseph took in the room, cataloguing the scene.

A single bed was pressed against the window and dressed in a faded floral duvet. On a cabinet next to the bed sat a dog-eared copy of *One Day* face down, its spine cracked from a lot of readings. A pair of worn trainers had been kicked halfway under the frame. In one corner, a laundry basket overflowed with T-shirts and faded jeans.

A corkboard hung above a tiny desk, dotted with scraps of daily life. There was a payslip from the restaurant, a torn bus timetable, a faded photo of three young women in sunglasses, laughing in a muddy festival field that could have been Glastonbury. Receipts littered the desk, alongside a bottle of cheap moisturiser and a very old tablet with a chipped screen that Megan was already heading over to.

In the corner, a battered canvas rucksack slumped against a chair. No laptop. No expensive electronics. No trace of the clandestine. Just the debris of a young woman getting by in Oxford.

Megan bent over the tablet and, with a gloved finger, pressed the button. Much to her surprise, it powered straight up with not so much as a password request. She took in the message that was open on the screen.

'Okay, this is interesting,' she said. 'This is part of a message exchange with a friend.' She scanned through them. Then she started to read from one. '"I saw Mr H with the sunglasses permanently welded to his face in the restaurant for lunch again today. Bloody hell, talk about a great tipper, and he's so much my type. I don't know what to make of his proposition, though. I mean, it's easy money, and I'm not about to turn down a thousand quid, but it's definitely a bit shady. What's a girl to do?"'

Joseph's eyebrows climbed up his forehead. 'Okay, what are you thinking?'

Megan scrolled down the page, frowning. 'Could be an indecent proposal, a bit like that film. Unfortunately, it's the last exchange with her friend.'

'Who we'll need to speak to as a matter of urgency.'

'Absolutely.'

Joseph looked at the room again, but nothing seemed to fit

with the idea of a radicalised terrorist. No pamphlets. No manifestos. No weapons of any sort. And certainly no vials of any obvious poisons. Just the trappings of the ordinary Oxford life of someone working hard just to make a living.

'I tell you what, if this is a cover story, it's one hell of a well-constructed one,' he said.

'I agree. Certainly, none of this fits the profile of the woman I'd built up in my head.'

'You and me both.' Joseph leaned over the tablet, took out his phone, and snapped quick photos of the messages.

'Doing Amy's job for her now?' Megan asked as she crouched to check under the bed.

As always, Joseph knew he had to deflect because the DC had no idea that the SOCO had been corrupted. 'Aye, better to get ahead of the curve and all that.'

'As long as we don't disturb a potential crime scene, or she'll have our heads mounted on spikes outside the St Aldates, as a warning to other officers.'

'Aye, don't I know it.' He took one last look at the room before turning to Megan. 'Okay, I think we're done here. Let's see how the boss is doing with the landlady.'

As they headed back down, through the open front door, Joseph caught sight of Amy and her SOC team in white suits assembling outside.

At least there's nothing up there for you to tamper with, he thought to himself.

At that moment, Chris emerged from the living room and closed the door behind him. The shrill edge of the landlady's anger had now faded into something calmer as she spoke with Emma.

'How did you two get on up there?' the SIO asked.

'Nothing useful, except a chat message mentioning a *Mr H*,

who always wore sunglasses. Sounds like he might have been a customer at the restaurant where she works.'

'And he offered her a thousand pounds to do something dodgy,' Megan added.

'Okay, that fits with what we know from the landlady,' Chris said. 'She said she saw him through the curtains, standing on the doorstep last night when he turned up here. After having locked herself in her room for most of the day, Sally seemed distressed when she saw him, but she went with him readily enough. The landlady thought they headed off to the pub on the corner, but Sally never came back. The landlady assumed she must have spent the night with him.'

Joseph nodded towards Megan. 'Indecent proposal, indeed.'

Chris gave him a questioning look as his phone rang, and he glanced at the screen. 'Sorry, I need to take this.' His expression darkened as he listened to the person at the other end. Then he took a deep breath. 'Okay, we'll head straight there.' He turned to face the two detectives. 'They've just found a woman's body less than two hundred metres from here.'

Joseph stared at him. 'Shite, that can't be a coincidence, can it?'

'It's not. The description matches Sally Green. What's left of her anyway.'

Megan's brow furrowed. 'What do you mean?'

'Her body's been discovered in the community hydropower station just by the lock. She was apparently sucked in by its turbine, and the bloody thing has sliced her up.'

Joseph shook his head. 'Fecking hell.'

Amy stepped inside. 'I've just been told about a woman's body that's been found close by,' she said.

'Aye, we just heard as well,' Joseph replied.

Chris's lips thinned. 'Then let's get moving, people. Amy,

you'd better come with us, and we'll let Emma and her team hold the fort here.'

A few seconds later, they headed back out onto the street. Despite the heat of the day, Joseph felt a chill settling in his gut. The one thing he was certain of was that whoever Mr H was, he almost certainly had something to do with the death of the young woman they were now heading over to investigate.

CHAPTER FOURTEEN

As Joseph and the others reached the far corner of the road, they passed The Punter. It was one of the DI's more favoured watering holes when he needed to really escape work. Unlike the Scholar's Arms, there was little to no danger of running into any of his colleagues. It gave him a chance to vanish into the background. It also served excellent vegetarian food, so that was always a bonus.

Next to the pub, another police cordon stretched across the road for the raid on Sally Green's home. Beyond it, a knot of onlookers had already gathered. Cyclists stood astride their bikes as dogs tugged impatiently at leashes. A female PC was trying her best to calm an elderly man who was loudly arguing with her that the cordon meant he couldn't get to his own home.

As they headed past the group, Joseph spotted John just ahead of them on the towpath on the other side of the hydro's perimeter gate. It was sealing off the approach to Osney Lock and the small community hydropower station standing beside it.

'So what exactly is the story here?' Chris asked as they approached the PC, with Megan, Joseph, and Amy in tow.

'One of the volunteers who helps maintain the Osney

Hydro came in about ten minutes ago to do some maintenance work,' John replied. 'He found the woman's body jammed into the mechanism and cut to pieces.' The PC shuddered, his face grey. 'What an awful way to die.'

Joseph could see it in his mind's eye, and his stomach was already turning. He slipped a Silvermint into his mouth, the sharp taste grounding him for whatever lay ahead. In contrast, Megan's eyes were glinting with anticipation. If there was a major difference between the two of them, it was that.

'Has the crime scene been disturbed at all?' Amy asked.

'Apart from Craig Watson, the man who found her, no. The hydropower station itself is enclosed, and no one else has been allowed inside.'

'Good, that will make my life easier and should help protect any potential evidence in there. Not that there may be a lot if she was in the water before she got sucked in.'

Joseph rubbed the back of his neck. 'But that doesn't make much sense.'

'Because?' Chris asked.

'Because from memory, there's a grate across the diverted channel from the Isis. That's meant to stop debris being drawn into the power station and damaging the machinery.'

'That would normally be correct, but the grate had been removed for maintenance,' John said.

Megan frowned. 'Then why on earth was the hydropower station left running?'

'It wasn't,' John replied. 'At least, not according to Craig Watson. He swears he shut it down last night and says someone must have broken in and deliberately activated it.'

'Then the lock to the power station is going to be one of the first things I check,' Amy said.

'If you want to talk to Craig yourselves, he's with PC Hale, giving his statement,' John added.

Chris nodded, his eyes travelling to the gateway where a very designer-looking single-storey cedar-clad building sat. A large window was built into one side. 'Is that Osney Hydro Station? It's not exactly what I visualised.'

'First time?' Joseph asked.

'To be honest, I didn't even know Oxford had a hydropower station.'

Megan nodded. 'You're not the only one.'

'Most people don't know anything about it because it's a community initiative, very much on the small end of the scale,' Joseph replied. 'It's designed to power only about sixty homes.'

Chris gave him a wry smile. 'Only in Oxford would you find a community project like this. Anywhere else it would be the usual mural, flower bed, or maybe a bronze sculpture at a push.'

'Aye, the folk of this city do love to march to their own beat,' Joseph said. But the ghost of any smile faded as they reached the inner cordon.

PC Laura Hale, a young officer with red hair and a kind face, stood there, notebook in hand. She was listening to a pale-faced man in his sixties who was trying his best to hold it together.

His eyes blinked rapidly, hands knotting and unknotting as he spoke to her. 'Whenever we work on the system, we shut everything down. Safety first. That's always the watchword round here.'

'So how did it happen, Craig?' Laura asked gently as they reached them.

'Some maniac must've deliberately started it up,' the man replied. 'And then, whoever it was, padlocked the station door for good measure. I had to fetch an angle grinder this morning just to cut my way in. Whoever it was, they wanted that poor woman to be dragged into the Archimedes' screw. How sick do you have to be to do something like that?'

Laura touched his shoulder. 'You've had a terrible shock.'

He gave a sharp nod. 'Damn right I have, and it will haunt me to my grave.'

Chris gave the man a sympathetic look before turning to the others. 'We'd better see this for ourselves.'

Amy and the detectives slipped under the tape and walked towards the cedar-panelled building. Joseph remembered coming here once before with Dylan during an open doors day. The volunteers who ran it, including Craig, whom he'd actually met before, had been there to talk with real pride about their project. If ever a project spoke of a strong community spirit, this was it. Never had the DI imagined returning under these sorts of circumstances.

Amy moved ahead of them as her sharp eyes swept the viewing window. But even with her usual utterly unflappable composure, she looked rattled as she turned back towards the detectives. 'Please stay outside for now as I make an initial assessment of the crime scene. But you can probably see everything you need to through the glass anyway. There's a clear view of the woman's body caught in the worm screw of the machine.'

'Of course,' Chris said, keeping his expression deliberately neutral.

Joseph couldn't help but wonder how long they would keep this dance up, pretending she wasn't a potential liability at a crime scene. If it were down to him, she would have already been in a cell. But right now, as this victim was potentially linked to the assassination of Chambers, they had bigger fish to fry.

He took a deep breath, bracing himself for whatever they were about to see as they crossed the small courtyard area. His gaze took in the human sundial markings on the ground that Dylan had previously demonstrated to him. By standing in the right spot, it showed the correct time. It was that attention to detail, including all the information boards, that made this the kind of place so welcoming for school visits and curious locals, as well as tourists who happened across it. It looked almost idyllic in the sunshine. But when Joseph reached the glass and took in the view beyond, any illusion of that peacefulness shattered.

Through the observation window, the giant blue Archimedes' screw, at least a few metres across, loomed before them, its massive blades stilled, water still dripping steadily from them into the sump below, casting little ripples of water across the surface. Strips of the victim's clothing still clung to the blades. But the body caught within them was scarcely recognisable as that of their missing waitress.

Joseph's stomach clenched. Megan muttered something under her breath, shaking her head. Even Chris briefly squeezed his mouth shut as he breathed through his nose.

But what struck Joseph beyond the brutality was the horror of it. This wasn't just a simple killing. It was a spectacle, a message, even. Was it from the Night Watchmen? If so, who was it for?

Even though Joseph managed only the briefest of glances to take all this in, it was more than enough to sear itself into his mind. He already knew it would return to haunt him in his nightmares. Sally Green's partly crushed face, tilted slightly to one side, almost looked peaceful with her closed eyes. But that was where any idea of serenity ended.

The Archimedes' screw had crushed and wrecked the woman's body. Her torso had been torn apart like an overripe fruit, the stomach cavity ripped wide open. One arm clung by little more than a flap of sinew and skin to her shoulder, the bone beneath stark white where it had splintered. A leg had also been torn away completely at the hip, leaving a ragged hollow.

Bile surged in Joseph's throat, and he turned his head away, fumbling another Silvermint from his pocket. Doubling over and breathing deeply, he crushed the mint between his teeth, forcing himself to focus on the sharp bite of menthol.

'Sweet Jesus,' he muttered. He braced his palms on his thighs, steadying himself with a long breath.

But Megan, as ever, showed incredible stoicism in the face of genuine horror. Out of the corner of his eye, Joseph saw the DC step closer, her expression alert, eyes hunting through the scene for every detail. The DI felt a flicker of pride as once again, it reminded him how far she had come.

Rob would be so proud of you if he could see you now, he thought.

Chris, to his credit, was also leaning forward, studying the ruined body with a steady gaze.

'No need to ask for the cause of death, I suppose?' Chris called through the glass to Amy, who was already descending the steps next to the downward-sloping Archimedes' screw for a closer look at the victim's body.

The SOCO turned briefly towards the SIO. 'If you mean, did she die in the screw mechanism, then my first conclusion is yes. The wound patterns make that obvious. The congealed blood also suggests her heart was still pumping when she was mangled to death. The crush fractures around the femur and pelvis are also entirely consistent with a body being forced through this machine.'

Joseph stared at her. 'You're saying she was alive when she went in?'

Amy nodded.

'Bloody hell,' Chris muttered.

Joseph forced himself to look for a third time, keeping his gaze fixed on Amy rather than the ravaged remains. 'I find that difficult to believe. If I were being sucked into something like this, I would be howling the place down. But she looks calm, almost as if she were asleep.'

Amy's head tilted. 'Perhaps she was drugged first. From what I can see, there are no defensive injuries or any other signs that she fought to save her life. That suggests she was unconscious before she entered the water. Even if this were suicide, and she were fully aware, I don't imagine she'd look as relaxed as she does.'

Joseph grunted his agreement, his eyes narrowing on her rather than risk losing his composure by looking at the corpse again.

'Can we be certain it's Green?' Chris asked. 'It certainly looks like our waitress, but looks can be deceptive.'

'We'll confirm with DNA material recovered from Martin Chambers's murder scene, as well as her home,' Amy replied.

Megan drew her lip over her teeth. 'Can we be sure this isn't some sort of extreme suicide?'

'Overdosing on sleeping pills is suicide, not this,' Joseph said. 'Assuming this is murder, I can tell you this for nothing, it was carried out by one sick little fecker.'

Chris nodded. 'It's like they went out of their way to mutilate her body rather than dispose of it discreetly.'

'Yes, why not simply weigh her down and let her sink in the river?' Megan said. 'This almost feels like it's been staged for us to discover.'

'I agree. Just like showing off by using two drugs to kill Martin Chambers,' Joseph said.

'But the thing that makes no sense to me is if she was working for Iron Dawn, why kill one of their own?' Megan said.

'Unless it's because her cover was blown, and she knew too much,' Chris said. 'Alternatively, maybe Green had no idea what she was caught up in. Either way, perhaps Iron Dawn needed to get rid of her before she could lead us back to them.'

'But once again, we come back to how she was killed,' Joseph said. 'This wasn't a quick knife between the ribs, a shooting, or even a killing by poison. So why'—he flapped a hand towards her body without looking at it—'put on this horror show of a death?'

The SIO held his gaze. 'Maybe because we're dealing with someone who's not only ruthless but also deeply unhinged. Perhaps this was their idea of enjoyment.'

Joseph slowly nodded as an unspoken conversation between the two men took place, that maybe it really was the Night Watchmen behind all of this.

'Aye, maybe it was a demonstration of just how far they're prepared to go; a message to their own to keep them in line.'

Megan, oblivious to any connection to the crime syndicate, gave them both a probing look. 'Then it sounds like we're dealing with a real psychopath in every sense here.'

The three of them exchanged looks as Amy reappeared in the doorway. 'This crime scene is going to take a long time to fully examine and catalogue. We'll also need divers to search the riverbed for evidence; maybe they'll find her phone. I've already done my best to check her body, but there doesn't seem to be one on her. My guess is it was taken from Green and, if we're lucky, discarded in haste by her murderer.'

'Surely, they are more likely to have taken it with them and deposited it as far away from the crime scene as possible,' Joseph said. 'With all due respect, that feels like a long shot.'

'Even so, we need to do this thoroughly,' Amy said. 'Somewhere this woman, even if she is a terrorist, may have parents, siblings, a partner, who'll mourn her loss. And we owe it to them to do this by the book.'

If Joseph hadn't known the truth behind the woman saying those words, he almost would have believed she meant it. But *hypocrite* was the first word that came to mind.

Chris nodded, turning to them. 'Our priority right now is identifying the man the landlady saw Green with last night. I don't think it takes much of a stretch of the imagination to believe that whoever murdered Green is also probably tied to Chambers's death. Right now, this man with sunglasses is our new prime suspect. We will need to put every resource we have into finding him.' He glanced back at Amy. 'Anything you discover, however minor, you need to report to me immediately.'

'Of course,' the SOCO replied, already signalling three of her team, who'd just arrived with cases and kit boxes, to set up.

Chris turned to Joseph and Megan. 'Okay, I've seen more than enough. We'd better go and brief Emma. We also need to get started on door-to-door enquiries. I'll probably get Ian and Sue to head up that effort, and also check every camera within a mile radius.'

They ducked under the cordon John had hung, and headed back up the towpath.

A nasal voice cut through the air from among the onlookers as they passed the outer perimeter cordon across the road. 'Would you like to comment on the murder of your chief terrorist suspect?'

They all turned sharply to find the man who'd spoken out.

Joseph felt a ball of anger in his chest as his gaze met the weasel-eyed face of Ricky Holt. The tabloid photographer with him was already snapping shots of the detectives.

Chris's eyes narrowed to slits. 'No comment,' he said.

The crowd stirred around Ricky as they lifted their phones, getting ready to post this exchange on their social media feeds however it went. Even the old man who'd been giving his state-ment to PC Hale, had his mobile out in readiness.

Ricky raised his chin. 'So you admit it then? That this so-called waitress was really a terrorist who belonged to Iron Dawn? And that you let her slip through their fingers only for her to wind up butchered on your watch? Bad show, guys.' His voice carried over the heads of the bystanders, pitched for maximum effect, as people around him began to murmur.

Joseph felt his hands tighten into fists. Every instinct screamed to vault the tape and throttle the smirk from the man's face. But he caught Megan shooting him a warning glance. Her head tilted a fraction as if to say, *he's not worth it.*

'Care to comment on whether you think Iron Dawn are laughing at you right now?' Ricky pressed on, his grin shark-like.

'Enough of this,' Chris snapped, his tone icy.

Ricky had angled his body towards the waiting phone cameras, playing the part of the fearless reporter holding the authorities to account. 'The people have a right to know if their local police force is failing them. They also have a right to know how many more bodies will end up in their river before their police force admits they are out of their depth with this case.'

Joseph's jaw worked furiously, his teeth grinding on the Silvermint still in his mouth. He stepped forward, just enough so his shadow stretched across Ricky's shoes.

'Like the SIO said, enough already,' he said, his voice low and dangerous.

Ricky's smile flickered, but only for an instant. Then the mask returned. He gave a lazy salute with his pen, his arrogant smirk back in place. His photographer snapped another burst, capturing Joseph's glare, no doubt destined for tomorrow's front page.

Chris's hand landed on Joseph's arm, steering him firmly away. 'Ignore him. You know how the likes of Holt thrive on this. Don't give him more ammunition than he already has to use against us.'

As they pushed back along the towpath, Joseph forced a breath out through his nose, steadying himself. He knew Chris was right. But every fibre of him whispered the same thing:

Ricky Holt is not just a nuisance, he's a fecking liability. If the Night Watchmen really had dug their claws into so many people, it struck him that someone like Holt would be the perfect mouthpiece. That thought settled in his gut like lead.

If the reporter was already dancing to the crime syndicate's tune, and the more he thought about it, the more it made sense, then every headline, every poisoned word in print, could be designed to not only mislead the public and stir them up, but also to set the entire investigation back.

Joseph glanced at the crowd beyond the tape, their phones raised. For the first time, he wondered if they weren't just chasing a killer, but fighting for the very story that the world would be allowed to hear.

CHAPTER FIFTEEN

A DAY after the discovery of Sally Green's murder, Chris had gathered everyone together in the incident room for an update. Emma stood at his side, while Derrick and Chief Kennan occupied their usual seats near the front. Their presence alone was enough to remind everyone of the gravity of this investigation. Doctor Jacobs was also there, his case at his feet, expression lined with fatigue. It was obvious to Joseph that the man had put some serious time into whatever he was about to tell them.

Chris held up a copy of Ricky Holt's paper, its headline screaming across the page in bold capitals: *From Poisoner to Prey —Police Fail to do Their Job!* Beneath it was a grainy photograph of Sally Green, paired with a zoom shot of Amy and her SOCO team at work at the Osney Hydropower Station, probably taken from across the river from one of the former warehouse buildings. A smaller inset showed Joseph mid-scowl, caught by Holt's photographer.

'I am sure you've all seen this,' Chris said, holding the paper as though it were a rancid turd.

Every head in the room nodded.

'Then you'll know that Holt is very well informed. Everything we know about the circumstances of Sally Green's murder —that's been confirmed by DNA as the same woman who posed as a waitress at Christ Church—is laid out in this article of his.'

Derrick's eyes swept across the room, narrowing. 'It is almost as though someone on this case has been feeding him information. If I discover it is anyone here, you'll be facing a disciplinary tribunal before you have time to blink.'

In the silence that followed, several officers shifted in their seats, expressions hardening as they glowered back at the big man. But Joseph kept his gaze level. Whatever Holt's source was, he was certain that it wasn't anyone sitting in this room. But the DSU's obvious anger was intriguing. Hadn't his paymasters kept him up to speed with what they were up to? It was notable that he hadn't looked at Kennan once so far in this meeting.

Derrick inclined his head towards Chris, signalling for him to continue now that the ball-breaking was out of the way.

'You'll also have seen the responses from the party leaders,' the SIO said. 'They're unanimous in condemning Iron Dawn for its involvement in these murders, and for its ongoing threat to target other ministers in the run-up to the election. If the pressure on us was already huge, it has now multiplied tenfold.' He gestured for Emma to take over.

She stepped forward. 'The Prime Minister has been emphatic that the general election will go ahead. She's presenting it as a test of our national resolve. But her message is clear that our democracy will not be held hostage by extremists.'

Joseph's jaw tightened as he thought, *Otherwise known as the fecking Night Watchmen.*

Kennan leaned forward in her seat. 'This decision will place every police force in the country under severe strain, including our own. Each candidate standing for election will need to be protected. That's why we need progress, and we need a breakthrough in this investigation, and we need it quickly, people.'

Chris nodded. 'So let's begin with updates. Ian, Sue, how did those door-to-door enquiries go around Sally Green's home?'

Sue stood, a notebook in hand. 'We had strong cooperation from the regulars at The Punter on East Street, where Sally Green was a familiar face to the patrons.' She nodded to Ian.

He took over, consulting his own notes. 'On the night she was killed, Sally was seen at the pub at approximately nine p.m. She was with a man in his forties with dark hair, sunglasses, and wearing an open-collared blue shirt. That is all the description we have. However, the timing fits what her landlady told us about the time Sally left the house with him.'

'And there's more,' Sue added, addressing the room. 'Two days after Martin Chambers was killed, several witnesses recall Sally appearing unsteady on her feet when she left the pub around eleven p.m. Apparently, the man with her joked that she'd had one too many. They then headed in the direction of the hydropower station rather than towards her home.'

A murmur rippled across the room as Joseph and Megan exchanged a knowing glance.

Chris reached for a printout, but looked instead towards Rob. 'Doctor Jacobs, perhaps you should share your findings.'

Rob stepped forward, placing the report on the table. 'Once again, thanks to the importance of this case, we were able to expedite the results from the lab. The toxicology results from them confirm Sally Green was drugged before her death. But it wasn't Rohypnol or any of the usual sedatives we might have expected, but a far stranger cocktail.'

The room stilled as everyone looked at the doctor expectantly.

'She'd been given a mild dose of opium combined with mandrake root.'

Low murmurs spread through the room before quickly fading back into silence.

Megan leaned forward. 'Mandrake? That sounds like something out of Harry Potter.'

Rob nodded. 'Precisely. In folklore, it was associated with witchcraft, but medically, it's long been known as a sedative and mild hallucinogen. When combined with opium, it produces a profound relaxation. The victim would have been compliant, perhaps semi-conscious, and certainly unable to resist as her murderer led her towards the hydropower station. It would also explain her calm appearance at the end. But make no mistake, the victim was alive when she was sucked into that machine.'

Dylan's previous words were echoing in Joseph's mind from their earlier conversation about the use of poison from a bygone era.

He raised his hand slightly, and Rob nodded towards him. 'Then this makes two poisonings that seem deliberately archaic. Aconite for Chambers, and now mandrake for Green. It feels like someone is reaching into the past here for their inspiration.'

Rob inclined his head. 'That's an important observation, Joseph. It suggests the killer is either steeped in historical knowledge or is deliberately staging it to look that way.'

Chris added, 'Either way, it makes this terrorist group extremely dangerous.'

'So, Sally Green really was one of them and was caught up in Martin Chambers's poisoning?' John asked, standing among the other uniformed officers.

'We believe so, but how involved remains to be seen,' Chris replied.

Joseph nodded, thinking back to the message on Sally's tablet. 'Aye, think about it. What better way for the real killer to keep their hands clean than by manipulating someone who might be a bit gullible and in need of some cash? Maybe her murderer spun her a story about how it would create great publicity for their cause if she slipped something into Chambers's food. I don't know, maybe it was some yarn about it being laxative powder, all the while reassuring her no one would actually get hurt.'

Joseph's mind was starting to really settle into this theory as he voiced it. 'So Sally Green does as she's told and then slips away before the so-called prank comes to light,' he continued. 'But when our murderer spots her AI-enhanced face being plastered all over social media, he realises Sally needs to be silenced before she can give the game away to anyone. That's why he takes her to a pub, drugs her drink, and once he's got her where he wants her, and having turned the hydro station on, pushes her into the water, making sure she's sucked into it.'

'Okay, I'll certainly credit you with a vivid imagination, DI Stone,' Chief Kennan said.

'I'm told it's one of my more endearing qualities.'

That drew a few chuckles from the team, even Derrick's face softened, though Kennan looked less than amused.

'I think Joseph's theory warrants serious consideration,' Chris said. 'But in many ways, it's immaterial right now. Our priority now is finding out who this sunglasses man is before another minister ends up in his sights, or one of his collaborators.'

Emma nodded. 'Based on Doctor Jacobs's findings, poisoning may be their favoured method. The NCA has already issued advice to ministers about what they consume. If at all possible, they should only eat from sources they can be confident haven't been tampered with.'

'But also, given the fact they just shoved a woman into a river to be pulped to death by a hydropower station, I think we can safely say they're not short of imagination when it comes to killing people,' Megan said.

Joseph shot her an approving look because he'd been about to say basically the same thing.

'Actually, as regards our perpetrator, we've already had a psychological profile drawn up,' Kennan replied. 'I'm going to read you all a section that I think is enlightening, particularly in light of this discussion.'

She scanned down the page and began. '"The suspect may have links to extremist or terrorist ideologies, with the poisoning and subsequent murder serving as a method to further a broader agenda. This could suggest a personality with a deep-seated grudge against a system they perceive as unjust. Their use of poison points towards someone both calculating and methodical, willing to rely on knowledge and planning rather than brute force. However, the subsequent death of Sally Green indicates a darker compulsion: a need not simply to elim-inate, but to shock, to horrify, and perhaps even to ritualise the act.

'"It is possible that the choice of such an overtly grotesque method of murder was intended as a message: either to allies, or rivals, or even anyone investigating. This suggests a perpetrator with a psychological profile leaning towards grandiosity, with a possible fascination for symbolism, ritual, or even the occult. The murder of the waitress may therefore have been collateral, eliminating a liability, or a deliberate act of theatre designed to heighten fear and reinforce control."'

Joseph gave the woman a long look. Was this some sort of deflection on her part to move suspicion away from the Night Watchmen, or did this actually underline the fact that they had nothing to do with any of this?

He kept his thoughts to himself, and nodded. 'And now we have new poisons out of folklore rather than a lab manual. That suggests to me a possible ritualised angle, like your report mentioned.'

Rob dipped his chin towards Kennan as well. 'Aconite and mandrake root have both been tied to witchcraft for centuries.'

Megan frowned. 'So what are we saying here? That we're dealing with someone who thinks they're some sort of occultist?'

'Or someone clever enough to use that symbolism to make himself look larger than life,' Joseph replied. 'Don't forget, fear's a weapon too. Maybe that's why they used the same symbol the Midwinter Butcher used; to get everyone really rattled.'

Chris shot him a look. 'That's an interesting angle. Without doubt, I think we need to make belief in the occult a serious focus for our investigation.'

'Actually, on that note...' Kennan began reading from the report again. '"Given the methodical nature of the crime and the escalation from poison to a brutal killing, the suspect's behaviour mirrors patterns seen in calculated, high-impact terrorist strikes. Investigators should consider potential ideological affiliations and whether the suspect's background includes a history of radicalisation or extremist involvement. The meticulous nature of the crime suggests a personality driven by both vendetta and a wider cause, with a strong potential for future violence."'

'So, are we really talking about a lone wolf who's pretending to be a terrorist organisation here?' Megan asked.

'We can't rule that out,' Emma replied. 'A one-man operation would certainly fly under the radar and would explain why the NCA or MI5 weren't able to pick him up.'

Joseph noted the steady way she said it, giving nothing away about their suspicion of any involvement with the crime syndicate.

Derrick leaned forward. 'So, the obvious question we all want answered is how do we track this bastard down?'

At that moment, the door opened, and Amy came in, an evidence bag clutched in her hand. 'I came straight here from the crime scene because the divers struck gold. They found a phone at the bottom of the river near the hydropower station. What's more, it was still working. We confirmed it belonged to Sally Green at the mortuary when we used her face to unlock it.'

Chris gave her an appraising look. 'Then please tell us you've got good news.'

'Potentially. We pulled up the call history from the phone. Sally received a call within the last twenty-four hours of her death.'

'And?' Kennan asked.

'It came from a burner phone. But we triangulated the signal, and two key locations came up. The last outgoing call from her phone was made right outside Christ Church College. That lines up with Sally leaving the college.' Amy paused, her eyes sweeping the room. 'But the last incoming call after that came from the Houses of Parliament at one p.m. on the day of her death and almost straight after you held the press conference with the AI-enhanced images of her.'

The silence was broken by a low whistle from Ian. Several detectives shifted in their seats as shocked looks were traded, Joseph and Megan among them. It also seemed like the DI's theory about the timing and reason for Sally's murder had just been validated.

Emma raised her hand. 'Alright, everyone, this is obviously an extraordinarily sensitive development. Due to that, I'm afraid that as of now, the NCA will formally have to assume control of the investigation, working with Counter Terrorism Command and MI5. But to be clear, this is in no way a reflection on any of you. Your work has been exemplary. But with Westminster itself now potentially implicated, this case has national security stamped all over it.'

Despite her supportive words, Joseph felt the ground shift

beneath him. The investigation slipping from St Aldates was one thing. But a burner call from Parliament? Marcus Blackwood? But if he was involved, why would Amy be allowed to throw him under the bus?

Ian finally voiced what most of the officers in the room were thinking. 'Are you seriously suggesting a minister might be involved in Chambers and Green's deaths?'

Emma met his gaze squarely. 'I'm not prepared to speculate. What I will say is that every possibility is on the table.'

Chris's frown deepened. 'Okay, everyone, get your reports up to date. We need to be in a position to hand this over formally by close of play today.'

Something flickered across Amy's face, too quick for most to pick up on, apart from Joseph, who knew just how corrupt she was. In that split second, he was certain of the Night Watchmen's involvement in this targeted murder. But she wasn't alone because the chief had also given something away—the faintest glimmer of triumph, gone almost as soon as it appeared. But surely the NCA and the other departments throwing their weight behind the investigation had to be bad news for the crime syndicate? The one thing he could be certain of, though, was that they were both up to their armpits in all of this. He was less certain about Derrick. Maybe he was being kept at arm's length, on a need-to-know basis.

Joseph kept his expression neutral, even as alarm bells rang inside his skull. If the Night Watchmen really were behind this, then Kennan and Amy were helping guide the investigation exactly where they wanted it to go. He realised he needed to voice his concerns to Chris. If they were being played, every move from here on out would be critical.

CHAPTER SIXTEEN

As they sat in Chris's conservatory at his home, a half of the boss's lethal homebrew was all the DI dared risk if he wanted to cycle home in a straight line. The black stout sat heavy in the glass, its creamy head lacing the rim. The taste, thick with roasted malt and bitterness, lingered on his tongue. It was certainly every bit as good as the pints he had nursed in Irish pubs over the years, though Chris's batch carried a rawer edge, with maybe a little more fire in its belly.

The wide-open doors of the conservatory let in the summer's evening air, laden with scents from the garden. House martins looped and dived beyond the garden hedge, slicing through clouds of insects as they fed. Somewhere down the lane, a dog barked and was answered by another. It was the sort of scene that should have settled Joseph's mind, but his thoughts were still churning too fast for that to happen anytime soon.

Chris leaned back in his chair, stout in hand, and studied his friend with steady eyes. 'All right. What's going on in that head of yours, Joseph?'

The DI turned the glass between his palms. 'My instinct is that the Night Watchmen are involved in this.'

'I agree, although I sense a "but" coming.'

'The *but* is I believe Emma may be making a mistake with this investigation.'

Chris didn't look surprised at hearing that. A faint smile tugged at his mouth. 'Go on.'

'Think about it. To put this into some sort of context, why have the Night Watchmen gone out of their way to target serving police officers previously to pull them under their control?'

'So they can turn a blind eye to the crime syndicate's operations, and lend them a hand when needed.'

'Exactly. But what if that's all been building to this exact moment with this general election rapidly approaching? You said yourself, their aim is to seize as much control as they can. So doesn't it strike you as odd that Amy just happened to hand us a mobile phone that supposedly links Green to a call made from Parliament? And when that came out in the briefing, I swear Kennan's expression wasn't exactly worried. She looked smug, if anything, almost like that was exactly what she wanted us to hear. Explain that to me.'

Chris lifted his glass, tapped it lightly against Joseph's, and drank. 'Which is exactly what I said to Emma after the meeting. Something doesn't stack up here. Especially when the Night Watchmen have no idea we know Amy's been compromised.'

'She certainly seemed focused on recovering that mobile. It was almost like she already knew it was there and what it would reveal. I can't help but feel we're getting played here.'

'That's precisely my suspicion as well.'

Joseph felt a surge of relief spread through him that he wasn't alone in reaching this conclusion. 'So what did Emma say?'

'She's already got a team pulling CCTV from Westminster to see who was around when that call was made. Even if the handset was a burner, the cameras may help narrow it down. But my suspicion is that someone is planting evidence to drag another MP into the mud.'

Joseph exhaled. 'Good. I was starting to think the Night Watchmen might have succeeded in pulling the wool over the NCA's eyes.'

Chris shook his head. 'No, I'm pleased to report the NCA's default setting is always one of suspicion. They trust nothing until they've torn it apart twice over.'

'I suppose there's still a chance the phone being left behind was an accident.'

Chris's forehead ridged. 'Not likely. Not when the killer went to such lengths to keep a distance between them and Chambers's poisoning. Whoever left that phone behind wanted it to be found. Everything that's been going on feels like a carefully crafted plan.'

Joseph leaned forward, his drink forgotten. 'If this is misdirection, who do you think really murdered Chambers?'

Chris stared out the window, watching the martins slice through the dusk. 'The obvious suspicion is that the Night Watchmen are pulling strings for Marcus Blackwood's benefit. We've had him under the microscope for months, but he's never taken a wrong step. Now, with an election brewing and Iron Dawn positioning themselves as a serious threat, Blackwood is in a prime position to profit from the chaos. I'm afraid all lines of our theory lead back to him. Let's just say, I wouldn't be surprised if one of the other party leaders is about to be framed for this.'

'Wheels within wheels...' Joseph rubbed at his jaw as he turned the thought over. 'Then this has the makings of something much bigger than just a murder investigation.'

'It does, but suspicion alone isn't enough. Without evidence that will hold up in court, we can't touch Blackwood.'

'But we can't just let him get away with it.'

'Agreed. That's why Emma's digging with the rest of the NCA agents. We just need to discover the crack in his armour.'

Joseph sat back, a sense of frustration filling his mind. 'I just wish I could help, but now the case has been taken from us, I'm going to be stuck on the sidelines like everyone else.'

Chris's brows drew in, his gaze sharpening on the DI. 'How serious are you about that?'

Joseph frowned. 'Why? What are you thinking?'

'Like every MP, Blackwood will need police protection in the run-up to the next election, especially now that the Iron Dawn threat is real. And you may not know this, but when Blackwood isn't in Westminster, he spends most of his time at his country home near Chipping Norton.'

'You're not suggesting...?' Joseph gave his friend a searching look.

Chris was already nodding. 'I am. You and Megan could be our officers on the ground for his protection duty assignment. Normally, we would plant our own agents in that role, but with the Watchmen's reach into Thames Valley, two familiar faces, one of whom they already think they've compromised, won't raise any suspicions.'

Joseph weighed the idea. 'In other words, the Night Watchmen still think they've got me in their pocket because they threatened my wife and daughter. So if I see anything dodgy, I can be relied on not to talk.'

Chris gave a firm nod. 'That's what I was thinking.'

'All right, then count me in. But if the Night Watchmen have anything to do with Blackwood, I don't want Megan caught in the middle of it. So if it's all the same to you, I'll do this alone. You just make sure my family is kept safe if the Watchmen manage to get a whiff of why I'm really there.'

'You have my word.'

Joseph drained the last of his glass. 'Then sign me up, and let's see what dirt I can dig up on Marcus Blackwood for you.'

When Joseph arrived back at *Tús Nua* on his mountain bike, Dylan and Iris were sitting outside on the embankment next to *Avalon*. Max and White Fang were stretched at their master's feet, asleep, while Tux was curled contentedly on Iris's lap. Even their resident squirrel, Raffles, had put in an appearance, scurrying back and forth to hoover up birdseed spilled by the greenfinches tucking into the feeder above its head. Dylan and the tree-rodent seemed to have finally reached a mutually acceptable feeding arrangement.

Spotting the DI, the two professors waved over to Joseph as he locked up his bike.

'Good, we were just going through your latest case, and wanted to discuss it with you,' Iris said.

'My former case,' Joseph corrected her.

'What do you mean?' Dylan asked.

'Let's just say it has been taken over by the NCA and leave it there.'

Dylan gave him a thoughtful look as he set his glass down on the table. 'It's become that serious, has it?'

'Very much so, but I really can't say more.'

'That's not like you.'

'I realise that, but I do have my reasons.'

Joseph longed to open up to them, to tell them everything about the Night Watchmen and the way they had wormed their influence into the very institutions meant to guard against them. But Chris had sworn him to silence long ago. The fewer people who knew, the safer they all were. And Joseph certainly wouldn't risk Dylan or Iris being dragged into this pit of darkness he was about to willingly descend into.

'That's a shame, because we have already put a lot of research into the poisoner,' Dylan said.

'You have?'

'Yes, and it meant a long trawl through the microfiche archives,' Iris added. 'And we came across something that might interest you.'

'Then you had better tell me, because if it is useful, I can always pass it along to the NCA.'

'Well, pull up a chair and have a drink with us,' Iris said.

Joseph smiled. 'Don't mind if I do. But what's in the jug, because after our last conversation, I'm guessing it's not some sort of gin cocktail, Dylan?'

A sour expression creased his friend's face. 'I wish. But I am under strict orders here.' He tilted his chin towards Iris.

She frowned at him. 'Oh, stop acting like a martyr. We're only talking about a few months here.'

Joseph immediately realised he had stepped into the middle of something else here, and he had a good idea what. 'So you're completely avoiding alcohol for now because of your cholesterol level?'

Before Dylan could answer, Iris squeezed his hand. 'Just cutting back and making sure he doesn't exceed his recommended fourteen units a week.'

'Which is going to put a serious dent in my gin habit, not to mention the gruel and water diet Iris wants me on.'

'It is hardly gruel and water. Cutting back on bread, white rice, and pasta, apart from the wholemeal variety, isn't exactly going to kill you. Although the alternative might.'

Joseph grimaced because Iris had always been a straight talker.

But then her expression softened. 'Besides, it's not forever, and it's worth trying as an experiment. It may mean you won't even need to go onto statins, and you'll see the benefits for your-self across the board.'

'And if anyone can tweak a recipe to make it cholesterol-friendly, it's you, my friend,' Joseph added.

Dylan's expression eased a fraction. 'Actually, I've already found a Turkish bread recipe that uses lentils instead of flour. Apparently, it's delicious.'

'There you go then. So, what are you drinking if not gin?'

'Just iced mint water with ginger,' Dylan replied. 'But I can get you a gin.'

'What sort of friend would I be if I did not stick with you in solidarity? Water's fine,' he replied, keeping quiet about the stout he'd already shared with Chris.

'There's no need, but I do appreciate the support. Anyway, back to that poison combination we found in the Oxford Gazette from the 1950s. There was apparently a spate of murders involving combinations of poisons across Oxfordshire, one of which exactly matched what Martin Chambers was poisoned with.'

'Really? And was the poisoner ever caught?'

'No, although the press gave them a name, the Alchemist. But there is one chilling postscript you need to know about. An investigative journalist, who was digging into the murders at the time, suggested there was a link to an occult group. Then she vanished after her house burned down, and all her research was destroyed.'

'It was suspected at the time she was silenced for getting too close to whoever this Alchemist was,' Iris added.

'You are not suggesting today's poisoner is the same person?' Joseph said.

'Unlikely. They're almost certainly long dead by now. But

maybe some maniac knows about the Alchemist's handiwork and was inspired by it?'

Joseph nodded. 'That's certainly a possibility. It also ties in neatly with something else we just found out. The waitress, who was found at the hydropower station, had been sedated with opium mixed with mandrake root. Nobody had heard of that being used before. It raised eyebrows immediately, because Rohypnol is normally the go-to drug for that sort of thing...'

His words trailed away when he saw Dylan and Iris exchange shocked looks.

'What is it?' Joseph asked.

'One of the Gazette reports described a young bank cashier whose drink was spiked in a village pub,' Dylan said. 'She was saved by her boyfriend before a man could bundle her into a car. He escaped in a Morris Traveller with false plates. When she was tested, the drugs in her system turned out to be opium and mandrake root.'

Joseph gawped at them. 'Fecking hell.'

'Precisely, and you'll be pleased to know we also researched their effects,' Iris said. 'Opium would leave a victim drowsy, but also euphoric. Mandrake has been used since antiquity for its soporific qualities. Together they make a person very compliant and easy to manipulate.'

'Shite,' Joseph muttered. 'That sounds very much like the Devil's Breath concoction that Catherine Kendrick used to control her victims.'

'Very much so. And it's too much of a coincidence the poisoner hit upon the same recipe as this Alchemist for it to be by accident,' Dylan said.

'Perhaps it's the Alchemist resurrected,' Joseph said, only half joking.

Iris gave him a straight look. 'Or, much more likely, someone who learnt about their methodology and was inspired by those old murders,' Iris said. 'But what I don't understand is why make their life so difficult with exotic combinations when simpler modern drugs exist that do the same job?'

'Maybe to show off,' Dylan suggested.

'Or, to quote from the psychological profile that's been drawn up, "a perpetrator leaning towards grandiosity, with a possible fascination for symbolism, ritual, or even the occult,"' Joseph replied.

Iris rubbed her hands together as though this was one great investigative craic. 'Now that *is* intriguing.'

But Joseph's mind was already turning again. Why would the Night Watchmen resort to such archaic methods? He suspected the answer mattered more than any of them realised.

'Anyway, I hope our efforts help cast some small light on the matter,' Dylan said, smiling at Iris.

'They certainly have, and like I said, I'll pass it on to the NCA. I'm sure they'll appreciate your efforts.'

'Then I shall drink to that,' Dylan said. He glanced at the jug, and his expression fell. 'Oh...'

'Just this once, one small gin, but no more,' Iris said with a sigh.

'That's the spirit,' Dylan replied, tipping the water away.

'Pun intended?' Joseph asked.

'Of course,' Dylan said with a wink.

Joseph smiled, but as the evening shadows stretched over the water, he was already imagining the implications of all of this. In his mind's eye, he saw ministers staring at their meals with paranoia as Holt's headlines helped spread fear among their ranks. Poison in the food, brutal murders. It felt like fear itself was being weaponized. And in the midst of it, he saw Marcus Blackwood looking calm and resolute before the cameras, telling the country that only he could keep them safe. Meanwhile, the Night Watchmen would be in the wings, pulling strings and getting their chosen man to the very top, whatever the cost.

In that moment, Joseph knew it was no longer just about finding a poisoner; it was also about stopping a story that was being spun to a nation to suit the twisted agenda of the Night Watchmen.

CHAPTER SEVENTEEN

JOSEPH PARKED the Triumph TR4 in front of a pair of towering wrought-iron gates. The tactical unit's unmarked BMW was just behind him, with the two armed officers inside who would be guarding the gate.

The TR4's top was down, but now that the vehicle was stationary, the heat of the summer air wrapped around him again. The gates before him were at least three metres high, flanked by stone pillars crowned with roaring iron lions. Between them sat a weathered coat of arms with some sort of Latin insignia beneath it, its details softened by centuries of being exposed to the elements.

All very National Trust, the DI thought to himself. Maybe he would be charged for a ticket to enter.

It felt odd to be there without Megan in the passenger seat, with sharp-eyed observations of what they were heading into. It certainly hadn't played well with her when Chris had insisted on keeping her back at St Aldates with a pile of paperwork she needed to do for him. Of course, the truth was this had all been part of the plan to keep her occupied while Joseph carried on with his undercover assignment. More importantly for him, it also meant Megan would be kept safe if things went south.

The DI nodded at the TU officers as they parked up outside the gate and began to set up shop and establish an armed perimeter. Both men had already been briefed by Sergeant Erol Kentli and knew exactly what they needed to do.

Joseph's eyes travelled to a tall white pole where an array of dome cameras had been mounted, their lenses like dark eyes looking down at the entrance. On the other side of a gate, a black Range Rover stood. Its passenger door was opening, and a man in a dark suit stepped out. He was straight-backed and square-shouldered, the type of man Joseph could spot a mile away. Without a doubt, he was ex-military. Probably one of the special forces team who worked with Blackwood back in the day in Afghanistan.

The man headed through a smaller side gate, and as he headed over to the TR4's driver's door, Joseph wound his window down.

'Detective Inspector Joseph Stone, Thames Valley Police, with the TU team in tow,' he said. 'I'm here to see Minister Marcus Blackwood about his security.'

'Identification, please,' the man replied.

Joseph held up his warrant card. But rather than give it a cursory glance, the guard snapped a photograph of it with his phone. Then he raised his radio to his mouth.

'Control, Gatehouse here. Running an ID check for DI Joseph Stone. Photo sent. The TU team have also arrived with the detective and are establishing an outer perimeter at the main gate.'

A man's voice crackled back. 'Copy that. Stand by.'

The guard's expression didn't change as they waited.

Definitely highly trained, Joseph thought.

The radio came alive again. 'The detective's identity is confirmed. Authorised for entry. Also, confirm identities of armed officers.'

'Roger. Out.' The guard gave a curt nod towards the Range Rover, before heading over to talk to the TU team. A moment later, the gates swung inward with a mechanical whine.

'Follow the drive to the main house and someone will meet you there,' the guard said.

'Thank you,' Joseph said.

With a wave to the driver of the Range Rover sitting behind the barely legal tinted glass, he began to head up the narrow drive bordered by ancient hedgerows and woodland. CCTV posts punctuated the verge at regular intervals, lenses tracking the vehicle as he drove past. The lane curved before opening up to reveal the main house coming into view.

Ellensmere Grange was even older than Joseph had realised from the TV coverage of the place. The thick oak beams running through the red brick walls were bowed with age. The heavy cover of ivy was also growing into the mortar where it could. It might have old bones, maybe sagging a bit with age, but the building was standing firm.

The DI parked before the pillared entrance where another figure waited. A tall man in a black T-shirt and jeans, his muscles bulging beneath the fabric, also had a radio clipped to his belt. His stance was relaxed, but his eyes were sharp, scanning Joseph as he stepped out of the car. Once again, the man screamed ex-military.

'Gareth Holgate, head of Mr Blackwood's security,' the man said, the Australian twang unmistakable. He shook Joseph's hand.

'You seem to run a tight ship here,' Joseph said, nodding at yet another camera dome mounted on a corner of the house.

'That's what I'm paid for. Still, we're glad for your help with the threat from these Iron Dawn lunatics.'

'Aye, no one can afford to take chances right now, and there's no such thing as too much security. Is Mr Blackwood available for a word?'

'He is, but before you go inside, we need to properly log you into our security system.' Gareth pulled a phone up to Joseph's face. 'The AI we're using here runs facial recognition across the whole perimeter. Quicker than badges or codes for identifying people. Stand still a second and try not to look too much like a criminal.'

Joseph raised an eyebrow. 'That will be the day.'

Gareth smiled as he took a series of photos. 'All right, DI Joseph Stone, you've been registered in the database. From here on, the system will know your face. It means the cameras will track you, but at least you will not be setting off alarms every time you head off for a piss.'

'That's comforting.'

'Think of it this way, if the system does light you up, we will know you've had a really bad day.'

Joseph allowed himself a small smile. 'Then I'll do my best not to give you any surprises.'

'I'd appreciate that, mate,' Gareth said. He gestured towards the heavy oak door. 'Come on in. Mr Blackwood's expecting you. He's currently with his deputy, Eddie McAllister. I'll let them know you've arrived.'

The front door opened onto a flagstone-paved hall. The coolness inside was a relief after the heat outside. Portraits stared down from the walls, which consisted of stern men in military dress, one even wearing a breastplate and clutching a musket.

It felt like stepping into a historical bubble. Megan would

definitely have loved it here with her passion for anything from history.

Gareth led him into a drawing room filled with family photographs and polished oak furniture.

'Please wait here for a moment,' he said. The head of security disappeared through a door from which a murmur of voices was drifting.

Joseph let his eyes wander, looking for any clue that might open up this investigation. After the discovery of the death sigil, not to mention the archaic use of poisons, the DI had promised himself he would stay alert for any hint of the occult with Blackwood or his circle. But aside from the expected trappings of wealth and heritage, there was nothing he could see that was out of the ordinary. Nothing, at least, except for an old-looking black lantern displayed in a glass case.

The DI headed over for a closer look. There was something familiar about the thing as he leaned in to read the engraved plaque. *For my dear friend and inspiring leader, Marcus Blackwood. Now let's create political waves together.*

Joseph frowned. What did a lantern have to do with anything? Casting light in the darkness? Some private joke, maybe?

The DI snapped a photo of it. If anyone might know anything about it and whether it might be linked to the occult, it would be Dylan.

His eyes shifted to a coat of arms mounted nearby. Beneath it, a plaque bore the Latin words *Non serviam nisi meis*. He was pretty sure it was the same inscription he'd seen over the front gate. Knowing this was exactly what Megan would do if she were here, he typed it into a translator on his phone.

The answer came back in seconds, and he read it aloud, "'I serve none but my own.'"

'Rather fitting for a family motto, but maybe less so for a statesman, don't you think?' a voice said behind him.

Joseph turned to see Marcus Blackwood standing in the doorway, with neat iron-grey hair. The man's penetrating grey eyes seemed to be measuring Joseph up, along with a smile that didn't quite reach his gaze. Beside him was Eddie McAllister, the deputy leader Joseph recognised from Chris's briefing notes, who had also served with Blackwood in Afghanistan. The man was smaller but well built, and with a much more open and friendly face.

Blackwood stepped forward, his hand outstretched. His grip was almost too firm, as though testing Joseph. 'I can't tell you how much I appreciate the police support for all of us politicians during these difficult times.'

Eddie nodded. 'And we know how stretched you all are with all these terrorist threats. That's something we intend to put right if we're elected to power, with a serious increase in funding to help strengthen your numbers.'

Marcus raised his eyebrows at his colleague before turning back to Joseph. 'You mustn't mind Eddie. He tends to turn every occasion into a chance for a political pitch.'

'I suppose that's part of your job description,' Joseph replied.

Marcus chuckled. 'Just so.' His eyes sharpened again on the detective. 'I hadn't realised you were Irish, at least I assume so based on your accent?'

Joseph gave a small shrug. 'Part Irish on my mum's side. My dad was from North of the border, but I grew up in Dublin.'

'A fine heritage for any man's background,' Marcus replied.

But the way the man's gaze lingered suggested to Joseph this was more than small talk. It was as if he were filing the detail away for later use. Perhaps he intended to pass it along to the Night Watchmen so they could find another of his relatives to use against him.

The DI's gaze was snagged by a large canvas dominating one wall. The painting was very much in line with the others in the hallway. But this one showed a man in a broad-brimmed hat with a feather, wearing a steel breastplate, and a rapier hanging from his belt. But the key difference was that, strip away the facial hair, and the man could have been Marcus himself.

'One of your ancestors, Mr Blackwood?' Joseph asked, nodding towards the portrait.

The man's smile softened. 'Please, call me Marcus, as we can afford to be less formal in my home. And yes, that's Sir Godfrey Blackwood of Ellensmere Grange. He was a Royalist loyal to King Charles, although he harboured ambitions of his own. The whispers—letters long since lost—spoke of private meetings and schemes to seize power. Hence the family motto. Somewhat ironic that he lost his life to Cromwell's Roundheads here on the estate, cut down with a musket ball whilst defending this estate during a skirmish.'

To Joseph's ears, it sounded like the perfect family background for a man who now appeared intent on carving his own path to power. And it seemed with the Night Watchmen at his back to ensure he got there by removing any obstacles in his path.

'And the estate's stayed in your family ever since?' Joseph asked.

Marcus shook his head, his look almost wistful. 'If only. Unfortunately, Cromwell did as he always did back then and seized the land to parcel it off to his allies. They then farmed the originally extensive grounds, but the house itself was left to rot for centuries. My grandfather bought it back in the 1950s for a thousand pounds, if you can believe it. It was a ruin back then, but he began the long restoration project. My father continued with it, and I've carried the work on ever since. It's certainly been a labour of love.'

'It must have cost a small fortune,' Joseph said.

Marcus's expression tightened. 'Believe me, a politician's salary barely pays to keep the lights on, let alone preserving something as magnificent as this house.'

Eddie leaned in with an easy smile. 'And that's partly why Marcus founded One Nation.'

'Sorry, you want a bigger salary to restore this house?'

Marcus laughed. 'Not quite. Eddie was actually talking about my family being on the wrong side of history. This is my chance to balance the scales, to unite our homeland, to make things better. Even the family motto inspired us, looking after your own. That's what One Nation stands for—unity, not division across our great, wonderful country.'

Joseph couldn't keep the scepticism from bleeding through. 'I mean no disrespect here, but that sounds like so much political spin, and telling people a fairy tale that can never be true.'

'I can understand your cynicism when our political system is so badly broken. However, the fourth point of our manifesto perfectly sums up the very real steps we would take if we were elected to power.' He dipped his chin towards his deputy.

Eddie picked up the baton without hesitation, suggesting to Joseph that the two men had rehearsed this speech countless times. 'We intend to end political tribalism and restore public trust in government. One united voice, free from division.'

Joseph raised a brow because to him, that sounded a lot like a pitch a dictator might make. 'A noble aim. But I can't see the other parties playing along nicely with that idea. After all, parliament's made an art of who shouts the loudest wins.'

Marcus's eyes hardened slightly, even as his tone remained calm. 'True. But look where that's got us. If we're serious about change, the disinformation poisoning public life must end, including those orchestrated by overseas actors. Social media must be properly policed. We can't allow lies and manipulation

—whether seeded by hostile states or extremists—to dictate the direction of this country.'

'Iron Dawn being the latest symptom of this malaise,' Eddie added.

Joseph studied the deputy. The man sounded sincere enough. Perhaps he even believed what he was saying. But that did not change the suspicion gnawing at Joseph, that Marcus's grand project was built on the Night Watchmen's blood money. Perhaps it was their funds that were actually paying to restore these decaying walls, and bankrolling a party dressed up with a positive reformist manifesto.

'And you truly believe you've got the answer to all of this?' Joseph asked.

Marcus spread his hands. 'We can only try. And try we will.' Then his expression lightened. 'Speaking of which, we've got a perfect opportunity to convince the public and tip the scales, with the leaders' debate next week live on TV. The other parties have finally agreed to it. It will be watched by millions.'

Joseph blinked. 'That's the first I've heard of it.'

'That's because it was only agreed upon this morning,' Eddie said.

'You do realise that's a security nightmare waiting to happen?'

'Everyone does, as it will require serious security cover,' Marcus said. 'Gareth's already tearing his hair out about it.'

'I'm not surprised. And talking about security matters, I'm going to need your full itinerary of every venue and every move-ment you're going to be making. And after what happened with Martin Chambers, I'd also advise everyone in your circle to avoid food from anywhere you can't control.'

Marcus shrugged. 'Sounds like no more takeaway curries for me.'

'Or Friday fish and chips for me,' Eddie added.

But Joseph caught the tension behind Blackwood's smile. The man actually looked like he was worried for his own life.

You really are a damned fine actor, Joseph thought. But whatever it took, the DI was determined to discover just what this man was up to, and just how far in the Night Watchmen's pocket he was.

CHAPTER EIGHTEEN

GARETH GESTURED to a steel door off the main hall as he and Joseph headed through the house for a tour. 'We'll start in here. Once you've seen the layout, you'll soon have a feel for how we run things here.'

The door opened onto a surprisingly compact control room. Banks of monitors filled a wall in a neat grid. On the screens were views of the lawns, the drive, and, of course, multiple views around the perimeter of the house. Two racks of equipment hummed quietly, their lights winking in patterns.

A man in a black T-shirt sat at the console, forearms inked from wrist to sleeve. A pack of cigarettes lay on the desk before him. But the man had the stillness of someone who could sit for hours without fidgeting. He didn't even look around when they entered. Instead, the man's eyes flicked from screen to screen.

'Blake, let me introduce DI Stone,' Gareth said.

Blake spared Joseph a glance and nodded. 'Afternoon, sir.'

'Can you show him the camera grid?' Gareth said. 'Start with the perimeter.'

Blake nodded and tapped a colour-coded keyboard. Six

monitors changed to show the high stone boundary wall from different angles.

Joseph immediately noticed that the tops of the walls were bristling with spikes. Behind the old stone wall, there was also a secondary wire fence with signs along it clearly showing it was electrified.

'You don't mess around with keeping people out, do you?' Joseph said.

'Damned right we don't,' Gareth said. 'As you can see, we have full coverage of the external perimeter.'

'So how are you for night cover?' he asked.

'Thermal at night, with IR flood lights for good measure,' Gareth replied. 'We also have motion sensors along the wall. If something moves that isn't the wind, Blake gets a ping here, and we get a buzz on our radios. We also run four-man patrols at night along the perimeter,' Gareth said.

'So what about the inner perimeter coverage around the house?' Joseph asked.

Blake tapped the keyboard again, and the screens all filled with external views from the house.

On one of the screens, a fox loped across the lawn, head down, tail low. The motion sensor flashed with a yellow box. Blake registered the wildlife identifier with a flick of his gaze. It really did seem that nothing could get near the house without being spotted.

Joseph stepped closer to the wall of screens, scanning for gaps in this tight security net. It was why he was meant to be here after all. The cameras' field of view overlapped generously, but he also knew no system was perfect. Then he spotted a possible loophole.

'You seem to have a dead spot between your two cameras on the northwest corner of the house,' he said.

Blake pulled a face. 'A camera went down there last night. We're waiting for its replacement.'

Gareth raised his eyebrows at the man. 'Make sure you get that sorted ASAP. Well spotted, Joseph.'

'Well, it's what I'm allegedly paid to help you guys sort out,' he replied with a smile. But mentally, he filed that titbit of information away; it could be useful. 'What happens if a would-be terrorist cuts the power to the house? In other words, if the lights die, do all the shiny toys in here and outside go down?'

Gareth pointed to the racks. 'UPS backups on every box of tricks. We've also got a diesel genny in the plant room with a three-day tank. It auto-starts if the mains trips. And before you ask, because you probably will, yes, we test it every week whether we need it or not.'

'Good man. And if they cut the phone lines?'

'Dual fibre feeds,' Blake said. 'Two different routes out to the main road to make sure we have redundancy built in if one is cut.'

'Sounds like you've thought of everything,' Joseph said, feeling impressed, but also concerned. For a private residence, Ellensmere Grange was a fortress in all but name.

'We've certainly tried, but as my time in the forces taught me, the trick is to not fall in love with your plan,' Gareth said. 'Even the best thought-through ones can go to shit during first contact with the enemy.'

'No doubt. I'm right in thinking you and your men are all ex-special forces, and that's how you know Marcus?'

Gareth shared a look with Blake before nodding. 'Obviously, we can't go into that in any great detail, but yeah. Half of the team here actually served with Blackwood and also McAllister in Afghanistan.'

'So, based on the fact you're all here, you must respect Marcus a lot as a leader.'

'Let's just say he pays well.' Gareth winked at Blake.

Even as he smiled back at the man, Joseph was wondering just how deeply that allegiance ran. Maybe all the way to the Night Watchmen?

'Okay, what about the other staff who work here?' Joseph asked.

'That's a short list. There's a housekeeper, two cleaners, one groundsman, and one handyman, all of whom only attend a couple of times a week. Marcus's wife, Alison, runs the kitchen like it's her empire. Apart from that, we do use the occasional agency help for events, but not this month. No one gets a pass with all the increased security we've put in place.'

Blake sat straighter as a delivery van appeared at the gate on one of the feeds. 'Groceries,' he said, scanning down a checklist.

'Same driver as last week,' Gareth added. 'Five minutes at the back door, and he'll be gone.'

'Okay, as I said, from now on, you'll need to source all your supplies through the police. We can't take any risks.'

Gareth pulled a face. 'That's not going to go down well with Alison. She normally deals with that side of things and is fiercely protective of her kitchen, along with where she gets her ingredients.'

'Then it sounds like I'd better talk to her.'

'If she's not baking, she's thinking about baking, so she's almost certainly in the kitchen,' Gareth replied.

Joseph caught the note of real affection in the man's tone, suggesting Alison kept him and his men well fed with her culinary creations.

'Then we'd better visit her next,' Joseph said. 'After that, I'll want to walk the grounds. On foot, not just with a screen.'

'You'll certainly get your steps in when it comes to this estate,' Gareth said with a smile, opening the control room door.

They stepped back into the cool of the hall, and the age of

the house closed in around them again. Rugs, polish, the distant tick of a grandfather clock, and a rich history were held within these four walls.

The kitchen lay at the end of a short passage, and the smell hit Joseph the moment the door was opened. Butter, sugar, spices, possibly cinnamon, and the warm hint of toasted nuts. The room itself breathed the kind of order that told Joseph someone really loved working here. Copper pans on a rack, knives on a magnetic strip, jars of flour and sugar aligned just so along open shelves, each with a neat label on. On the table in the middle sat a cake on a cooling rack. It had been covered high in a pale frosting, pecan halves arranged in a ring across the top like little boats.

A woman in her forties, wearing an apron, her sleeves rolled up, turned at the sound of their entrance. Her hair was the colour of autumn leaves and had been coiled up with a tie. As the woman's gaze alighted on Joseph, her face lit up with a warm smile.

'You must be DI Stone. Marcus told me you'd be coming.' She extended a warm, flour-dusted hand. 'Welcome to Ellensmere Grange.'

'Thank you,' he replied as he shook it. 'And please, call me Joseph. I've been told this is very much your empire.'

Alison's smile tugged wider as she glanced at Gareth, who grinned back at her. 'Empire's a bit grand, but yes, the kitchen is mine. Marcus can have his politics and speeches. But I hold court here, with butter, flour, and the occasional burnt finger.'

Joseph smiled as he glanced around again. Every surface gleamed, but nothing felt sterile. This was a lived-in kitchen, one that breathed comfort and effort. He thought of Dylan; his old friend would adore this woman and especially her kitchen.

But even as the DI soaked in the atmosphere, he wondered how much Alison actually knew of what her husband might be caught up in. If Marcus Blackwood could fool an entire elec-torate, couldn't he also fool the woman he shared his bed with? Or was the politician like how he and Kate were together, sharing everything? If so, did that mean Alison was embroiled as deeply as Marcus was in whatever the Night Watchmen were up to?

Alison was gesturing towards the cake on the table. 'So what do you think of my latest creation?'

'Well, it certainly looks delicious.'

'It's called a hummingbird cake,' she replied.

'Are there actual hummingbirds in it?' Joseph cracked a smile.

Alison chuckled. 'Thankfully not. But it does have banana, pineapple, and, as you can see, toasted pecans. I've been working on the recipe for weeks. I like to imagine the judges on those television cake shows would faint at the sight of this, but I still keep trying to perfect the recipe.' She picked up a knife and cut a generous wedge. 'Tell me the truth when you taste it. Gareth and his men flatter me shamelessly, but they'd eat wall-paper paste if I told them it had butter cream inside it.'

Gareth snorted. 'Probably true.'

Alison slid the slice onto a plate and placed it before Joseph. 'Go on. I want an honest opinion.'

Joseph hesitated, aware of the absurdity of the moment. Was this some sort of test? Here he was, a detective on an undercover mission to probe a politician suspected of corruption and worse. He was also meant to be protecting him from all threats, including poisoning. Hadn't he just given Gareth a speech about making sure that all food and ingredients in the Grange were vetted first? And now here he was being offered cake as though it were the most casual thing in the world. But surely, the Night Watchmen wouldn't risk poisoning him? Or would they? Maybe this was even a test.

Joseph took the proffered dessert fork, cut through the dense crumb, and braced himself as he raised the smallest possible piece to his mouth. The faintest hint of bitterness, and he would be off to the loo to shove his fingers down his throat, faster than any of them could blink. Thankfully, instead of that, the taste of sweet banana and pineapple hit him first, followed by the warm undertone of spice, and finally the pecans, rich and nutty. The cream cheese icing had a tang that balanced everything out.

'Well?' Alison asked, hands on hips, eyes bright.

Joseph swallowed, then let the corner of his mouth curl upwards. 'That, right there, is the taste of heaven.'

Her relieved laugh filled the room. 'Thank you, Joseph. I suspect everyone else around here is far too biased to be objective anymore. Anyway, you didn't come here to discuss cake with me.'

'No, I didn't,' Joseph said, setting down his fork, though the cake begged for another bite. 'Where do you source your food and drink supplies from?'

'In the main, from a deli in Chipping Norton, and the market there on Saturday. I always prefer to use fresh, local produce, flour, butter, and the rest. I also like to know who I'm buying from. Why?'

'Because Iron Dawn has already shown themselves willing to use poison,' Joseph said. He studied the woman's face as he spoke, searching for any flicker of recognition, of complicity, but he could see nothing there other than concern.

'Good Lord, yes, that poor dear man, Martin Chambers, such a loss,' she said. Then her gaze sharpened. 'You don't honestly think they might try to tamper with what we eat here?'

'It's certainly a possibility,' Joseph said. 'And not just slipping something into a bag of flour from the market destined for you, either. They could follow you, watch for opportunities, even abduct a member of Marcus's family, including your good self. That's why I'd prefer you not shop yourself until this threat is over. If you draw up a list, we'll have trusted officers collect what you need from vetted suppliers.'

Resolve hardened in Alison's eyes as she nodded. 'If that's what it takes, then so be it. Marcus might bluster about liberty and freedom, but this is about keeping us all safe, so I'll do whatever you ask.'

To Joseph's ears, her words had the ring of truth to them. She certainly believed in her husband, that was evident. But just how deep did that loyalty run? Of course, if she did know what Blackwood was really up to, then she would also know there was no chance of Iron Dawn targeting them in their own home.

'Thank you for being so understanding,' Joseph said, giving nothing away. 'And I'd advise the same for your staff. No one should leave the grounds without clearance, and certainly not for groceries.'

'This kitchen's my territory,' Alison said with a wry smile, resting one hand on the worn wooden counter. 'Marcus jokes, I rule it like a kingdom, but someone has to keep this house fed and sane. And if that means sharpening my own knives and keeping the pantry stocked, so be it.'

Joseph allowed himself a small smile. 'I'm sure it's all going to be fine, but we can't be too careful, can we?'

'We can't,' Alison replied with a smile.

The cake was good, and her welcome seemed genuine. But Joseph knew better than to be lulled by that sort of thing. To start with, he could already tell things weren't quite what they seemed here. Ellensmere Grange was a fortress as much as a home, and very likely to be hiding secrets. And until he uncovered what those were, nothing here could be taken at face value.

CHAPTER NINETEEN

WHATEVER ELSE A POLITICIAN did in the run-up to an election, one thing had become abundantly clear to Joseph—they spent a staggering proportion of their lives locked in meetings or staring into cameras on an endless cycle of video calls that never seemed to end. There had been a constant stream of advisors coming and going to meet with Eddie and Marcus. The two ministers had set up shop in the large drawing room of Ellensmere Grange for hours, papers spread across the polished walnut tables, the murmur of their voices rising before falling back to a low hum.

That suited Joseph just fine. So long as the two men stayed inside the house, his job to keep them both safe remained straightforward. No vehicle transfers to worry about, no crowded venues, no risk of an ambush in Oxford's narrow streets. The fewer movements they made, the fewer ways things could go wrong. That was assuming that the Night Watchmen weren't actually behind it all, because if that was true, it made all of it a moot point.

But what made the day pass more easily was Alison Black-wood. She insisted on feeding him and the rest of the security team as though they were her own family. Plates appeared like clockwork. Sandwiches stacked high, fruit tarts still warm from the oven, flasks of coffee with the lid steaming when you twisted it off. She even made sure offerings were sent down regularly to the armed officers at the gate. Gareth had told Joseph she always looked after the men like that. Once again, he couldn't help but feel that Dylan would greatly approve.

Despite all that pleasantness, as well as finding anything incriminating against Blackwood, Joseph was also painfully aware that he needed to keep security as his prime focus, if only to keep up appearances.

As the saying went, *an Englishman's home is his castle*, but in the case of the Grange with its high walls, locked gates, a cordon of cameras, and men in black T-shirts with radios clipped to their belts, it was more like a fortress. In comparison, the DI couldn't help thinking about his equivalent, *Tús Nua*. Could an Irishman's narrowboat, moored in the middle of Oxford, be his equivalent of a castle? He liked to think so. Okay, his boat might not have wrought-iron gates or an army of security men, but it was his and Kate's home, and that counted for everything in his world. And on quiet evenings, with the water tapping gently at its hull, it felt just as safe as Blackwood's ancient family pile.

On his first night there, as Ellensmere Grange finally began to settle, Joseph had a cottage pie in front of him, steam curling up into his face. He dug in with the kind of hunger that came after long hours of observing and waiting for nothing to happen. Alison had made it with turkey mince instead of beef—*better for the heart*, she'd said with a smile—and while Joseph had doubted her choice, one bite proved her right. Rich tomato, herbs cut just right, vegetables softened down to sweetness. It was the kind of dish you didn't realise you needed until it was gone. He made a mental note to get the recipe from her before he left. Dylan would thank him for it with his new crusade to lower his cholesterol.

Later, after clearing his plate and thanking Alison, Joseph checked in by radio with the tactical officers on night shift. He gave them simple instructions—if the team saw even the faintest flicker of anything unusual, he wanted to be called immediately without hesitation, even if he was asleep.

The floorboards creaked beneath his weight as the DI headed upstairs to the attic bedroom he'd been assigned. As he reached the top of the house, the air up there was heavy with the heat of the day still trapped beneath the rafters. To anyone watching, it looked like he was retiring for the night, just as Marcus, Alison, and Eddie, who was also sleeping at the Grange in the run-up to the election, had done earlier. But Joseph wasn't there to sleep. He had something else to do, something Chris had trusted him with.

The DI sat on the edge of the bed, letting the minutes stretch past. Five minutes became ten, became thirty. Through it all, he listened to the house emptying itself of sound, the closing of doors, the faint hum of pipes, the muffled bark of a fox somewhere across the valley. By the time a full hour had passed, Ellensmere Grange lay in silence, and that had been the cue Joseph had been waiting for.

Joseph slipped a hand into his pocket and felt the small, weighty shape of the listening device Chris had issued him. The other pocket held his phone, already dimmed to its lowest light setting. He eased open the bedroom door and stepped into the corridor.

The sudden darkness pressed in on him, and the DI let his eyes adjust before he moved. He knew from Gareth's earlier explanation that there were no cameras monitoring the inside of the house, and that suited him just fine.

But three steps in, he grimaced as a floorboard betrayed his movement with a long, low groan.

Joseph froze, his ears straining for even the smallest sound, like a door opening or a person shifting in their bed. Nothing but silence. Slowly, and this time he kept to the edges of the floor where the support from the joists was strongest. Then it was down the staircase, one careful step at a time. It wasn't until he reached the ground floor that he let himself release a long breath. He'd made it without another squeak.

Creeping around like this makes me feel like a fecking burglar, he thought.

If anyone caught him now, that was exactly how it would look, and that wouldn't play well for him. But Chris had been blunt about why planting the listening device the DI had hidden in his pocket was necessary because it was the only real option they had if they were going to find out what was being discussed behind closed doors. A wiretap on Blackwood's phone was effectively useless because if Marcus really was in bed with the Night Watchmen, then he'd be using burners that couldn't be traced. But here, within these old walls, it was a different matter. Blackwood and McAllister spoke freely within the Grange, confident in the safety of their security. That arrogance was what Chris hoped the bug would capture.

Joseph opened the door to the drawing room. Gareth or one of his men had stationed themselves outside to guard it during the day, making sure nobody lingered in an attempt to overhear what was being said. Did that little detail in itself suggest they didn't fully trust Joseph yet? And what exactly were they worried about him overhearing?

Inside, the room was a web of shadows. Sofas sprawled across the carpet, heavy with cushions, the faint gleam of polished wood catching what little moonlight made it through a crack in the curtain. Joseph's eyes paused on one of the sofas pressed against the wall. He crossed to it, slipping his phone from his pocket. With the door closed behind him, he could risk the torchlight. He turned it on and it lit up the narrow gap between the sofa and wall, revealing a net of cobwebs strung like silver thread. Clearly, the cleaner's work stopped short of dusting there. And it was perfect for what he needed.

The DI peeled the backing from the bug's sticky pad and reached into the gap, fingertips brushing the spun cobwebs. He pictured fat-bodied spiders scuttling towards his skin and tried not to shudder. With a firm press, he fixed the device to the wall, switched it on, and pulled his hand back out as fast as possible.

That was when he saw it, a sharp pinprick of light through a gap in the curtain. Then another, smaller but steady, both distant. It looked like torchlight somewhere within the grounds.

Joseph killed the beam of his own phone as he watched, making sure he didn't draw attention to himself. If it were one of Gareth's men patrolling, fine. But something in the rhythm of those lights didn't feel like patrol torches. Too irregular, and they also seemed to be too focused on one area.

He stepped back from the curtain and tapped a message to Chris—*Nothing to report here.*

The code was simple and actually meant the bug was live. The TSU van parked in the valley beyond the estate could now start recording, catching whatever might be said in this room over the coming days.

But as for this latest development, Joseph's eyes stayed fixed on the window, where the distant lights still moved faintly in the darkness. The DI's instinct was already screaming at him that he needed to investigate this and quickly before whoever it was disappeared into the night.

An idea had already formed in his mind. Joseph slipped out of the drawing room and moved fast down the corridor, now not worrying about the loudness of his footsteps. A moment later, he pushed through the door to the security office.

'Hi, Blake, still at it, I see,' the DI said as he entered the room.

The tattooed man swivelled in his chair, lit by the glow of the monitors in the darkened room. 'Yeah, at least until my relief gets here in about thirty minutes. I thought you'd turned in for the night?'

'I almost had, but I thought I'd take one last look at the feeds,' Joseph said, making his tone casual. 'It will help me to sleep easy, not to mention looking professional in my reports back to the boss.'

Blake grinned, showing crooked teeth. 'Oh, I hear you, brother. And once a paranoid policeman, always a paranoid policeman, hey?'

'Aye, something like that.' Joseph leaned closer, studying the bank of night-vision cameras. The house, the walls, the tree line of the surrounding woodland were all covered with night vision clarity. 'You haven't noticed anything unusual going on out there?'

Blake gestured at the screens. 'If there is, damned if I've seen it.'

'Right...' Joseph let his gaze wander deliberately over the monitors. He paused on the feeds showing the edge of the woods and the same spot where he thought he'd seen the lights.

Blake's eyes followed his. 'You saw something?'

This was as good a time as any to test the man and whether his allegiances lay. 'Yes, I spotted two pinpricks of light from my room.' He watched the man for any flicker to give away anything he already knew about them.

'Close by?' the man asked without so much as a flicker.

'I can't be sure, but they could have been further off, I suppose,' Joseph replied.

'That might explain it then. I do occasionally catch flashes on the cameras at night from the ridge opposite. Probably dog walkers with torches. At least, I think they're dog walkers. Hard to be sure. Well, you never know these days.' He arched his eyebrows.

'Aye, I hear you. The middle of nowhere, no street lamps, far away from prying eyes.' Joseph gave the security man a sidelong look. 'Sounds like a dogger's paradise. And I'm talking in my professional capacity here, not personal experience, you understand.'

Blake snorted. 'Right you are, brother. Want me to send a couple of lads to check it out though?'

Something in the man's tone snagged in the DI's mind. He'd spent years watching people squirm in interview rooms when they were lying. But most of all, it was those giveaway micro-facial expressions his subconscious picked up on and relayed to him in the form of instinct. Yes, something was off. Blake had responded too quickly, his gaze momentarily breaking contact with the DI's.

You're definitely hiding something, Joseph thought.

He just shrugged. 'Don't worry about it. Just keep an eye on those cameras. Anyway, you wouldn't have a spare cigarette, would you? I could murder one right now. I gave it up, but...' He shrugged.

Blake shrugged. 'Of course. But you'll have to smoke it outside. House rules, I'm afraid. Alison doesn't let anyone light up inside.'

That was exactly what Joseph had been banking on. 'Fair enough. Have you got a match on you as well?' He realised he needed to make this look convincing.

Blake reached into his jacket and handed over a cigarette and a single red-tipped match.

'You're a scholar and a gent,' Joseph said. He raised the cigarette in salute and headed for the front door.

Outside the house, the night was quiet, the air heavy with the scent of grass and rose bushes. A sliver of summer's new moon hung low, silvering the tops of the surrounding woodland.

In full view of the door camera, Joseph made a show of striking the match against the brickwork and shielding the flare with his hand. He sucked in a lungful of smoke, grimacing at the acrid taste, and exhaled in a plume that drifted in the still air, trying not to cough. Then he gave a thumbs-up to the camera, before beginning a stroll around the house.

As the DI walked, his eyes flicked to the wall cameras he knew were there. Then he spotted the missing camera on the northwest corner of the house, just its mount left behind.

Okay, let's pray this works, he thought to himself. If it didn't, he would know about it soon enough.

The DI ambled casually into position, flicked the stub to the gravel, and crushed it under his heel. Then he lengthened his stride as he walked straight out along the northwest blind spot between the adjacent cameras. His heart rate only began to decelerate when he reached the shadows of the woods and slipped into them.

The lights of the house fell away behind him as he started to circle back to where he'd spotted the two torch beams. Thankfully, he also knew the range of the night-vision cameras. They were sharp within a few dozen metres, but were effectively blind further out. This far out in the woods, and without a torch, he should effectively be invisible to them. At least he hoped so.

The ground was uneven underfoot, roots snaking under the leaf litter. Without anything to light his way, he nearly fell when his boot snagged the edge of a badger sett. He caught himself just in time by grabbing hold of a tree trunk, swallowing a curse.

Joseph pressed on for another minute without seeing

anything and was about to give up when, ahead of him, he caught a faint flicker of light between the trunks.

The DI slowly moved towards them, using the cover of the trees wherever possible. His heart thudded hard against his ribs when he saw a second point of torchlight. Yes, they seemed to be converging on something.

Then he felt the surface beneath his shoes suddenly change from soft earth to something harder. He crouched, pressed a hand to the ground. The surface felt compacted, a track maybe? But as far as he could remember from a map of the grounds he'd gone over earlier that day with Gareth to check for any security loopholes, there'd been no other road in the woods apart from the main driveway. Was this track too new to be included?

The lights ahead disappeared, and he heard car doors clunk closed. Suddenly, two harsh headlights flared to life in the wood, driving the night away around him.

As an engine roared into life, Joseph flung himself sideways, pushing his body against the rough trunk of a tree. His pulse roared in his ears as a black Range Rover lumbered into view, bouncing along the track he'd just discovered.

The detective held his breath. If this were Gareth's men, why were they out here? Did Blake know about it? Something to do with why this track was missing from the maps?

Joseph's breath caught as the vehicle passed less than a couple of metres from the tree he was hiding behind. His mind was racing, trying to come up with a plausible excuse for why he was this far away from the house. But then the tyres crunched past as the vehicle carried on away down the track. Only when the Range Rover's lights vanished into the distance, did Joseph dare take a breath.

Okay, what the feck were you up to out here? he wondered.

The DI jogged along the track in the direction the Rover had come until a structure loomed out of the darkness.

It was an old dovecote built on top of an outbuilding, half-forgotten, its pitched roof sagging under corrugated panels that had been used to patch a once pristine slate tiled roof. Shielding his phone's torch with his hand, he risked using it to examine the building before him. The churn of tyre tracks in the dirt around the building, along with hundreds of boot prints compacting the ground, confirmed whatever this place was, it was well used.

Joseph headed towards the old building where double doors had long since rotted away. Beneath the sagging timbers of the roof, inside was an old, rotting log pile covered with moss.

The DI swept his phone's beam across the piles of wood. Nothing else was in there. No crates, no obvious hint that anything dodgy was being stashed there. But the marks on the ground outside told him that it was anything but a forgotten outbuilding. Had he simply been too late, and whoever had been driving the Range Rover had just moved the last of what had been stored here? Maybe narcotics for the Night Watchmen. Guns even. He could certainly see the advantage of the crime syndicate using the minister's private estate to hide the tools of their trade. But that was still supposition on his part, and Chris needed hard proof if the NCA was to do anything about it.

He glanced at his watch. Already eight minutes had passed since he'd left the house. Blake would start wondering, if he wasn't already, where the DI was.

Joseph cast one last look at the dovecote, at the shadows hiding whatever truth lay within the building.

Then he turned and jogged back through the woods, heading for the lights of the house, wondering exactly what it was he'd uncovered here.

CHAPTER TWENTY

Inside the security room, Joseph's radio crackled into life, and one of the tactical officer's voices came through it. 'The last two vehicles on the list have just arrived at the main gate for Blackwood's strategy meeting. Please advise. Over.'

'Roger that, we've got eyes on them,' Joseph said, leaning closer to the monitor showing the entrance feed. 'Hold them there while we confirm the passengers.'

On the screen, one of Erol's officers spoke to the driver of a black Mercedes while another checked the dark blue Jaguar idling behind it, all under the gaze of Blackwood's guards who were still manning the gate as backup.

Any gathering of senior party figures and wealthy donors was always going to be a security headache. With a supposed terrorist threat hanging over the country, it was doubly so. But once again, the irony wasn't lost on Joseph that this whole security setup could be totally pointless if Blackwood was as corrupt as they suspected.

Beside the DI, Blake Thomson ticked names off a clipboard, his eyes flicking between the monitor and the list.

Joseph nodded to him. 'Who are we expecting in those vehicles?'

'In the Mercedes, it should be Minister Michael Mercer. The Jag's registered to Sir Reginald Harrington.'

The DI's spine straightened. The first name meant little to him, but the second rang a very loud bell indeed.

They'd interviewed Harrington after Chambers's assassination. He'd been at the fundraiser and had been backing Chambers for party leader. So, why was he at Blackwood's strategy meeting for the One Nation party?

Guess I'll just have to ask him, Joseph thought.

On the monitor, two of Gareth's men crouched with mirrors on poles, sweeping beneath the Mercedes and the Jaguar before popping each boot. It was thorough work, at least for the benefit of the cameras.

The DI's radio chirped.

'All checks complete,' the TU officer said. 'I can confirm the passenger in the Mercedes is Minister Michael Mercer, and in the Jag, Sir Reginald Harrington. Do I have authorisation to let them through?'

'Affirmative,' Joseph said, pressing the transmit button. 'Send them on up. Out.'

Blake tapped a switch on the console. The iron gates groaned and slid open. Both vehicles rolled forward onto the drive and made their way towards the house.

Joseph left the control room and headed through the hallway. Voices murmured behind the heavy double doors of the drawing room, where the earlier guests had already assembled. He slowed as a softer sound reached him, a whisper from the half-open kitchen door at the end of a short corridor he glanced at as he passed.

Alison Blackwood was standing close to Eddie McAllister,

her hand resting on his shoulder. Eddie nodded, head bent, listening carefully to whatever she was saying. But they were standing so close it almost suggested an intimacy between them. An affair? If so, then Alison was playing a dangerous game here. Risking something like that right under the nose of a man with ties to the Night Watchmen was playing with fire. Of course, there might be an innocent explanation, but Joseph still filed that titbit away. Chris would definitely want to know about it either way.

But right then, there was someone else Joseph was far more interested in, namely Sir Reginald Harrington.

The DI stepped out through the front door into the rapidly warming morning air. Gareth was already waiting at the entrance, earpiece in place as he spoke quietly into his mic. The sound of tyres on the driveway grew louder as the two cars climbed the final stretch to the house.

The head of security nodded as Joseph joined him. 'Are you happy with how things are going?' Gareth asked.

'I've seen nothing to raise any concerns so far,' Joseph replied.

'That's good to hear. I just checked in with the two teams patrolling the border wall. They've got nothing to report either.'

As though you're even remotely surprised by that, Joseph thought. Out loud, he said, 'Good to hear. Security-wise, the more boring this day is, the happier I'll be.'

'That makes two of us.'

Some movement through the drawing-room window caught Joseph's eye. He turned to see that Alison and Eddie had now joined the rest of the guests. She was smiling broadly, handing out slices of her hummingbird cake, while Eddie leaned close to Marcus Blackwood, already deep in discussion. To anyone watching, it looked like the picture of a united team. He certainly hoped so for her and Eddie's sake.

Joseph's gaze swept over the rest of the room, the donors and party men laughing and gesturing, full of the easy camaraderie of people who were convinced they were on the winning side.

'It's going to be a long day for them, and for us,' Gareth said, following Joseph's gaze.

'Aye, there's a lot to organise in the run-up to an election.'

'Like you wouldn't believe. Marcus says that apart from all the logistics, they need to make sure their message reaches every doorstep to tug at people's hearts and minds. Mind you, he wouldn't expect me or my men to vote for him. He's good like that. That's why we probably all will.'

Joseph gave him a shrug. 'Nothing wrong with being loyal to the boss, I suppose.'

But Gareth shook his head. 'No, it's not that. One Nation actually has its head screwed on when it comes to national security. They're serious about defence spending at the international level. And on the home front, they're pledging to double the police budget over the next five years.'

'You won't get an argument from me against any of that,' Joseph said.

Gareth nodded. 'At least you can see why people like me find his arguments persuasive.'

Joseph nodded. 'Of course, I can. But when it comes to the ballot box, people weigh up a whole mix of things, especially how well-off people feel.'

'True,' Gareth agreed, glancing back toward the house. 'Still, I hope those men and women in there manage to get their message across. Because it is a message worth hearing.'

There was conviction in the man's eyes, the kind Joseph recognised straightaway. Gareth wasn't just doing a security job here. No, the man was a true believer in every sense of the word. And part of the DI could see why. Blackwood's appeal was obvious. But that only deepened the question gnawing at him— where did One Nation end and the Night Watchmen begin?

And how did Iron Dawn fit into the picture? What was the real endgame just about to begin?

The crunch of tyres on gravel pulled him back. The Mercedes and the Jaguar rolled into view, emerging from behind the hedgerow, and both cars slowed to a stop at the entrance.

Gareth stepped forward to open the rear door of the Mercedes, but Joseph moved deliberately toward the Jaguar first. He reached it and pulled the passenger door open.

Sir Reginald Harrington looked up at him, a crease forming between his brows. 'Don't I know you from somewhere?'

'Actually, you do. I'm DI Stone. You might remember me from the night of Martin Chambers's assassination. I was one of the officers who attended the scene.'

Joseph saw Gareth heading over but lifted a hand. 'I've got this.'

The security chief hesitated, a faint frown crossing his face, but then turned away to escort Minister Mercer inside.

Sir Reginald Harrington climbed out of the Jaguar, his expression already sombre. 'Yes, I never forget a face. It was a damned bad business with Martin. He had a serious political career ahead of him, which was cut short far too soon.'

'You were planning to back him, weren't you?' Joseph asked.

The older man gave him a straight look. 'Indeed, I was. But how do you know that?'

'It came to light during our investigation when his wife mentioned it,' Joseph said. 'But what puzzles me is, if you were so invested in Martin Chambers, why are you here now? Supporting Marcus Blackwood for the top job? If you don't mind me saying, it seems like one hell of a change of mind.'

Harrington's eyes narrowed slightly. 'Are you asking me that in your official capacity, Inspector?'

'No, just a personal interest, trying to get a handle on how the world of politics works,' Joseph said, holding the man's gaze.

The hedge-fund billionaire exhaled through his nose, the faintest curl of disdain flickering across his face. 'Inspector, I'm nothing if not a pragmatist. Martin Chambers was his party's best hope—intelligent, driven, electable. But with the current prime minister still at the helm, that same party's got no chance. None. They're dead in the water, and that's the political reality for you.' He gave a small shrug, as if brushing aside something distasteful. 'The One Nation Party, on the other hand, is a breath of fresh air. Their proposals are bold and forward-looking. This country needs vision, not dithering. Marcus Blackwood has it. I'd rather back a man who looks like the future than cling to the ruins of the past.'

'But they're trailing badly in the polls.'

Harrington's gaze flicked away for a fraction too long before returning. 'At present, yes,' he admitted. 'But polls are fickle things. They can swing overnight, as I'm sure you know. And I don't measure politics in weeks. I measure it in decades. One Nation could surprise everyone in this election, but even if they don't, there's always the next one.' He gave the DI the smallest of smiles. 'That's where I'm placing my bets.' He tilted his head towards the door, where muffled voices rolled through. 'Now, if you'll excuse me, Inspector, I've a meeting to attend.'

'Of course, and thank you for your time, Sir Harrington. Let me see you in.'

Joseph led the man across the gravel and into the hall, his mind dwelling on every word Harrington had just said. He'd certainly said them with the ease of a man who'd rehearsed his lines, as though he'd given this justification before, if only to himself. But as far as Joseph knew, his name had never been linked to the Night Watchmen. But that didn't mean the syndicate wasn't circling the man. After all, they had their claws in plenty of others, so why not a billionaire kingmaker too? The fact that he was here at all already suggested he would be a major feather in Blackwood's hat.

As he swung the heavy oak door closed behind them, Joseph lingered for a moment in the hallway, staring at the portraits from the past. In the drawing room, voices rose and fell. What was being plotted in there? *And how much of it,* he wondered, *already carried the fingerprints of the Night Watchmen?*

CHAPTER TWENTY-ONE

WHATEVER JOSEPH HAD IMAGINED the job of a proxy NCA agent might be, it certainly wasn't this. The reality had been another long, grindingly dull day. With Marcus and Eddie locked away in their marathon strategy meeting with the inner sanctum group of their party, and the outer perimeter patrolled by Gareth's squad of former soldiers, Joseph's grand assignment had boiled down to little more than sitting in the security office beside Blake, who seemed to thrive on little to no sleep. Together, they'd watched CCTV feeds that showed absolutely nothing of interest. The major highlight of their day had been the Hummingbird cake that Blake had just eaten, and Joseph was saving to have with a cup of coffee later.

But the real place he wanted to be was in the heart of the action inside the drawing room, listening to what was said behind those closed doors. But hopefully, one of Chris's specialists inside the NCA surveillance van on the other side of the valley was tuned into the listening device he had hidden behind the sofa the previous night. That thought offered a crumb of comfort, but little in the way of alleviating his sense of restlessness. He couldn't help but feel he shouldn't be just sitting on his arse as time ticked away, but actually doing something.

On the monitors, the most exciting activity consisted of a pair of blackbirds stabbing at grubs in the lawn as they hopped back and forth. Hardly the stuff of terrorist incursions and not exactly a David Attenborough documentary either. The monotony rolled on, and Joseph finally decided this was as good a time as any to slip away and make contact with Chris. Their arrangement was still texts only, safe, discreet, and with no chance of being overheard by the wrong ears.

'I am heading off for a pee,' Joseph said, pushing back his chair. 'If a pickup full of terrorists happens to storm the gate in my absence, do me a favour and give me a shout.'

Blake grinned as he sipped from his water bottle. 'Deal. As long as you grab us a coffee from the kitchen.'

'Done.'

Joseph deliberately took the long route to one of the upstairs loos, winding through the hallway again. The kitchen stood deserted now, no stolen moments unfolding between Alison and Eddie. On the table, the platters of sandwiches, which had found their way to him and the security detail earlier, had been stripped bare. On the counter lay the empty gold plate where Alison's hummingbird cake had sat, reduced now to nothing more than a scattering of crumbs. Clearly, Marcus's inner circle had fallen upon it with enthusiasm, perhaps grateful for sustenance after so many hours of talk.

Beyond the heavy drawing-room doors, Joseph caught the muffled ebb and flow of voices. The pitch was lower now, more subdued, the tones of men and women weary after six relentless hours of debate. However grand their ambitions, surely even the most fervent politician must tire of the sound of their own rhetoric eventually.

The DI climbed the stairs slowly, listening for any stray

movement that might betray an unexpected encounter, before slipping into the first-floor toilet. Privacy mattered, and not just so he could relieve himself. If he were to text Chris, he needed to be absolutely certain no one could see what he was up to or interrupt.

Opening the door to the loo stopped him in his tracks. Lavish tropical wallpaper lined the walls, and a vase of freshly cut roses stood upon the counter, their scent filling the air. Next to the sink sat a woven basket neatly filled with small hand towels, each folded, with another basket beside it to collect the used ones. The lotions and creams lined up on a glass shelf could have stocked the spa at the Randolph. If the toilet itself turned out to be solid gold, like the infamous one stolen from Blenheim Palace down the road, he wouldn't have been surprised. This smallest room in Ellensmere Grange was still larger than the whole of his living space aboard *Tús Nua*.

How the other half live, he thought, turning the key in the lock and sealing himself into this oasis of toilet luxury.

One pee later, and having availed himself of the ridiculously posh amenities, Joseph set to work. Sitting on the closed lid, phone balanced in his hand, he began tapping out the text, carefully pasting in the number plates he'd discreetly noted from the visitors' cars.

Then he got to the key piece of information he needed to relay to his boss.

Something I think you're going to be interested in. None other than Sir Reginald Harrington has turned up here for One Nation's election strategy meeting. I've already tackled him about why he switched allegiance away from Martin Chambers's party to Blackwood's One Nation. His reasoning boils down to this—he thinks, even if they don't win this election, they're on the ascendant for the next one. Regardless, we can't overlook the fact that he happened to be at the same charity dinner as Chambers the night he was poisoned. If the NCA haven't kicked the tyres on Harrington yet, I suggest they make a start.

Joseph frowned, his thumbs moving faster.

Hopefully, you're getting a decent feed from the bug I planted. I've seen no further hint of movement around the old dovecote out in the woods, but I'm keeping an eye open just in case. Also, and you'll decide if it's even relevant, my hunch is Eddie McAllister might be having an affair with Alison Blackwood. If Marcus really does have ties to the Night Watchmen, then his deputy is playing a dangerous game there. That makes me think Eddie may have no idea what his boss is tangled up in. Either way, I thought you should know. Anyway, please let me know if the bug's giving you anything juicy. You owe me a pint either way.

He hit send, but instead of the comforting chime, the message hung there, unsent. He scowled at the screen. Then he spotted the distinct lack of signal bars.

That was strange because earlier on, he'd had full reception. Could the thick stone walls of the Grange be killing the signal? The unease prickling the back of his neck said otherwise. This wasn't the sort of place you wanted to suddenly feel cut off. Even with Gareth's team patrolling the grounds and the tactical team at the gate, backup was further away than Joseph might have liked.

Pocketing the phone, he unclipped his radio to check with the TU officers.

'Are you there? Over.'

Only static hissed back. He tried again. 'Come on, for feck's sake, pick up.'

Nothing, just the cold, empty crackle from the radio.

That trickle of unease thickened into a knot in the DI's gut. Plenty of years of experience had taught him to listen when his instinct kicked in that something was wrong, and right now that feeling was growing stronger by the second.

He shoved the radio back onto his belt and yanked open the toilet door, stepping out onto the landing.

The silence hit him first. No hum of voices from the drawing room, no clink of glasses, not even the faint shuffle of guards' boots outside the front door. Just stillness.

Joseph moved quickly down the stairs, alert for anything. At the bottom, he reached for the drawing-room door. It wouldn't budge; something heavy pressed against it from the other side.

'What the feck?' he muttered, putting his shoulder into it. The old oak groaned as he heaved it, millimetre by millimetre, open. A gap appeared, and through it he caught the shape of a man slumped sideways. Gareth. His dead weight had wedged the door shut.

Joseph squeezed through the opening, his pulse pounding in his ears.

The sight that met him stole the breath from his lungs.

Everywhere he looked, from Marcus Blackwood to Eddie McAllister, to Alison, Sir Harrington, all the donors and party ministers, they had all collapsed in their chairs, heads lolled, glasses spilled, their bodies motionless.

The DI's mind was racing as he did his level best to remain calm. Were the people simply unconscious, or was this something worse? He rushed to Marcus first, who, like many of the other victims, had a plate lying at his feet, a half-eaten slab of cake next to it on the rug, and a spilled cup of his tea beside it.

When the DI pressed his fingers to the man's neck, a surge of relief swept through him at the steady thump of the man's pulse. A similar check of Alison revealed the same thing. That was confirmed as he checked a few other people, including Gareth.

Okay, so they aren't dead, but they are unconscious, the DI thought. Questions began spinning around his head, but he knew he needed to get backup and fast. Blake had told him that there were twin phone lines in case one was cut. That should mean...

Joseph ran back into the hallway. His heart lifted when he spotted an old-fashioned telephone, complete with a rotary dial. But when he grabbed the handset and lifted it to his ear, he didn't hear the reassuring crackle of a phone line. A quick check confirmed the phone was still physically wired to the wall.

Whatever else was going on, the DI knew he needed situational awareness and fast.

Adrenaline surged through Joseph's veins as he sprinted back through the corridors towards the security office. The door banged against the wall as he shoved it open.

Blake was slumped sideways in his chair, a half-eaten slice of Alison Blackwood's hummingbird cake still clutched in his limp hand, crumbs dusting his shirt. Joseph's slice lay untouched next to where he'd been sitting. The man's chest rose and fell faintly, but his eyes were closed, the glaze of drugged unconsciousness written all over him.

That settled it; the cake had been the delivery mechanism for whatever it was that had knocked everyone out. And here he was awake, only by the grace of God.

The DI scanned the bank of monitors, relieved that the feeds were still up. But then his chest tightened as one camera showed the front gates opening. The two TU officers lay sprawled on the tarmac, their weapons lying just beyond reach. A white transit van tore through the entrance and raced up the drive.

The Range Rover that had been parked as a guard position was abandoned too, and both security men were collapsed against its wheels, motionless.

Joseph's pulse kicked harder. Whoever was coming, they'd

planned this to the split second. The first step had obviously been to drug everyone. The second? And here he was unarmed except for his baton and some pepper spray. He had thirty seconds before the van reached the house.

The DI bolted from the office and flew through the hall, shoving the heavy front door open before him. The heat of the afternoon smacked him in the face. Beyond the steps, the rows of guest vehicles gleamed in the golden sunlight. Bentleys, Mercedes, a Jaguar, all with their drivers slumped over steering wheels or alongside them.

Just how much fecking cake did Alison hand out? Joseph wondered. The other burning question was, had she known anything about the drug it obviously contained? That seemed unlikely, since she too was passed out in the drawing room, but he still couldn't rule it out.

In an ideal world, he'd have gone for one of the heavier vehicles for what he had in mind. A Range Rover would have stood a chance against a van. But every chauffeur was out cold, and he didn't have the seconds to lose to search for the keys. Which left him with just one option.

The Triumph.

The TR4 sat at the edge of the row, nose angled towards the drive. Small, fast, fragile, but his only card to play.

The DI sprinted towards it, fumbling his keys with slick hands, the growl of the van already getting louder as it closed on the Grange. He jammed the key into the ignition and twisted hard. The engine caught at once, with a reassuring throaty burble.

Joseph slammed the accelerator down. The rear wheels spun, squealing on tarmac, before biting. The Triumph fish-tailed wildly, rear end slewing out, but Joseph caught it with a sharp twist of the wheel, his heart pounding. He missed the flank of a Bentley by millimetres as the car snapped straight and hurled forward, gravel spraying in its wake.

The world narrowed to the drive ahead. He tore through the gears, hand braced on the door handle, deliberately keeping it unlatched. The engine roared, and Joseph's whole body thrummed with it. He'd only get this one shot.

Fifty miles an hour, sixty... The hedges blurred at the edges of his vision.

Then the van burst into view, white paint catching the light as it screamed towards him. Two men in balaclavas stared out from its windscreen at the fast-approaching vintage sports car. Even with their faces hidden, Joseph saw their mouths open.

Fighting every instinct, Joseph rammed the throttle flat to the floor, pushing the Triumph harder. At the last possible instant, he wrenched the door wide and hurled himself sideways.

Time fractured in his mind in that moment: the TR4 hurtled onwards: the van swerving right with its tyres shrieking; a crunch of metal bending and glass shattering; the Triumph slamming into the van's corner bumper; the van tipping as its wheels slipped over the embankment and then starting to roll sideways off the road.

Branches whipped at Joseph's face as he crashed through a laurel hedge, small branches tearing at his arms, leaves slapping his face. Pain flared across his ribs as he tumbled through the tangle, and everything else was swallowed from view. Then his body burst out the other side, his momentum carrying him, tumbling down the steepening slope, sliding and bouncing, earth and stones flying in all directions. A stream glinted below as he skidded to a bone-jarring stop.

Joseph's whole body groaned as he rolled onto his side, his lungs heaving, skin stinging from a dozen cuts and scrapes.

For a moment, he lay still, stunned by the violence of it all, but a quick mental inventory reassured him he was in one piece. There was no stabbing pain in his ribs, no grinding of broken bones, just the deep throb of bruises already blooming beneath his skin. He'd been lucky, far luckier than he deserved, considering he'd thrown himself out of a moving car travelling at least seventy miles per hour at the time.

Using the trunk of an oak sapling for support, he dragged himself upright. The world tilted as his vision swam, but he forced it into focus.

Below him, at the base of the ravine, the van had landed on its roof, its wheels still spinning lazily. Even through the smoke, Joseph saw the passenger door groan open, a black-gloved hand pushing against it.

Then came the sound.

A low whoosh, almost gentle at first, before the van erupted. A ball of fire surged skyward, the blast slamming into the DI with a wall of intense heat, making him shield his face.

When he looked back, blinking through smoke and sparks, he saw the van had become a raging inferno. The outstretched arm that had been reaching from the passenger side now hung lifeless, already being swallowed by the blaze. Whoever had been inside the van hadn't stood a chance.

Joseph staggered forward again, the roar of the fire filling his ears. Then he realised there were sirens and they were growing closer, followed by the sound of tyres skidding to a stop nearby. Doors slammed, voices barked orders, and heavy boots pounded on the ground, getting closer. But Joseph barely registered any of it. His gaze stayed locked on the fire as he stumbled down the slope towards the van, legs heavy but moving anyway. He didn't know what he meant to do. There was no saving anyone from that furnace, but instinct still drove him towards it. He had to try to help them.

But then a hand gripped his shoulder, strong and steadying.

'It's too late for them,' Chris's voice said behind him.

Joseph turned to find his boss standing there. Chris was strapped into a stab vest, with Megan at his side, her face pale in the firelight as he looked at him. Behind them, tactical officers fanned out in arcs, rifles ready as they scanned the woods for any accomplices.

The only words Joseph could find were hoarse. 'How did you know?'

'Ricky Holt,' Chris said grimly. 'He called the station and claimed he'd been tipped off that Iron Dawn were planning to hit Ellensmere Grange to take Blackwood out. We scrambled everyone available, but—' His eyes flicked past Joseph to the burning wreck. 'Were there any more of them?'

'Not that I saw,' Joseph replied. 'But everyone in the house has been drugged out. I think it might have been the cake they all ate, including Alison, who made the fecking thing.'

Chris nodded sharply. 'Okay, we'll get medics in there immediately.'

Joseph caught his sleeve. 'What about the officers and the others at the main gate? Please tell me they're alive.'

'They all are. The terrorists used tranquilliser darts to bring them down.' But then Chris's mouth tightened. 'Whoever planned this, they wanted the TU and Blackwood's people unconscious, not dead.'

Joseph exhaled, a relieved sigh of relief. 'Aye, that's one blessing at least.'

'Why aren't you flat on your back like the rest of them?' Megan asked, gazing at him.

The DI gave her a wry look. 'Let's just say I passed on the cake.'

'Good thing I wasn't here, then,' Megan said.

Joseph managed a tired smile. 'Aye, you wouldn't have stood a chance.'

A pair of armed officers headed past them carrying extinguishers, but even as they angled hoses towards the blaze, Joseph knew it was too little too late. The van was already an oven, flames clawing at the tree line with enough heat to make his skin prickle.

Chris helped Joseph, with Megan assisting, back through the torn hedge to the driveway. But the DI's stomach sank when he spotted the Triumph. The right wing was crushed in, the wheel dangling grotesquely from its axle. The battered engine ticked and groaned with the indignity of being turned into a metal missile.

Joseph winced. 'Oh shite. I'm so sorry about your car, Chris.'

The DCI gave him a sideways look, then a small smile. 'Don't worry about her. We'll sort her out in no time. The important thing is you're still in one piece.'

Megan glanced between them, eyebrows arched. 'Bloody hell. Talk about getting off lightly.'

Joseph chuckled softly. 'If only. I suspect I'll be putting in most of the work to help fix her.'

But even as he smiled, he caught Chris's eye. The barest flicker of a nod passed between them, unseen by Megan. There were bigger secrets here, about Blackwood, the Night Watchmen, the hint of the occult, what had been happening on the estate in the middle of the night, and where Alison fit into all of it.

But most pressing of all was Iron Dawn's raid on Blackwood's home, and what that meant for their investigation.

CHAPTER TWENTY-TWO

'WELL, this is one hell of a shit show,' Derrick said flatly, leaning back in his chair. His office at St Aldates felt smaller than usual, the blinds half-drawn, casting bars of shadows across the room. His gaze fixed first on Joseph, then Chris, like he was daring either of them to contradict him.

Chris spoke before Joseph could. 'If it hadn't been for Joseph's quick thinking, it could've been a lot worse. Those terrorists weren't messing about. We recovered two Kalashnikovs from the back of that van with full magazines and a rucksack full of cable ties. If Joseph hadn't acted when he did, we could be talking about a mass hostage situation, or worse. Maybe even a massacre at Ellensmere Grange.'

Derrick turned his head slowly, his stare settling back on Joseph. The hard set of his jaw said it all before he'd even uttered a word. 'But it should never have been allowed to get that far in the first place. If you'd been doing your job properly, none of this would have happened.'

There it was. The opening salvo. Predictable as rain falling in Kerry back in Ireland. Joseph felt his pulse spike, but he forced himself to draw a long, steadying breath. As usual, the big man was looking for a scapegoat.

'With respect, there wasn't exactly a lot I could have done beforehand,' Joseph said, his voice tight. 'Everyone in that house was drugged up to the eyeballs. And the men on the gate were taken down with tranquilliser darts. Short of developing clairvoyance, I wasn't in much of a position to stop it beyond what I did.'

The DSU scowled at him and turned toward Chris. 'How are all the victims doing now?'

'The effects wore off Blackwood and his guests after about thirty minutes,' Chris said. 'The tranquillisers used on our men were veterinary-grade. Strong, but not lethal. They have been checked over at hospital, same as Blackwood and his guests. They've all been discharged with no lingering after-effects.'

But the troubled crease between Chris's brows stayed.

'There's still a problem, isn't there?' Joseph asked, before Derrick could cut back in.

Chris hesitated, before nodding. 'The question I can't shake is, why didn't they use those Kalashnikovs on the armed officers? They had the weapons and the element of surprise on their side. But they went for darts and sedatives. That isn't normal behaviour for terrorists. They're not usually selective like that.'

'Maybe they meant what they said in their manifesto,' Joseph replied. 'That they were only targeting politicians. Not the public, or in this case the police, just the so-called *enemy*.'

Derrick tapped his pen against the desk, a sharp, repetitive click that set Joseph's teeth on edge. He looked up, and for once, the usual hostility in the man's stare wasn't there. Something else sat behind his eyes, confusion even.

Joseph felt a flicker of surprise at that. Once again, Derrick seemed genuinely out of the loop. Surely they would have kept him briefed, even with the barest details. Unless they only told him what they wanted him to know. Maybe they were still testing his loyalty.

But then the mask slipped back on as Derrick's expression hardened, the open hostility back as he leaned forward.

'What I want to know, Joseph, is how you allowed everyone in that house to be drugged in the first place.'

The DI felt the surge of anger building in his chest. He clamped it down, but his voice still came out sharper than he intended. 'Once again, I'm not a fecking psychic, am I? How the hell was I supposed to know the cake was laced?'

Derrick's eyes narrowed to slits. 'We don't know that for certain until the toxicology comes back. But rather convenient though, that you were the only one who didn't eat any.'

He peered at the man. 'What exactly are you insinuating here?'

Derrick leaned across the desk, his eyes flinty. 'Why don't you tell me?'

Of all the directions Joseph had expected this meeting to take, this certainly wasn't one of them. The DSU knew full well the Night Watchmen had put the squeeze on him before by threatening his family, forcing him to play along. As far as they were concerned, and Derrick too, for that matter, they'd backed off ever since.

So what the hell did this mean? Was Derrick bluffing, trying to rattle him? Or worse, did he actually believe Joseph had crossed the line and slipped all those people a Mickey Finn himself, carrying out the Night Watchmen's orders as their inside man working with Iron Dawn?

The thought turned Joseph's stomach cold as his anger burned.

But before he could erupt, Chris cut in before he could destroy his career forever.

'Obviously, there was no way Joseph could've known the cake might have been drugged,' the SIO said.

But the DSU wasn't letting go just yet. His gaze locked on Joseph like a hawk watching its prey. 'I just find it very convenient that of all the people in that house, you were the only one who didn't eat a slice of the cake.'

Joseph felt his jaw clench. 'Must have been my lucky day,' he shot back. But the irony wasn't lost on him. This attack on his character was coming straight from a man who'd already bent the knee to the Night Watchmen. Who was Derrick, of all people, to judge him? But maybe all this righteous bluster was nothing more than a smoke screen, a performance to throw them off the scent.

Derrick leaned back, shaking his head. 'So Joseph's massive cock-up aside, what do the NCA have to say about whoever was behind this, Chris?'

'Even though this isn't strictly their case, I reached out,' Chris replied. 'Alison Blackwood maintains her innocence, but can't explain how any drug might have found its way into her cake.'

A thought struck Joseph then, and he leaned forward. 'Actually, I can back Alison up on that. She gave me a slice when she first baked it, on the day before the strategy meeting. I didn't suffer so much as a dodgy tummy. That suggests whatever was slipped into it must've been added later.'

Chris gave a short nod. 'Your experience supports the NCA's theory that someone at the gathering slipped the drug into the cake. They're now scrutinising everyone who had access to the house both before and during the meeting.'

'In that case, they might want to take a closer look at Sir Reginald Harrington,' Joseph said.

Derrick's eyes narrowed. 'Because?'

But Chris was already nodding, already on board with

Joseph's train of thought. 'Because Harrington also happened to be sitting very close to Martin Chambers during the charity dinner at Christ Church the night the minister was poisoned.'

Derrick frowned. 'Are you suggesting Sally Green wasn't the one who poisoned Chambers?'

Joseph felt the possibilities tumbling together in his mind. 'When I asked Harrington why he'd turned up at Blackwood's strategy meeting when he'd previously been backing a rival party, he told me One Nation was the future, and that they had a real chance to change the country. What if that wasn't just pragmatism? What if Harrington made sure of it by poisoning the one man who could've blocked Blackwood's rise to power?'

The silence in the room thickened. Even Chris didn't answer right away.

Finally, Derrick leaned forward, his brow furrowed. 'Let me point out the obvious flaw here. Why would Harrington then turn around and drug himself along with everyone else at One Nation's strategy meeting, if his goal was to help get them into power?'

Just like that, the theory that had started to gather speed in Joseph's mind stuttered to a halt. He let out a breath through his nose. 'Aye, you're not wrong. It doesn't exactly stack up.'

'Maybe not, but I'll mention it to Emma anyway,' Chris said. 'Better it's on their radar than not.'

Joseph felt that familiar knot of frustration settle in his gut again—the helplessness of knowing he was only ever seeing one small part of the bigger picture.

'So what happens now?' he asked.

Derrick pulled a face like someone had shoved dog shite under his nose. 'You're going back to Ellensmere Grange to continue your minister protection duties.'

Joseph blinked. 'I am?'

'Yes,' Derrick said, his tone sour. 'Marcus Blackwood

insisted on it. He even suggested—and I'm quoting here—you should be put forward for the King's Police Medal for gallantry for what you did to save them all.'

Joseph stared at him, caught between disbelief and amusement. The very man he suspected of being tied to the Night Watchmen was recommending him for a medal.

'That would certainly get my support,' Chris said without hesitation.

Derrick swung a glare his way. 'We're certainly not on the same page when it comes to that.' Then his eyes came back to Joseph, hard and unblinking. 'For reasons lost on me, the man seems to think you've got the sun blazing out of your arse. Because of that, he wants you by his side until the election is over. So that's where you'll be.'

Joseph forced himself to keep his tone level. 'I've no problem with that. But surely Marcus and Eddie would be safer in a more secure location?'

'Which is exactly what I suggested to Chief Kennan when I spoke to her,' Derrick snapped. 'But apparently, Marcus is insisting he won't be driven out of his own home. He's ordered that the meeting schedule goes on as planned. His house, his rules, and all that nonsense.'

Joseph shook his head slowly. 'I can understand the politics of it, but it's going to make everyone's lives a lot more difficult. I don't imagine the NCA are exactly thrilled either?'

'No,' Chris said, his voice carrying the weight of what he wasn't saying. The look in his eye hinted to Joseph that a long conversation between the SIO and Emma had already been had.

Derrick's nostrils flared so wide he gave a reasonable impression of a bull. 'Then let's make damned sure there are no more cock-ups this time round.'

'I'll do my best,' Joseph replied with a glare, stopping himself just short of throwing in a finger.

'Good. Now get out of my sight. You've given me enough of a ballache for one day.'

Chris traded a look with Joseph before the two of them turned and walked out. As soon as they were clear of the office, Chris rolled his eyes. 'You really didn't deserve any of that.'

Joseph gave a humourless smile. 'Aye, I know. But here we are, anyway.'

They stepped into one of the open-plan rooms where Megan, Ian, and Sue were gathered around a television. Joseph instantly recognised the commanding voice booming from the speakers. Marcus Blackwood.

Megan spotted them and beckoned them over. 'Timed to perfection; you're going to want to see this.' She hit rewind on what had been a live stream, and pressed play.

Joseph and Chris moved closer, their gazes fixed on the screen.

Marcus Blackwood stood outside the John Radcliffe Hospital, surrounded by TV crews and cameras. Two armed officers flanked him in the background, along with several of his personal security, their dark suits and earpieces making the whole scene look like something staged for broadcast.

'I would like to single out DI Joseph Stone for his astonishingly quick thinking,' the leader said. 'If he hadn't rammed the terrorists' van, we would almost certainly be looking at a very different outcome today.' The camera zoomed in slightly as Marcus Blackwood delivered the line with just the right amount of solemnity. The pause, the tone, the almost reverential nod, it was all pure political theatre.

In the incident room, every head turned towards Joseph.

'Look at you, getting name-dropped,' Ian said.

Joseph grimaced. 'Trust me, I'd much rather I hadn't.'

'Rubbish,' Sue said. 'This is exactly the sort of thing that puts an officer in line for promotion. You'll be polishing that medal before long.'

Chris gave her a dry look. 'You didn't see what he did to my car.'

A ripple of laughter went around the room, although Joseph didn't join in. He was still watching the screen, his jaw tight. Whatever Blackwood was about to say, he knew the man wasn't one to turn down an opportunity like this.

Sure enough, the politician's tone hardened. 'This sort of incident underlines how our police and security forces are so underfunded. The men and women, as DI Stone so aptly demonstrated, frequently go far above and beyond, often putting their own lives on the line. And they do that despite a serious lack of resources. These cracks in the system are what terrorist groups like Iron Dawn exploit. However, make no mistake, these threats to the very existence of our democracy will only increase over time. We need to act today before it's too late.'

The leader leaned closer to the microphone, his eyes glittering. 'That's why, if our party, One Nation, is elected to power at the next election, we'll triple the budgets for the police, security services, and armed forces. A vote for us is a vote for safety. A vote for us is a vote for strength. A vote for us is a vote for security.'

In the room at St Aldates, Megan folded her arms. 'That didn't take him long, did it? Barely survived an assassination attempt, and he's already milking it for campaign points.'

'To give him credit, he's rather good at it,' Sue said reluctantly. 'I'll give him that.'

He's also fecking dangerous, Joseph thought.

On the screen, a reporter called out, 'And is this one of the topics you'll be covering at the televised live debate with the other leaders in two days' time?'

'You can count on it,' Marcus replied smoothly.

'And what words do you have for your rivals?' the reporter asked.

Blackwood turned squarely to face the cameras, the late-afternoon sun glinting off the silver in his hair. A slight smile played at the corners of his mouth.

'I'd say this. While they squabble over ideology and point fingers at each other, we're the ones with a plan. The public doesn't want more talk, they want action. They want leadership that won't flinch in the face of danger. So to my rivals, I say, step aside, or step up, because One Nation is ready to lead. Thank you, everyone, for your time.'

With a beaming smile, he strode towards the waiting Range Rover. Gareth held the door open and swung it shut the moment he was inside. A few moments later, the convoy began to move away.

The camera swung back to the reporter, who wore the sort of earnest expression only television news could produce. 'And there you have it. Marcus Blackwood, unbowed after last night's shocking attack. He's not only reassured his supporters, but also put rival parties on notice. And his message is clear, the One Nation's leader didn't only just survive an assassination attempt, but his determination to seize the political initiative has crystallised, and is ready to lead the country.'

Chris reached for the remote and clicked the TV off. The sudden silence was heavy in the incident room. 'You might want to think about going home to grab some things before you head back to Ellensmere Grange,' he said to Joseph.

Megan stared at him. 'You aren't seriously sending Joseph back there alone after what happened? If you are, then I want to be by his side.'

Joseph cut in before Chris could answer Megan's protest. 'Don't worry about me. They're doubling the number of armed officers on site. Besides, I bet you're loving the chance to catch up on all your paperwork while I'm babysitting politicians.'

The DC scowled, then her mouth broke into a wide grin. 'You know me way too well. But promise me one thing, don't get yourself into any more trouble.'

'I'll try my best,' Joseph said, though the dryness in his voice made it clear even he didn't believe it.

Chris gave them a small smile. 'Sounds like you've got your orders, Joseph. But before you head out, I need five minutes.'

'Of course,' Joseph said, falling into step with him.

A short while later, the two of them were tucked away in one of the small meeting rooms. Chris closed the door firmly, shutting out the low hum of voices from the incident room.

Joseph leaned back against the table, frowning. 'So what's the NCA's take on everything that went down?'

'That it may have been staged, at least in part, by the Night Watchmen to push Blackwood closer to power,' Chris replied. 'That's the question, though, isn't it? Was he really unconscious? Or, and this is the scenario they've been gaming out, maybe the plan was that he was seized along with the others, but then somehow managed to slip free. Imagine the optics of that. A would-be prime minister escaping from his captors, and then raising the alarm himself, to save the day.'

Joseph's stomach clenched. He could picture it all too clearly: the headlines screaming Blackwood the Survivor, rolling news looping his miraculous escape, talk shows hailing him as the man destiny demanded.

'Jesus, the public would've lapped that up,' he said. 'He'd have gone from candidate to folk hero overnight.'

'Exactly, and he and his party would've become unstoppable as a political force,' Chris said. 'Sympathy, admiration, fear, all collapsing into one powerful narrative. And judging by how fast his party's poll numbers jumped off the back of this *attack*, they know exactly how to exploit it.'

Joseph rubbed the back of his neck, a sense of unease gnawing at him. 'Which means Marcus might've been playing everyone in Ellensmere Grange. Pretending to be a victim, when all along, he was centre stage in the action. If he'd pulled off a stunt like that, the whole country would be eating out of his hand right now.'

Chris nodded grimly. 'That's why the NCA is convinced we haven't seen the endgame yet. Either this was a dress rehearsal, or something went sideways thanks to your unexpected intervention. But one way or another, Blackwood walked out of hospital looking stronger than he went in.'

The thought lodged in the DI's gut like a stone. 'And the debate will only help amplify his message.'

'Oh, trust me, I more than realise that.'

'But surely the NCA's got enough by now to bring the whole lot of them down,' he said.

'Not quite,' Chris admitted. 'Not if they want Blackwood himself in the net. That's why we need you back there. Eyes and ears inside their citadel until we know more.'

Joseph's mouth twisted. 'I take it that means the bug didn't catch anything useful?'

'In one. Just hours of dull political chatter. The only thing of note is how laser-focused they all are on this debate. Every briefing, every rehearsal, all seem to build toward it.'

Joseph grimaced. 'Which is going to be a fecking security nightmare.'

'Agreed, MI5 and the NCA both recommended scrapping it, but none of the leaders want to be the first to blink. So it's happening as planned.'

'Bloody politicians.' Then a thought occurred to him. 'So

what about that CCTV footage from inside Westminster relating to that call from the burner phone. I'm guessing from the fact you didn't come and arrest Blackwood, it didn't prove anything?'

Chris gave a humourless smile. 'Exactly. Unfortunately, all it caught was a gaggle of ministers gathered together in the bar. Blackwood was among them, but there was no clear view of whether he used his phone at the time of the call. So, unfortunately, other than suspicions, we still have no hard evidence to pin on him. Maybe combined with other evidence, it might be enough to convince a jury he was somehow involved, although that's a bit of a stretch. That's why you being there is so important—if there's anything useful you can dig up... Talking of which, we should discuss your last text.'

Joseph stared at his hands. 'Like I said, there's no sign of any links to the occult in the Blackwoods' home. As for the activity around the dovecote, if it is being used for anything clandestine by the Night Watchmen, like drug storage, I've yet to find evidence of it.'

'Then keep digging, you still are our best chance of a breakthrough with this case.'

'Don't worry, I will. Hopefully, Alison won't lace my tea in the meantime.'

'Don't even joke about that,' Chris replied. 'That's why I want you to be extra careful with anything you eat or drink.'

'I was already planning on packing a thermos with me,' Joseph said.

'Don't worry, we'll handle catering,' Chris told him. 'Fresh supplies, vetted daily, and no risks this time. And strictly no cakes.'

'Glad to hear it, although Alison won't be happy,' Joseph said.

'Maybe not, but this has got far too serious to allow her to play hostess to everyone, however well intentioned she is. Anyway, just watch your back. And until we know otherwise, trust no one. Not Blackwood, Eddie, Alison, or anyone else in that house.'

'Paranoid will be my middle name from now on.'

That earned the DI a weary smile from the SIO. 'Then you'd better get moving, and head home to grab those fresh things. But please, Joseph, no more heroics. First whiff of trouble, you call it in. Do you understand me?'

'You've got it.' Joseph dipped his chin before heading for the door.

CHAPTER TWENTY-THREE

ONBOARD *TÙS NUA*, Kate was hugging Joseph so hard he thought one of his ribs might crack. Every bruise gained from leaping out of a moving car screamed in protest. He had to grit his teeth not to groan.

'Honestly, I'm fine,' Joseph said, trying to prise her limpet-like arms loose from around him.

'Maybe you are, but only by luck and not judgment,' Kate replied, pulling away just enough to stare at him. 'I'm certainly not happy about you heading back to Ellensmere Grange. Surely Chris can assign someone else?'

'Not on this occasion.'

'But I don't understand why it has to be *you?*' Her voice cracked on the last word.

Joseph's chest tightened. He was sorely tempted, as he so often was, to tell her everything—the NCA's involvement, the fact he was working as their eyes and ears inside Blackwood's camp. But if Kate knew that, she could easily become a target, and he couldn't risk that. Not now, not ever.

He shrugged, trying to avoid her searchlight gaze. 'Those are just the breaks for a serving officer. You know that.'

'Yes, but knowing you, I expect you were probably more than happy to accept,' she said.

Joseph grimaced, not bothering to deny it. 'Anyway, in a desperate attempt to change the subject, how's your own digging into Chambers's death going?'

Kate held his gaze for a moment, then sighed as the edge in her expression softened. 'Actually, I might be onto something with Sally Green. A source contacted me. They said their dashcam picked up someone on the night Sally Green died.'

Joseph stared at her. 'Proof of who murdered her?'

'Maybe not a smoking gun, but it was a man fleeing the scene at the right time. The car the dashcam was fitted to was parked near Osney Mead lock on the main road. It recorded a man running away from the alley that leads from it. The timing is apparently almost exact for when Sally died at the hydropower station.'

'And did the camera get a clear look at his face?'

'Apparently.'

Joseph gawped at her as he took her hands in his. 'Jesus H. Christ, this is dynamite, Kate. So hand over the footage already and we'll get on with the business of hauling the bastard in for questioning.'

Kate raised both hands. 'Not so fast, I'm afraid. The owner of the footage wants to be paid for an exclusive.'

'Fecking mercenary!'

'Maybe he is, but unfortunately, they know they've got a big story on their hands. The man in the footage is apparently someone significant.'

Joseph's ears pricked up at hearing that. 'I don't suppose they gave you a hint of who?'

'No. They just said the name's worth a lot of money to the right bidder. I'm trying to negotiate them down because their expectations are ridiculous. If they don't budge, I may need to split the exclusive with one of the broadsheets. The Gazette's pockets aren't deep enough for this.'

Joseph scowled. 'You do know we could arrest this person for obstructing an investigation. I could probably shake the name out of them in five minutes flat.'

Kate folded her arms, her chin lifting. 'Maybe you could, but over my dead body. As you well know, journalists, even ones who have boyfriends who are policemen, have a professional duty to protect their sources. Even if they are money-grabbing little shits.'

Joseph smiled. '*Boyfriend* now is it?'

'Well, life partner is a bit of a mouthful.'

'Don't worry, I'm just as happy to settle for love of my life.'

Kate's scowl dissolved away into a laugh. 'What am I going to do with you?'

'Oh, I might have some ideas.' He pulled Kate in and gave her a lingering kiss.

'If you think you'll get around me that way, you might just succeed, so please stop.'

Joseph pulled away, grinning despite the ache in his ribs. 'You can't blame a man for trying.' Then the smile slipped from his face as a sense of seriousness took hold again. 'But obviously the sooner you can get that video to us, the better it'll be for all concerned.'

'Don't worry, I'm working on it,' Kate said, though her frown lingered. Then, her expression shifted slightly. 'Whilst I have you, I need to bring you up to speed about Ellie.'

Joseph braced himself. 'Oh God, what drama is it this time?'

'No problems for once,' Kate said, her voice softening. 'Quite the opposite, in fact. We've got reason to feel very proud. Despite everything that's been going on, Ellie's still managed to get her head down. She's on track to submit her thesis by the end of the week.'

Joseph's chest swelled with parental pride. 'And she's happy with how it's gone?'

Kate gave a wry smile. 'Of course not. You know what she's like; she's an absolute perfectionist. But from everything she's told me, she's more than got this.'

'I'd expect nothing less from our golden girl,' Joseph said. 'Send her my love and tell her I'm incredibly proud of her.'

'I think she already knows that,' Kate said. 'And whilst I'm bringing you up to speed again, the other thing I need to tell you is about Dylan. Iris confided in me, he's really miserable at the moment.'

Joseph rubbed his temple. 'I assume, something to do with this high cholesterol business?'

'It's everything to do with it. After being resistant to the idea, he's now swung to the opposite extreme and gone completely overboard with his new diet. No gin, no proper food, no little indulgences at all. Iris says he's turned into a complete food zealot. She wouldn't worry so much if he wasn't making himself miserable in the process. And by proxy, her too.'

Joseph let out a slow sigh. 'I'm not surprised if he's cut out everything he used to enjoy. Sounds like he's taken it too far.'

'That's what Iris thinks as well. She said the whole diagnosis has really rattled him. For the first time, I think Dylan's really having to confront his own mortality.'

Joseph nodded slowly. 'Something that comes to us all eventually. But there could be another explanation for the way he's reacting this way.'

Kate tilted her head. 'Which is?'

'Like I said to him, because he's got Iris in his life now,' Joseph said.

Kate blinked, then a flicker of surprise softened her expression. 'You're saying he has someone else to live for?'

'I wouldn't quite put it as dramatically as that,' Joseph said, giving her a small smile, 'but yes, a reason to stick around. Don't forget, he's waited for that relationship for years. And now he's got her, well...'

Kate finished quietly for him. 'He wants to be with her as long as possible.'

'Just like my good self,' Joseph replied. He reached out and squeezed Kate's hand.

Her face lit up with a smile. 'You old romantic.'

'Aye, guilty as charged. Anyway, it sounds as if Dylan's gone a bit off the deep end with this diet of his. I'll have a quiet word when I get the chance. I'll suggest he doesn't need to be quite so puritanical.'

'Already done,' Kate said. 'But I think hearing it from you might help. He's also making far too big a deal out of taking statins.'

'Ah, now I can sympathise with that,' Joseph admitted. 'You know I hate the idea of medication. It always feels like a failure of some sort.'

Kate shook her head. 'You two are as bad as each other. Iris and I have already told him the research is clear. Statins work. He just needs to ease up on the diet and accept the pills.'

Joseph nodded. 'Then consider it done. I'll talk to him before I head back to Ellensmere Grange. Speaking of which, I'd better get my things together. Including a good supply of coffee. Do we still have any of those Sumatra beans from the Covered Market?'

'About half a tin left.'

'Then I'll take the lot if you don't mind.'

Kate arched an eyebrow. 'They don't have decent coffee of their own?'

Joseph hesitated, then decided there was no point in lying because Kate would see through it anyway. 'It's not that. We're taking extra precautions in light of what happened last time.'

Kate's eyes widened. 'You mean to make sure you don't get drugged?'

'That's about the measure of it. We're still waiting on lab results, but everything points to the cake being spiked, and unlike everyone else, luckily, I didn't eat any. Because of that, all food and drink are going to be monitored. Hence, taking my own coffee with me.'

Kate's hand went to her mouth. 'Do you seriously think Iron Dawn will try again?'

Joseph's jaw tightened. 'I honestly have no idea. But we'll carry on as though they will.'

Kate slowly nodded. 'The problem is they've already scored a major propaganda coup. Ironic, isn't it, that it's helped the very party they supposedly targeted surge in the polls?'

'Isn't it just?' Joseph tried to keep his expression neutral.

A knock came at the door. 'Joseph, are you there?' Dylan's voice called out.

'I am, and your ears were obviously burning,' Joseph replied as he opened the door for his friend.

The professor stepped in, White Fang and Max at his heels. They immediately spotted Tux perched on the arm of the sofa. The cat stretched languidly, then hopped down to saunter over, rubbing himself down their sides, before leaping onto the worktop to avoid their more enthusiastic greetings.

'Good to see you're okay after your mishap,' Dylan said.

'Barely,' Joseph replied. 'But since you're here, there's something I needed to talk to you about.'

'If you don't mind, I'd like to go first,' Dylan replied. 'I wanted to get you up to speed about my research on that mark you found on Martin Chambers's serviette.'

Kate's gaze immediately zeroed in on Joseph. 'What mark?'

Joseph weighed whether this was the right moment to tell

her. But then Dylan, as though reading his mind, gave him the barest encouraging nod.

The DI sighed and took Kate's hand in his. 'Look, I don't want you to go off the deep end about this, but we found something significant that seems, on the surface at least, to draw a connection to the Midwinter Butcher case.'

Her eyes widened. 'What exactly?'

'They found Azrael's symbol drawn onto a napkin we believe Sally Green gave him,' Dylan said.

Kate's face paled as she looked between Joseph and the professor. 'You're saying you didn't actually catch the real Midwinter Butcher last time?'

Joseph quickly shook his head. 'No, that's not what I'm saying. All the evidence pointed to Aaron Fearnley and Helen Edwards being the ones responsible for what happened back then. But our guess is that either someone was inspired by them, or maybe more likely, Helen came across the Azrael symbol on that dark net forum she hung out on.'

Dylan nodded. 'And now someone else is using Azrael's mark again. But in the context Joseph discovered it, given as it was moments before Chambers died, it basically looks like they used it as a death sigil in this instance.'

Kate's lips parted. 'You're saying this Iron Dawn group literally cursed him and then carried through with their threat?'

'That's the implication,' Dylan admitted. 'I started digging deeper into the meaning of the Azrael symbol. There are fragments in some of the grimoires, whispers of the mark being used in rites of passage. It also crops up in different cultures under different guises, but always tied to death, endings, and transition. But there's something older about the symbol. It's actually pre-Christian, and the angel's name only came later. Whoever scrawled it, there's a good chance they know their history and maybe even want it recognised.'

Joseph stared at his friend. 'That actually tallies with the psychological profile for the murderer, which says pretty much exactly that. It also struck me from the start that there's almost been an element of theatre to all of this. Using two drugs combined on their victims, the way Sally Green was murdered, and also the use of the sigil... This is someone wanting to make a statement.'

Kate held up her hands as she looked from one to the other. 'You're saying Chambers wasn't just poisoned, he was ritually murdered?'

Joseph gave her a grim look. 'That's what it's starting to look like.'

'And if this mark ties to Azrael, it might explain more than Chambers's death,' Dylan added. 'Think about Sally Green. The brutality of what happened to her down at that hydro station. Seen through the eyes of someone who believes in the occult, tearing a body apart can serve a purpose. A ritual of destruction. A way to bind the death to something larger.'

Joseph's gaze tightened on the professor. 'So, once again, we need to seriously consider that this is somehow linked to the Midwinter Butcher case. But if they *are* using the same methodology, we didn't find a sigil on Sally Green's body...' His words trailed away. Of course they hadn't, if Amy had successfully hidden it, just like she'd almost certainly intended to do with the napkin, if Joseph hadn't spotted it first. Another piece of critical evidence would have gone missing, which would have linked these murders to the Night Watchmen.

'Am I thinking what you are?' Dylan asked.

'Are you?' Joseph replied, concerned he'd somehow given something away.

'Yes, it could have been lost in the river when she was pushed in.'

Kate nodded, but the colour had drained from her face.

'You're saying that, just like the Midwinter Butcher case, the victims weren't just killed, they were sacrificed to Azrael?'

Dylan's expression became grave. 'That's my guess. Which means Chambers and Sally's deaths might not be isolated at all. They're both part of the same thread.'

'One that extends all the way back to the Midwinter Butcher murders, you mean?' Joseph asked.

The professor nodded slowly. 'Yes. Different victims, different stages, but maybe the same hand guiding it in the background. Perhaps Helen Edwards was even put up to persuading Aaron Fearnley to use Azrael's symbol by a group she belonged to. Regardless, I believe that it's the same darkness running through all these cases.'

Joseph felt the weight of it settle on his chest. If Dylan was right, they weren't chasing separate crimes at all. They were staring at something far wider, and with the use of the Alchemist's poison, and maybe even something much older.

'Anyway, that's all I have for you,' Dylan said.

'Thank you for all of this, and I'll make sure it's passed on to Chris to share with the NCA.'

Dylan nodded. 'And don't worry, we'll keep digging. But you mentioned there was something you wanted to talk to me about? A new nugget of information you need to share about the case, Joseph?'

The DI turned his thoughts away from the darkness of the subject, and took hold of his friend by the shoulders. 'Now what's all this about you being something of a martyr about reducing your cholesterol?'

Dylan gave a sheepish smile. 'I know, I know.'

'Come on then, let's get you sorted out on all of this. Enough with this whole going off the deep end, already.'

'And now you've got both of us on your case,' Kate added.

Dylan sighed. 'Not to mention Iris.'

'Exactly. So make yourself comfortable, because we are so going to have *the talk*, my friend.'

Kate squeezed his hand as Dylan sank into the chair and Tux leapt from the counter onto his lap, with the dogs settling at his feet.

It looked to Joseph as though this was going to be a family effort.

But even as he got ready to give his friend a well-needed lecture, he couldn't shake the fresh significance of the sigil from his mind. Azrael's mark, etched in ink and blood across the years. Was this the missing piece that bound all these events together, and now to the Night Watchmen? And how many more victims had already been claimed under its shadow, and how many more would follow before they stopped it?

CHAPTER TWENTY-FOUR

After the chaos of Joseph's previous stay at Ellensmere Grange, the contrast this time was striking. The constant comings and goings had been replaced by an almost eerie calm. It was partly down to the new rules MI5 and the NCA had laid down. They had insisted that until further notice, Marcus Blackwood's meetings were to be conducted remotely by video. That condition alone had allowed the minister to return home following the so-called *terrorist* attack.

But the changes didn't stop there. To Marcus's evident horror at anyone meddling with his precious family home, heavy security shutters now covered every window and door. He'd been reassured they were temporary, but Joseph could see why he worried about damage to the Jacobean building that he'd so painstakingly helped restore. The steel looked brutally out of place against the old brick and oak, a twenty-first-century prison bolted onto seventeenth-century bones. Even the DI found himself quietly agreeing with him.

Inside, there was another surprise. The door to the drawing room, the chamber that had become Marcus's private nerve centre, stood wide open. Whatever they were discussing evidently no longer required secrecy, which meant the listening device Joseph had hidden for the NCA was redundant. More than that, he was now sitting in the room itself. It appeared Marcus had approved him to enter the inner sanctum of his kingdom.

In a rehearsal for the imminent leader political debate, Joseph watched as an observer as Eddie and Michael Mercer, another of the One Nation ministers, stood in for rival party leaders. They'd been verbally sparring with Marcus, as Alison played the part of moderator. The walnut coffee table had been shoved against the wall to be replaced by a camera on a tripod, its feed linked into a monitor. Two box lights glared from opposite corners, flattening out the shadows cast by the thickening storm clouds beyond the shuttered windows. It looked less like a family drawing room and more like a makeshift TV studio.

Marcus was centre stage in all of this, wearing a crisp navy suit, his tie knotted just so, his hair trimmed to a precise line. Even his wardrobe was clearly being rehearsed. A lion-shaped lapel pin gleamed every time he shifted. He looked like he'd been born for this. Eddie sprawled opposite, his ankle hooked lazily over his knee, while Alison sat ramrod straight, a folder of notes in her lap.

'Let's keep this as close to the real thing as we can,' Alison said. 'Marcus, would you like to start with your opening?'

The leader inclined his head as though already acknowledging the applause of millions of unseen viewers.

'I'm here to tell you that Britain stands at a crossroads. Division in our politics. Rising threats to our safety. A loss of trust in those meant to lead. The One Nation Party offers a clear plan.' His hand moved in time with his words, like a conductor marking the beat. 'One Vision. One Voice. One Nation. We will protect this country from those who would harm it, unite Parliament behind a shared purpose, and restore our pride. This isn't about left or right, it's about every citizen's safety and future.'

Joseph caught himself leaning forward despite his better judgment. The rhetoric was polished, and the delivery strong. Corrupt as hell or not, Marcus Blackwood knew how to work a room, even one with only a handful of people in it. On TV, this same performance would be electric.

Alison checked her notes. 'Mr Blackwood, your manifesto proposes next-generation surveillance and AI-enhanced analysis. Critics say these will erode civil liberties. How do you respond to that?'

Marcus's voice didn't waver. 'Our liberty means nothing if we cannot defend it. Advanced technology, responsibly applied, saves lives. But those who threaten our way of life must know we'll stop them swiftly.'

Eddie leaned forward. 'Or you'll build a surveillance state that spies on everyone.'

Marcus dipped his chin. 'I hear your concern. Many watching, will share it. But when we stop a terrorist before they act, we don't just save lives, we defend the very freedoms you're afraid of losing. That's unity, not division. And I'd welcome cross-party oversight to guarantee it.'

Michael took his turn, frowning at the cameras. 'You say you'll end tribalism. How exactly do you intend to do that with tensions in Parliament already at boiling point?'

'By focusing on what unites us. People are sick of all the point scoring and personal feuds. My first act as Prime Minister would be to create a National Unity Committee on terrorism and infrastructure, with every party represented.'

Joseph could almost hear the imaginary applause swell.

But Alison's eyes narrowed, because she wasn't letting him off the hook that easily. 'But you frequently call your opponents weak, even dangerous. How does that help unity?'

Marcus offered her the faintest smile. 'I'll always challenge policies that endanger Britain. But I won't trade insults for the sake of theatre. Collaboration builds strength, not conflict. And we'll invest where we must, to achieve that.'

The words were rolling almost too smoothly, and Joseph's scepticism started to build. Before he could stop himself, he addressed the obvious elephant in the room. 'So where exactly does the money come from to pay for all of this?'

Alison smiled at him, as if she'd been waiting for the interruption. 'It seems an audience member has a question. Would you like to answer that, Marcus?'

Marcus turned that polished gaze on Joseph. 'We'll cut waste. Streamline bureaucracy. Partner with the private sector. Every pound spent will be transparent, published for the people to see. It won't be easy. But it *is* essential.'

Eddie smirked, tipping Joseph a conspiratorial wink. Then he looked back at his leader. 'So basically you're promising everything, and paying for it with smoke and mirrors.'

'Oh, trust me, we'll have a full breakdown of exactly how we'll be able to pay for all of this available in our full manifesto. As of tonight, that will be live on our party's website. Every figure, every pound and penny, set out for the public to scrutinise.'

Marcus leaned forward in his chair, his gaze locking onto the camera lens, the box lights catching the silver threads in his hair. 'Britain doesn't need another five years of division. It needs leadership that protects, unites, and inspires. One Vision. One Voice. One Nation. Vote for a Britain that stands together.'

The words hung in the air like the last note of an anthem.

Then, Marcus turned to Alison. 'So, how did that sound?'

Alison began to clap, a smile tugging at her lips. Eddie and Michael followed, their applause filling the room.

'Bravo,' Alison said. 'Deliver that tomorrow, and the public will be eating out of your hand.'

Even Joseph had to admit the man had presence. Blackwood might be as crooked as a bent nail, but he could work an audience as if he were born to it.

Eddie slapped Marcus on the back. 'Forget the rehearsal. Start picking out fabric for the curtains in Number Ten.'

Marcus snorted. 'Let's not get carried away just yet. If the polls are right, third place is the best we can hope for. But if we play this well, we'll shape the narrative and set the stage for the next election. That's when our real chance comes.'

'Unless we end up with a hung parliament,' Michael chimed in. 'Then we might just hold the balance of power.'

Alison sighed, flicking through her notes again. 'If you're serious about achieving that, we'd better keep at it. Tomorrow's live political debate isn't about clever lines, it's about hearts and minds, Marcus. You've got to be ready for anything.'

The leader adjusted his cufflinks, confidence radiating from every pore. 'Oh, I'm more than ready.'

At that moment, Joseph's phone buzzed in his pocket. Chris's name lit up the screen. He gave the room an apologetic look. 'Sorry, I need to take this.'

Nobody objected as Joseph slipped out, closing the door quietly behind him. He quickly headed up to the luxurious loo, before closing the door behind him.

'Hi, Joseph, are you alone?' Chris said.

'Yes. Fire away, but I thought we agreed to avoid phone contact.'

'This is important enough to forget that. First things first, we've identified the source of the drug used during the Ellensmere Grange attack.'

'In the cake, I assume?'

'No, not even close. The house's main water supply was

tampered with. A manhole cover outside had been lifted. Inside, we found an empty cylinder fitted with a time-release valve. It discharged straight into the pipe feeding the property.'

Joseph swore under his breath. 'Feck, so the tap water itself was contaminated?'

'That's what it looks like.'

The DI thought of the tea that everyone else had been served, as well as Blake drinking from a steel water bottle. And he'd just been about to make a coffee for the two of them from that same infected water.

'So what drug was used?' Joseph said.

'This is where it gets stranger. The substance used to knock everyone out was henbane.'

Joseph felt a strange prickle running down his spine. 'And what the hell's that when it's at home?'

'According to the toxicology report, henbane's a sedative plant. The Greeks and Romans used it in rituals. It apparently turns up in witchcraft, too.'

'Why am I not surprised? Okay, you factor that with the other poisonings, and it's hard not to see a pattern here, especially with a possible link to the Midwinter Butcher killings as well. Maybe Dylan's theory about someone taking inspiration from the Alchemist murderer isn't so far-fetched, after all.'

Chris exhaled slowly. 'Funny you should say that. I mentioned that to Megan. She's at the Oxford Record Office in Cowley right now, digging through their archives. Old case files, news cuttings, anything that might connect the dots.'

'Even though she's meant to be off the case?'

'What can I say? She's like a dog with a bone, and just can't leave it alone.'

'That's not really a bad trait in an officer. Not that I'm one to talk.'

'No, you're certainly not,' Chris replied. 'Anyway, the

important thing is this, if the water was contaminated, then technically everyone in Ellensmere Grange that day, including Blackwood himself, was at risk. On the surface, at least, that puts the whole room in the clear, at least for that incident.'

Joseph's mind was already racing ahead. If that was true, then the poison hadn't been targeted. It had been indiscriminate. But in a house full of ministers, donors, and party figures, maybe that was the point.

'Maybe that's what we're meant to think,' Joseph said. 'No doubt, I expect it has bumped One Nation's popularity in the polls.'

'It's done exactly that. The NCA is already working on the assumption that this was staged precisely for that purpose. A political theatre dressed up as terrorism.'

Joseph gave a dry laugh. 'Wheels within wheels.'

'That's politics for you,' Chris said. 'There's something else you should know. What's now being seriously discussed is that maybe Marcus Blackwood doesn't work for the Night Watchmen. Emma has been championing this theory, and I tend to agree with her.'

Surprise pulsed through Joseph. 'Sorry, I don't follow. All the evidence—'

'Is correct,' Chris interrupted. 'Just maybe we had it the wrong way round. Rather than being the Night Watchmen's man, maybe Marcus Blackwood is actually the one who pulls all the strings behind the crime syndicate.'

The idea slammed into the DI's mind. In an instant, it all made perfect sense. 'Jesus, I can see exactly where you're coming from. It all fits, doesn't it?'

'I'm afraid it does; it also explains an awful lot. We may have finally discovered our man in the shadows, who's been controlling the crime syndicate all this time. And that's why I need you to keep your head down and your ears open. So, how's it going there?'

'I'm afraid there's nothing much to report, other than the fact they're putting some serious effort into preparing Blackwood for tomorrow's debate at the Blavatnik. Talking of which, I'm sure that has to have people worried there with all the leaders gathered under one roof.'

'Yes, especially after what just happened at Ellensmere Grange. For all we know, Blackwood might try to stage something in an attempt to boost his numbers again during the run-up to the general election.'

'I'm not sure he'll want anything to get in the way of his performance. Based on what I've just seen, he's going to put on one hell of a performance—maybe good enough to swing an awful lot of voters.'

'Then let's just hope he doesn't try anything underhanded. But if he and the Night Watchmen try anything, we'll be ready. The NCA and MI5 have been working with TVP for weeks. There'll be a rock-solid security ring around the event tomorrow. Counter Terrorist Specialist Firearms Officers with rifles will be on every rooftop within range, and there'll be a helicopter in the sky at all times. The outer cordon will be covered by our TU, and armed escorts will be ready to extract the ministers at the first hint of trouble. We've even had teams crawling through the sewer network to make sure Iron Dawn hasn't left any surprises underground. Anyone going in will be screened at checkpoints. If you so much as sneeze in a funny way, you won't get through.'

'Okay, that covers the obvious threats,' Joseph said. 'But what about poison being used again?'

'That's already been accounted for. Water will be tested on site, and there'll be no food served at the venue. Not even so much as a sandwich platter in sight. The leaders will eat at their secured residences beforehand.'

'Yes, better not to take any chances. And have you considered gas or an aerosol release? I can't help thinking of Catherine Kendrick and the stunt she pulled at the New Theatre, dropping an entire audience into that bloody trance.'

'Don't worry about that. Every air conditioning and ventilation system in the Blavatnik School of Government has already been inspected, and it'll be done again in the hours before the debate. If there's so much as a loose screw, it will be flagged.'

'So in other words, you've thought of everything.'

'Collectively, I certainly hope so,' Chris said. 'But if I had my way, I'd skip all this and have Blackwood in custody tonight. But Emma insists we're not there yet. The problem is, and it's hard to argue against, beyond circumstantial links, there's still nothing we can pin on him. Not yet, at least. But that's why, if you come across anything, anything at all, that could implicate him, I need to know immediately. Because, I'll tell you this much, if One Nation makes a splash tomorrow in the debate, it'll be harder than ever to bring Blackwood down. These next twenty-four hours are the moment when he's most vulnerable. If we miss this opportunity, we may not get another chance.'

'No pressure or anything then,' Joseph muttered. 'But I'll do what I can.'

'Good man. And good luck to all of us.' The line went dead as Chris ended the call.

Joseph lowered the phone, staring at the screen. Outside, thunder rumbled far off in the distance, the storm the weather forecast had promised was drawing nearer. And here he was, alone in a house with Marcus Blackwood, Alison, Eddie, and the rest of his inner sanctum. Right now, it felt like he carried the entire weight of the investigation on his shoulders. All he could do was his best. And he just hoped that, when the reckoning came, it would be enough to bring Marcus Blackwood and the Night Watchmen, and everything connected with them, all tumbling down.

CHAPTER TWENTY-FIVE

IF THERE WAS any incriminating evidence in Marcus Blackwood's home—occult, poison, or otherwise—Joseph was damned if he could find it hidden anywhere. Under the pretence of checking that all the windows were secure, he'd walked the entire house, quietly pulling open desk drawers and cupboards, even checking in Marcus's study desk. Nothing had been locked or hidden. The only thing even faintly questionable in any of them was a stack of classic Victorian pornography in the library. Maybe a little bit dodgy, but hardly evidence to incriminate Marcus and the Night Watchmen.

Night had finally fallen on the eve of the political debate, and Joseph had retired to his attic room in Ellensmere Grange. The storm that had been threatening all day had finally broken, and the first great rumbles rolled in after midnight. Now, as the time rolled towards one a.m., each thunderclap grew closer and deeper, like cannon fire closing in across the hills, almost like an echo from the First English Civil War that had once ravaged this estate.

Unable to sleep, the DI watched lightning flare against the low clouds over the surrounding woodland, throwing the bedroom into relief a heartbeat at a time. And then the rain came, a sudden, unrelenting downpour that hammered against the tiles and drummed on the attic window left open to release the relentless heat trapped in the room.

With no chance of sleep, Joseph picked up his phone, examining the photograph he'd taken at the high table in Christ Church of the sigil scrawled on the serviette. He flicked to the next photo and paused. He found himself looking at the photo he'd snapped in the drawing room of the black-shuttered lantern sitting in its glass case.

It had completely slipped his mind, and he'd forgotten to show it to Dylan. Joseph quickly tapped forward, attaching the image to an email. *'I took this in Blackwood's drawing room. I don't suppose you happen to recognise it?'* He hit send, but because of the lateness of the hour, he realised he wouldn't get a reply until morning.

The DI set the phone back down on the bedside table, the glow of the screen fading into darkness. But his mind kept circling, caught between the roll of thunder outside and the feeling that somewhere inside Ellensmere Grange, actual evidence was still hidden, waiting for him to find it.

A hidden safe somewhere, maybe?

The one thing he knew for certain was that sleep wouldn't be coming easily tonight with the political debate looming tomorrow. Without damning evidence to bring Blackwood down, the NCA investigation, which had partly relied on him, would be out of time. By the close of play tomorrow, there was every chance that the future of the country would be in Blackwood's hands.

The luminous hands of an alarm clock told him it was two-thirty. He was deep in the grip of grogginess when he saw it. A pinpoint flash of light caught the glass of the open window. Too sharp and clear to dismiss it as lightning.

Joseph was at the window in an instant, his eyes fixed on the tree line.

Another flash.

This one had come from the same place in the woods as before. It was definitely coming from the direction of the derelict dovecote building.

His heart rate hitched up a fraction. It was the only hint that something strange was going on at the estate. If it was nothing, so be it, but he was damned if he would let another chance to get an answer slip away.

Within minutes, the DI was dressed and heading downstairs.

'All quiet?' Joseph asked as he headed into the security office.

'Apart from the storm, not a murmur out there,' Blake replied, gesturing at the monitors. 'The gate's quiet as well. Everyone's sleeping snugly in their beds, safe in the knowledge that I drew the short straw for tonight's shift. Well, apart from your armed officers, and our own lads patrolling the perimeter.'

'Good to hear. Any chance of blagging another smoke?'

Blake gave him a frown. 'Ever thought of buying your own?'

Joseph shrugged. 'Trying to give it up. Easier if I don't keep a packet in my pocket. You know how it is.'

The guard chuckled and dug into his packet. 'I do, brother.' He handed him one with another match.

'I owe you,' Joseph said, already heading for the door.

'You certainly do,' Blake replied with a crooked smile.

Joseph stepped out into the night. Rain lashed across the drive, plastering his shirt to his skin within seconds. The sky above was a churning bruise of cloud, alive with flashes of silver that lit the house and grounds ghost white in strobe bursts.

The DI lit the cigarette beneath the camera, gave a thumbs-up to Blake, then strolled away as if he had nothing more pressing on his mind than keeping out of the rain. The moment he reached the blind spot between cameras, he left the house and headed for the trees.

The woodland was a riot of noise. Rain pummelled the canopy and cascaded from leaves in little waterfalls. Every footstep sank into the soft earth, his shoes sucking at the mud, rain running down his collar. He strained his eyes looking into the gloom of the wood, punctuated by the flashes of lightning, and saw a Range Rover parked outside the dovecote again.

Joseph ducked behind a tree, his breath quickening, as the rain soaked his hair and ran down into his eyes. He was already working on excuses for why he was out here in the middle of the night, but then he heard it. At first, it was almost drowned out by the storm. Then it came through clearer, threading through the noise of thunder.

A low chant, rhythmic, of voices rising and falling together.

The hair on Joseph's arms prickled. Whatever this was, it had to be significant. The chant rolled on as the lightning flared, deeper now, almost a vibration he could feel through the sodden ground. Although he couldn't quite catch the words, it had the feel of a religious ceremony to it. So what the hell was this about then? Could this be the missing evidence linking Blackwood to some sort of occult ceremony?

Joseph drew the telescopic baton from his pocket, thumb resting on the catch. A glance at his phone showed full bars.

For a moment, the DI considered radioing the team at the gate. But what exactly would he tell them? That in the middle of a storm, he had heard a strange hymn being sung in the middle of the wood?

Whatever this was, he needed to see it for himself first, before calling it in.

Step by step, rain running down his back, the DI moved closer, until he paused behind the trunk of a large dripping oak.

The derelict dovecote loomed ahead, its sagging roofline silhou-etted against the storm's flares of light. The low thrum of voices was definitely coming from inside it. Five, maybe six people, their chanting rising and falling in rhythm.

The DI held his breath as, step by careful step, he closed the distance, teeth clenched against the squelch of his boots in the sodden earth. The smell reached him next. Not the bite of burning wood but something sweeter, cloying. The smell of sandalwood and scorched herbs. Sage, maybe?

This—whatever the hell it was—could be the very thread Chris and the NCA needed to bring Blackwood and the Night Watchmen down.

Joseph put his phone away, thumbed the telescopic baton open with a muted snick, and crept closer.

Then everything fell into place as he was finally able to take the scene before him in. A section of the dovecot's floor had been built as a sliding panel with the logs on top of it to disguise the opening. It had been drawn back in hidden runners, taking the pile of timber with it. Beneath it yawned a basement at least ten metres by five, dug into the earth. Its walls were lined with hessian sacking, held in place by wooden posts.

So this was why the tyre tracks converged on this ruin, the footprints. The building was obviously very much in active use, but for what exactly? Joseph couldn't help but think of the Azrael sigil. Was that linked to what was going on in there?

As the voices swelled together, he took a half step forward to get a look at whatever was going on in the excavated chamber.

Then he spotted the candlelight guttering in the breeze, and illuminating the edges of crimson robes of six people chanting. At the centre of a semicircle stood a man stripped to his waist, his bare chest gleaming with sweat. The man's face was hidden behind a horned mask, wrought into a grotesque parody of a devil.

Joseph felt a surge of elation. Based on the muscled physique of someone who had to be ex-special forces, the man standing in the middle of this madness had to be Blackwood. In that context, the demon mask seemed entirely appropriate. This man was a demon in every sense of the word.

The scarlet-robed figures swayed, hoods shadowing their faces. Their voices were weaving together in something that sounded like broken Gaelic, the syllables warped and twisted enough that Joseph couldn't follow it.

Between them and the masked man, stood a crude table, presumably some sort of altar, draped in black cloth. On it sat a shallow bronze bowl, steam coiling upwards from it. The smell hit Joseph harder now, herbs scorched in oil. Yes, sage and maybe rosemary, mingled with something else. Then he knew exactly what that was—the iron smell of blood.

The DI's pulse sped up as a hooded woman stepped forward. She dipped a bundle of rushes bound in red thread into the bowl, then flicked droplets in an arc across the man's chest. The beads glistened like red jewels as they traced lines down his skin.

The chanting deepened, mingling with the roar of the storm above.

One of the figures stepped towards a brazier glowing with coals to one side, and with tongs lifted something from it. Even through the sheeting rain, Joseph could see the shape clearly. It was a metal disk, faintly glowing, with a diagonal line carved across its face. If this was another sigil, it certainly wasn't one for Azrael.

The figure walked calmly up to the bare-chested man. 'Are you ready?' the man asked, in good old-fashioned English.

The man nodded and held out his left wrist.

With a swift movement, the robed figure grabbed hold of the man's arm as two others broke from the semicircle to take hold of his shoulders. In a sudden fluid movement, the first robed figure pressed the heated disk hard against the man's wrist. The man writhed as the metal hissed, his teeth bared visibly beneath the line of the mask. Blue wisps of smoke rose from the symbol as it burned, sizzling into his flesh.

Even though there was some distance between Joseph and the group, the sickening, cloying smell of something like pork burning on a barbecue hit his nostrils. The DI watched with growing astonishment when the man didn't scream his lungs out. His pain threshold had to be through the roof.

Then, at last, the robed figure pulled the disc away, as the others supporting the man patted him on the back.

A woman, based on the sway of her hips, stepped out from the semi-circle, moving forward, and pressing a pad of moss against the angry welt that had already risen on the man's wrist. Steam hissed faintly as the green soaked into the raw wound.

'This will help numb the pain,' the woman said.

Joseph instantly recognised the voice of Alison Blackwood.

So she wasn't a bystander in whatever was going on here. There she was, right up to her fecking eyeballs, leading this whole weird circus. And if that was Marcus before her in the mask, he had been what, exactly? Anointed? Was this some sort of occult blessing as he got ready to seize control of the country?

Whatever Alison's true role was here, one thing was clear to the DI. This wasn't politics, it wasn't even crime in the way he understood it, this was something darker, and much more sinister.

'You are now welcomed into the Order of the Midnight Sun,' Alison's voice rang out over the fading chant. She pulled back her hood, the candlelight catching the sharp gleam in her eyes, removing any doubt about who she was.

The others headed towards the man in the centre,

murmuring their congratulations. A hand on his shoulder here, a brief clasp of a forearm, as they all congratulated him.

'From this night forward, we will raise you higher than you have ever dreamed,' Alison said. 'You have ascended, not only to the summit of the Night Watchmen, but onwards to the pinnacle of this nation's power. The country will be yours to command. And when you speak, the people will listen. And through you, our reach will know no bounds.'

Like a series of dominoes, thoughts started to cascade in the DI's mind: the serviette sigil left for Chambers's table; the exotic use of poisons; Dylan's talk of the Alchemist; and the brutal tearing apart of Sally Green's body at the hydro station. Could this be where it all traced back? Not to Marcus but to Alison herself, the real power behind the throne of an ambitious man? And with her rituals and use of the occult, had she helped her husband rise to power?

Alison turned, raising a single gloved hand. One of the other tall masked figures standing at the edge of the circle stepped forward and inclined their head towards the far side of the basement.

Joseph followed the movement with his eyes.

There, he saw them. Stacks of crates sat in the shadows, partly hidden beneath a heavy canvas blanket. A hooded figure strode over to it, hooked a finger under the edge, and pulled the tarp back.

The stencilled markings on the wooden sides glared in the candlelight, making Joseph's stomach clench into a tight ball.

C4 – Semtex – High Explosive.

Joseph's phone suddenly lit up with a message from Dylan, illuminating his face as well as any torch. As he stabbed the button to darken it, he still had time to take in the message.

'We saw that lamp together in the Ashmolean Museum. It's a replica of Guy Fawkes' lantern from the Gunpowder Plot.'

Joseph's stomach lurched as he stared at the crates of explosives. The C4 was meant for the political debate, where the rival party leaders would be sitting ducks under the glare of the lights and TV cameras. It was going to be a massacre, all the rival party leaders taken out in one massive strike.

Alison had moved closer to her husband. 'All the tools are here, my love. The moment is almost at hand. And when it arrives, nothing and no one will be able to stand in your way.'

Whatever this was, Joseph knew one thing for certain: it wasn't just theatre, it was preparation to seize control of the country.

Then, suddenly, headlights flared briefly through the gaps in the boarded walls, followed by the low rumble of engines. Several cars, headed straight down the track towards the old dovecot.

Joseph scrabbled backwards into the darkness as the vehicles drew close enough to make out. There were at least two of the black Range Rovers of Blackwood's security team. But behind them was a white Mercedes. He'd seen that vehicle before somewhere. Then he knew where. Back in the Old Ink Press pub car park, where he'd discovered Chief Kennan offering a bribe to Derrick. Then his heart sank as he recognised the final car in the convoy, a BMW 7 Series. The same car that Derrick owned.

Even though Joseph knew the man had been corrupted, part of him had hoped he wasn't part of this. But watching him step out of his car with Amy, no less, and both head up to Kennan to shake the chief's hand, finally swept away any doubt. Much to his surprise, he actually found tears beading his eyes before fiery anger surged through his veins to burn them away.

Well, feck you, Derrick, he thought as he pressed the dial that would connect him instantly to the TU officer on the main gate. The time to call in the cavalry had finally arrived.

The DI had started to back away in the darkness of the wood when his phone screen lit up as it connected. Then, he felt something hard pressed into the small of his back. He knew with cold certainty that it was a pistol.

'If you take that call, she'll fucking die,' Gareth's voice said.

'Hello, Joseph?' the TU officer's faint voice said from his phone.

From behind the DI, Gareth held another phone screen in front of Joseph's face so he could watch it. On it was a video of Kate, sitting gagged in a dark room.

'So here we are again,' Gareth whispered into his ear. 'We really thought you'd get the message after the last time we abducted Kate. But no, it seems as though you still haven't got it through your thick skull. So watch this live feed of the consequences when you don't do what you're told. Go ahead...'

Joseph saw a man enter the room, whom he immediately recognised as DCI Greg Charlton, another officer corrupted by the Night Watchmen. The man raised a Glock to Kate's head, grinning towards the camera.

'Are you there, Joseph?' the TU officer asked again.

'Just one word from me, and Greg will finish her,' Gareth hissed into the DI's ear. 'Do you understand me?'

'Yes,' Joseph said, cupping his hand over the mic of his mobile as a bitter tang filled his mouth.

'Now be a good boy and deal with your TU officer.'

It felt like a stone was filling the DI's throat as he raised the phone back to his mouth.

Gareth pressed the tip of the pistol harder into the small of the DI's back.

'Sorry, I just got called away for a moment,' Joseph said into his phone. 'I was just checking in to see if it was all quiet down there?'

'Not so much as a car passing on the main road.'

That snippet meant that wherever this convoy of vehicles had come from, they had somehow avoided driving past the main gate entirely.

'Good, then let's hope it stays that way,' Joseph said.

'Is there any reason for it not to?' the officer asked.

Gareth held his phone with the video feed of Kate and Greg closer to the DI's face.

'Sorry, just making conversation. Goodnight.' The moment he pressed the call-end button, the phone was snatched from his hand.

'Now, that's more like it,' Gareth said. 'But time for you to have a little nap as we work out what to do with you.'

Joseph started to turn, but up against an ex-special forces operative, he was too slow.

Gareth brought the pistol down in a brutal arc, the metal cracking against the back of the DI's skull. White light seared Joseph's vision with the numbing blow. The ground rushed up to meet him, and darkness swallowed everything.

CHAPTER TWENTY-SIX

THE VOICES BLED into Joseph's fogged mind, distant at first, as though carried on the wind. Then they slowly began to sharpen into focus.

'Everything's in place for tomorrow night's debate,' a woman said. The tone was clipped, authoritative, and instantly recognisable as Chief Kennan.

'Yes,' came another voice, with the rough impatience of Derrick. 'And the manhole covers will be left clear for your men to enter through.'

'Good, because we'll need to be in and out sharpish to place the C4 and be ready for it to blow at nine-thirty,' Gareth Holgate replied.

Joseph's brain struggled to process what he was hearing. A throbbing pain pulsed at the back of his skull, hot and raw where Gareth's pistol had struck. He became aware of the cold, wet, uneven ground beneath him, the rustle of branches overhead, and the plastic zip ties biting into the skin of his wrists secured behind his back.

At least he was still alive for now, that was something he would not have expected.

Joseph forced himself to breathe slowly, shallowly, as though still unconscious, while his mind scrambled to catch up. He needed to work out how deep in the shite he'd landed himself in, and quickly.

Through slitted eyes, he risked the barest glance. He'd been dumped where he fell, close to the derelict dovecot. Kennan, Derrick, Amy, and Gareth stood only a few yards away. Beyond them, Gareth's men worked in an ordered line, transferring the crates of C4 from the hidden basement beneath the building and loading them into the waiting Range Rovers. Candlelight still guttered faintly from the chamber below, throwing grotesque shadows across the clearing.

'That's one hell of a lot of explosives,' Amy said, eyeing the crates as they were carefully placed into the vehicles one by one.

Holgate gave a short, humourless chuckle. 'Enough to flatten the entire building, and everyone inside it.'

The words sliced through Joseph's grogginess. Not that he needed any, but there it was. The debate at the Blavatnik School of Government really was the target.

'Just make sure he's out of there by nine-thirty, before it detonates,' Kennan said. 'If he lingers, he'll be caught in the blast.'

'Don't worry about that,' Gareth replied. 'I'll brief him fully on the way there.'

Joseph's heart hammered against his ribs. So they were planning to make sure Blackwood escaped, while everyone else burned in the rubble.

The DI slowly moved his gaze further out. There was no sign of Blackwood and Alison, or her cult members, anywhere.

'You do realise a lot of innocent people are going to die in that blast?' Derrick said, his voice quieter now.

Kennan's reply was sharp. 'You cannot make an omelette

without breaking a few eggs, Walker. Not getting cold feet, are you?'

'I just think it's unnecessary,' Derrick growled.

'Not when you want to effect real change, it's not,' Holgate shot back.

Joseph couldn't just hear the iron in his voice, but the conviction of the man, too. But he was at least pleased to see that Derrick's glare at the man was pure venom.

'You really are a true believer, aren't you?' Amy said, also looking less than impressed.

Holgate shrugged. 'I've been with him every step of this journey. So yes, you could say that. All my men are. But it seems some of us are more motivated by the money. Isn't that right?' His gaze zeroed in on Amy.

The SOCO shrugged. 'What you get up to is your business. All I'm looking for is to be very well paid for all the crap I've done for you. Talking of which...' She put her hand into her pocket and took out a smartwatch. 'This is Chambers's. All you need to do is plant it somewhere in the house, and I guarantee the police will be very interested when they find it, presuming it's something he had taken from the crime scene, to complicate the investigation.'

Derrick's jaw clenched, but he didn't say anything.

Kennan shook her head with a dry laugh. 'Don't mind them, Gareth. They might lack your conviction, but they also don't lack greed. They both know as well as I do that this is the payday of a lifetime. Enough to disappear, start over, and live the life of a king. Let the country tear itself apart in the ashes. That's not our problem.'

Joseph felt anger rising inside him, stronger than the pain in his skull. For his colleagues to sell their souls for something like this beggared belief.

Derrick shook his head. 'Maybe I'm corrupt, but it doesn't mean I have to like it.'

'I'm sure you'll cry all the way to the bank,' Gareth replied. 'Anyway, what are we going to do about your problem?' He jutted his chin in Joseph's direction.

'Since when has DI Stone been *my* problem?' Derrick replied.

'Since you gave us your word you had him in line and he wouldn't be an issue.'

'Which, by his presence here, suggests you monumentally screwed up on,' Kennan added.

Derrick glared at her. 'Joseph had absolutely no idea about any of what was going on here, because you wouldn't let me brief him.'

'And you're sure about that?' Amy said, narrowing her gaze at him.

Kennan nodded. 'Yes, it seems one hell of a coincidence that on the night we move the explosives, Stone just happens to stumble across the C4 as we're getting ready to shift it.'

'What can I say?' Derrick muttered. 'Stone's got a nose on him, and has a knack for always sniffing out the truth. Besides, you're the one who signed off on him being assigned to Blackwood's protection detail. If you want to point a finger, it's just as much on you for hiding the bloody explosives on this estate, where he might trip over them. And anyway, you know he's one of yours.'

'I'm not so sure about that. He's only played along because we dangled the lives of his family over him. But if you want my honest opinion, we don't really have any use for him anymore.'

'But you've got Kate,' Derrick said, his tone warning. 'Take it from me, while you've got her, he'll do anything you ask of him.'

Kennan made a scoffing sound in the back of her throat. 'I wouldn't be so certain. Unlike you, he still clings to that wretched sense of duty of his. And that makes him dangerous to us, especially now, with everything so close to the line.'

'Then leave that to me,' Gareth said. 'I can have a shallow grave waiting with his name on it, and your ex-wife's too, Walker, if it comes to that.'

Derrick's voice came out as a growl. 'Don't you fucking dare touch her.'

The DI's mouth became bone dry. To hear them trade Kate's life like a bargaining chip—his Kate—was almost worse than if they executed him right there and then. A knot of rage and fear clenched in his throat, so tight he could barely breathe past it.

'Will you stop the squabbling?' Kennan said. 'We all know it'll be our leader's decision, and no one else's.'

Gareth gave a low laugh. 'Are you sure about that?'

Kennan's eyes narrowed. 'What exactly do you mean?'

'You've seen it yourself. The hold Alison and her travelling band of freaks have on him. Don't tell me you haven't noticed.'

Kennan shrugged. 'It's his choice how he gets his kicks and who he shares his bed with. Yes, her little cult's a distraction, and insisting she leaves those bloody occult marks at the crime scenes has been a complete pain in the arse, but Alison still brings something useful to the table.'

'Useful?' Gareth spat on the ground. 'Her potions and poisons, maybe, but he believes every crazy word she utters these days. You all saw him when we first arrived tonight. That's not the man I know. That woman's got inside his head, I tell you.'

'As long as his extracurricular hobbies don't interfere with the Night Watchmen's business, who cares?' Kennan replied. 'He wouldn't be the first powerful man with a taste for the occult. And so far, it hasn't slowed him down.'

Joseph risked a sideways glance. Derrick's face was a mask

of confusion, as if half of what he was hearing was news even to him. Amy's far less so. It seemed the DSU wasn't privy to the full depths of the Night Watchmen's occult connections.

'And if she does cross the line?' Amy asked.

Kennan's lips curved into something like a smile. 'Then maybe we give her one of her own poisonous concoctions and make it look like an accident.'

Gareth let out a humourless laugh. 'Fuck. You're as devious as I am. But we still have that *other* problem. What are we going to do with Stone in the meantime until the boss tells us what to do with him?'

'Maybe get that insurance policy underway,' Amy said, with a hard expression.

'Good idea, better to be prepared to draw together those loose ends if we need to in a hurry,' Holgate said.

'What do you mean by that?' Derrick said, looking between them.

'Better you don't know,' Kennan said. Then she turned towards Joseph. 'You can stop with the playacting now. I can tell by the way you're breathing that you've been awake for the last five minutes. Isn't that right, Stone?'

For a heartbeat, the DI considered keeping his eyes closed and playing dead. But what good would it do? They already held all the cards, especially in the form of Kate.

He slowly rolled into a sitting position and, fighting the dizziness still pounding inside his skull, opened his eyes fully.

Kennan smirked at him. 'Now that's better. So, what are you going to do to plead your case?'

Joseph met her gaze as his jaw tightened. 'Oh, you'd like to watch me beg, wouldn't you?'

'Only if you meant it. But something tells me you're too principled to compromise those lofty standards of yours. Am I wrong in that assessment?'

'Normally you wouldn't be,' Joseph said. 'But you're holding Kate, and we both know that gives you power over me, whether I like it or not.'

'Maybe, but even then I'm not sure I can really trust you,' Kennan replied. 'So do your best to convince me.'

Joseph felt the words burn his throat. 'Because I couldn't live with myself if Kate was hurt because of something I did, or something I failed to do.'

'That does have a familiar ring to it,' Kennan said, shooting a glance at Derrick.

Joseph glanced at the DSU, whose face had hardened. 'Look, it's the same for both of us. Neither of us is stupid enough to stick our necks out knowing the consequences.'

Derrick's face gave nothing away, but Joseph didn't need to be a mind reader. The man might be separated from Kate, but it was obvious he still carried a torch for her. Just as the DI himself had through all the years he and Kate had been apart.

Amy's eyes locked onto his, a thin smile on her lips. 'That's where you're wrong, Joseph. I don't believe you can sit on your hands while you know what's coming. Hundreds of people at the Blavatnik School of Government blown sky high? You might want to hold back, but we both know you won't be able to resist acting the hero yet again.'

A ready lie sprang to Joseph's lips, but Kennan was already raising her hand, silencing him before he could even start.

'Please don't insult our intelligence by bothering to deny it.'

The words dried in Joseph's throat, evaporating before they could leave his mouth. He simply nodded.

Kennan's mouth curved in something that wasn't quite a smile. 'You see, right there is your problem, Stone. You're a good copper through and through. Too bloody honest for your own good.'

Joseph gave a small shrug, though his chest was tightening.

'Guilty as fecking charged. But whatever else you do, leave Kate out of this.'

'We both know I can't do that,' Kennan said. 'She's leverage, and I need to make sure you're both silenced once and for all, however we get there.'

Holgate's hand shifted, already curling around the grip of the Glock on his belt.

Derrick stiffened. 'Wait, we agreed.'

Kennan turned her head slowly, one brow arched in quiet amusement. 'Yes, I suppose we did.' Her hand slid over and rested lightly on Holgate's arm. 'As I said before, Joseph and Kate's fate is in our leader's hands and no one else's. But make no mistake. We're not letting this man run loose when his conscience will get the better of him. No, we keep him quiet until after the dust settles and One Nation's on its way to power. Then we'll decide what happens to him, and to the woman he loves.' Her eyes narrowed. 'And just in case you're thinking of being clever, Stone, remember, we've still got one more ace up our sleeve. Your daughter.'

Joseph's blood iced. 'Don't you fecking dare touch a hair on Ellie's head.'

Kennan's lips curled. 'There's the real man at last. And what exactly is that promise worth to you?'

The implications roared through him. Ellie and Kate, on one side of the scales, hundreds of souls on the other. How could he ever be expected to choose between the two?

Kennan must have guessed at the thoughts raging through his mind, because she gave a slow nod. 'Don't worry, I'm not asking you to choose now, Stone. That comes later when we release you, and we ask for your loyalty. Refuse to work for us in body and soul, and you'll all die. Take your time to think about it. Think hard, while we get on with the business of changing the future of this country forever.'

Joseph's voice was little more than a rasp. 'But you know I'll be missed when I don't turn up by Blackwood's side for the debate.'

Kennan's smile widened, a flash of teeth. 'Oh, you mean by Chris Faulkner? The loyal DCI at St Aldates. The one you've been confiding in. The one who's been guiding you. You mean him, don't you?'

Joseph felt the ground tilt beneath him. 'What the hell do you mean by that?'

Derrick's head jerked around. He was staring at Kennan, eyes wide. 'Yes. I'd like to know that too.'

'You didn't know because Stone here wasn't allowed to confide in you,' Kennan said, her tone flat, matter-of-fact. 'I've only just learnt this myself, but the truth is, as well as myself, you've been under investigation from the start. Faulkner didn't show up at St Aldates on some miraculous fast-track DCI program, Derrick. He was placed there to expose you, and anyone else working for the Night Watchmen. And of course, we played along and gave them just enough rope. All the while, we had our own mole inside the NCA who, earlier today, filled in the gaps of what we suspected might be really going on.'

Derrick blinked once, twice, three times, as though his brain was refusing to process the words. He turned slowly towards Joseph, disbelief etched into every line of his face. 'You were investigating me?'

Joseph already knew denial wasn't even an option. He drew a breath and forced the words out. 'We were, and it seems for good reason.'

Derrick blinked several more times before raw anger erupted out of him. 'And to think I fucking trusted you.'

'Which is exactly how I fecking feel, you great festering arsewipe of a man,' Joseph snapped back.

Gareth grinned as he watched their exchange. 'Look, as amusing as this all is, children, we've got a job to do.'

Kennan tilted her head in acknowledgement. 'Yes, we most certainly do. Okay, Stone, here's what's going to happen. We're giving your phone back for one call. You're going to tell your buddy, Chris, you've found something incriminating on Blackwood, and that you'll be retrieving it during the debate while the Grange is empty. That will have him chomping at the bit.'

Joseph's stomach twisted. 'And if I don't agree to play nicely?'

Kennan's smile didn't reach her eyes. 'Then you already know the consequences.'

Joseph could see it in her eyes that she wasn't bluffing. He knew he'd been outplayed. 'For fuck's sake, pass me my phone.'

Gareth slid it from his pocket and handed it over. Joseph's reflection stared back at him from the dark screen. For a heartbeat, he just looked at himself, wondering if this was the last time he'd see his own face. One call and maybe one last chance.

'Make it convincing,' Kennan warned, folding her arms. 'If Faulkner suspects anything...' She inclined her head towards Gareth, whose hand rested lazily on his Glock, 'Then you'll be the first to pay, followed by Kate.'

Gareth added, almost cheerfully, 'Put it on speaker so we can all hear.'

Joseph turned on the phone, his pulse thundering in his ears. He could almost hear Chris's voice already, hopeful that he'd finally found the critical evidence they'd been waiting for. Which he had, of course, just he couldn't tell because he couldn't risk the consequences to his family and even the SIO himself.

'All right,' Joseph muttered, and pressed call.

As the ringing continued, the DI felt Kennan's eyes boring

into him, Gareth's fingers tightening around the pistol. Then Chris finally picked up.

'Joseph? You must know it's the middle of the night, and you're breaking protocol by ringing. That must mean you've found something.'

Joseph swallowed hard. He had to pitch this exactly right, urgent enough to sound real, but not so much that Chris would smell the setup. 'I'm afraid I haven't found a thing yet. That's why, during the debate, I'm going to stay back at the Grange to tear it apart, looking for proof the man's guilty. It's probably going to be our last chance to dig up any dirt on Blackwood before he becomes untouchable.'

The pause that followed stretched like piano wire as Joseph's mouth dried.

'So you're saying we're going to have to let the debate go ahead as planned?' Chris asked at last.

Joseph's eyes flicked to Kennan. She gave the smallest nod, her eyes razor sharp.

'Aye, I'm afraid so,' Joseph replied with a measured tone, fighting every instinct bellowing at him to scream out the truth.

'In that case, I'll have a team on standby tomorrow during the debate in case you find something. Just call me when you're ready to bring in the cavalry.'

'Don't worry, I will.'

'Then, good luck.'

To us both, Joseph thought bitterly. Out loud, he said, 'I'll be in contact soon.' He ended the call and handed the phone back.

Kennan gave him a thin-lipped smile. 'See? That wasn't so hard. Even a man like you, with the right motivation, can be brought to heel.'

Joseph clenched his hand into a fist, fighting the urge to wipe that smug look right off her prune-lined face.

Gareth took the mobile, slipped it into his pocket, then

jerked his head towards the hidden underground chamber. The Glock was already in his other hand. 'Personally, I'd be happy to put a bullet in you now. Your choice, Stone.'

Joseph glowered back at him. His only option was to stay alive, buy time, and find some crack in their plan. If he were dead, there was no hope for Kate. Or Ellie. Or the hundreds who'd be at the Blavatnik School of Government.

He dipped his chin. 'All right, all fecking right...'

Each step towards the dug-out basement felt like a walk to the gallows, where there was every chance of them killing him regardless of what he did. When Joseph reached the bottom of the stairs, he turned back, looking up at the four of them— Kennan, Derrick, Amy, and Gareth. Three of those people were about to betray everything they were sworn to uphold, for what? Money. Power. A twisted vision for their country.

The DI squared his shoulders as he looked back up at them. 'History won't remember you as heroes. Just cowards with blood on their hands.'

'I thought it was the winners who wrote the history books,' Kennan said, smirking. Then she nodded to Gareth.

With a grunt, the head of security shoved the woodpile back into place over Joseph's head with a squeal. The DI held Derrick's gaze to the last, silently begging him to wake the hell up, to see what he'd become, but the big man just looked away.

Velvet blackness swallowed the DI as the roof slammed into place, sealing him in the dug-out chamber like a man trapped inside his own coffin.

CHAPTER TWENTY-SEVEN

With a start, Joseph awoke, disorientated in the stifling blackness of the hidden room beneath the dovecote, his skull pounding. At some point, the adrenaline had ebbed, and exhaustion had dragged him under. Before he'd reached the point of utter exhaustion, he'd fought to move the roof until every muscle screamed, his throat was hoarse from shouting for help that never came.

How much time has passed? he thought as he tried to gather himself in a fresh attempt to escape.

The DI craned his neck up. Between the heavy boards that made up the ceiling of the basement room, were the faintest slivers of sunlight from outside the dovecote.

He pressed his ear to the boards, straining for footsteps, voices of anyone he could try appealing to. But all he could hear was muffled birdsong outside, broken only by his own shallow, rasping breaths.

For one long, terrible moment, the urge to curl up, to close his eyes, and wait for it to end almost overwhelmed him. But the DI forced those thoughts down. He couldn't give up. If he did, hundreds of people would die at the Blavatnik debate. Kate would also die, maybe even Ellie too, if Kennan and Holgate decided she was also a liability.

Joseph could see it clearly now; of course, they had no intention of freeing him. Blackwood would rise to power, the Night Watchmen would thrive, with Alison Blackwood the one really pulling the strings. Meanwhile, Joseph Stone and those he loved would simply rot in forgotten holes in the ground.

He did his best to fight the despair, to hang on, as the hours rolled past, bleeding one into another. But the stubbornness that defined Joseph Stone to the marrow of his bones still flickered deep inside the man. He wouldn't die here. He couldn't. For all their sakes.

The daylight just visible through the cracks turned molten gold to purple as the sunset began to fade. It was the evening that would redefine the future of the country. That was when he heard the crunch of tyres on the track, followed by a slamming door and approaching footsteps, hesitant at first, but then more certain.

Joseph pulled himself upright, pressing his mouth to the boards. 'Hello! For God's sake, let me out of here!'

As the footsteps grew closer, his pulse raced. Had Derrick come to his senses and was ready to help him? Or was it Gareth Holgate, come back to finish the job?

Joseph braced himself at the top of the steps, every muscle taut. If it were Holgate, he'd throw himself at the bastard. Trained SAS or not, Joseph would fight like a cornered animal, if only to leave the bastard a few mementos to remember him by.

A bolt scraped across, and suddenly intense light speared into the chamber, briefly blinding him and forcing him to shield his face with his hands.

Then, as his eyes began to adjust, he saw the last person he expected to see peering down into the dark at him.

'Joseph, are you okay?' Megan asked, her expression etched with concern as she hovered above him.

The DI was so shocked, it took him a moment to find his voice. 'How the feck did you find me?' he eventually said as the DC helped him climb out of the chamber.

'Derrick pulled me into his office and told me you were trapped here. He also told me you'd been kept prisoner, and I had to hurry.'

Joseph didn't know whether to laugh or cry at hearing that. 'And he told you everything?'

'Only that I had to avoid Blackwood's security team keeping guard at Ellensmere Grange. He also told me to use a track up through the woods to avoid the main drive. But even finding the gate to the track was a bloody nightmare because it had been deliberately disguised with bushes. I had to clear those before I could drive up here.'

'Of course it was, which is why the rest of us didn't know it was even there. That's how they could move the explosives without being spotted.'

Megan frowned. 'What the hell are you talking about?'

'I'll tell you on the way, but first, what time is it?'

'Nearly eight o'clock.'

Joseph's blood ran cold. 'Shite. That means the political debate is about to kick off at Blavatnik.'

'Yes, but what about it?'

'I'm as sure as I can be that a crime syndicate backing Marcus Blackwood has placed explosives beneath the building in the sewers, intending to kill all the other political leaders.'

Megan's eyes grew wide. 'And all the people attending.'

'I know.' He looked at the Volvo V90 Megan had brought. 'And you're driving.'

'Of course, but we should ring ahead and warn Chris.'

'Do it.'

Megan started to take her phone from her pocket when Joseph heard the unmistakable snick of a trigger being cocked.

'I don't think so,' Blake's voice said.

The two detectives turned to see the security officer standing in front of them, a Heckler and Koch MP5 submachine gun in his hand, pointing at them.

'I'm afraid I'm going to have to rain on your little rescue party attempt,' he said.

'How the hell did you know I was even here?' Megan asked, staring warily at the MP5.

The man grinned and jabbed a finger up the trunk of a nearby oak where, half-hidden by leaves, a security camera watched them from above.

'For feck's sake, you mean you saw me both times I came out here?' Joseph asked, his voice tight.

'Oh, we saw you all right,' the man said. 'And Gareth was intrigued by what you were up to with your little nighttime wanderings. That's why we took your girlfriend as insurance, luring her in with the promise of some dashcam footage that would help prove who murdered that stupid waitress. Truth is, we already knew everything about your movements, Stone. You see, we were tipped off that Chris Faulkner, who is really an NCA agent, sent you here on a clandestine surveillance mission, trying to dig up dirt on Marcus.'

Megan snapped her head around to stare at Joseph. 'What the hell is he talking about? Chris is an agent? And you, going bloody Mission Impossible behind everyone's back?'

'Later,' Joseph said, keeping his attention squarely on Blake.

'As if you think there's going to be a later.' The man smirked, swinging the muzzle of his MP5 up. 'Now, do me a favour and get back into that pit. I don't want to waste a round unless I have to. Gareth wasn't happy about you being left alive, Stone. He left strict orders that if you got out, I had to shoot you on sight. So here we all are. Sorry that you managed to get caught up in this, Miss.'

'If you'll pardon my French, you can go fuck yourself,' Megan replied.

Blake grinned even wider at her.

'And how do you expect to explain our deaths?' Joseph asked, forcing his voice to keep level.

'That's easy. We'll pin it on our favourite bogeymen, Iron Dawn.'

'What do you mean, *bogeymen*?' Megan demanded.

The man's grin widened. 'Iron Dawn never existed. It's been the Night Watchmen all along, pulling on a useful disguise.'

'The NCA already guessed as much,' Joseph said. 'But you won't get away with it. Chris and the others already know the truth.'

'He might know, but not for long? He'll be dead soon enough, along with every other NCA agent nosing into our affairs that our informant has told us all about. They're all being pulled into tonight's debate. Easier to clean the house in one go.'

Joseph's mind reeled. 'An informant?'

'Oh yes, NCA Chief Emma Lawson. Compromised nice and early on. She's been feeding us intel for months, but still doing just enough to look like she was seriously looking into the Night Watchmen. Anyway, I need to dash. Don't want to miss the fireworks when that C4 goes off. Should make one hell of a show.'

Joseph's eyes narrowed. 'You sick little fecker.'

'We all get our kicks where we can,' the man shrugged, and turned to Megan. 'But I do have one last question: how the fuck did you know where to find him?'

'Wouldn't you like to know,' the DC shot back.

Blake's slap came fast across her face, its crack echoing through the trees. Megan staggered back, but managed to keep her balance.

That was the opening Joseph had been waiting for. His wrists might still be bound, but his body was still free to move.

The DI hurled himself forward, his shoulder smashing into the man's ribs. They hit the ground together in a blur of limbs, with Joseph somehow managing to end up on top. He crushed the man's forearm against the ground with his knee as Blake's hand reached for his weapon.

His opponent's finger tightened on the trigger, and a burst of gunfire spat sparks off the Volvo's flank.

'Megan!' Joseph shouted as Blake's other hand clawed at his eyes.

The DC was already moving. Her baton snapped out and came down hard on Blake's temple with a sickening crack. The man grunted beneath Joseph, but still he fought on, his fingers inching towards the soft tissue of the DI's eyeballs.

'Again!' Joseph bellowed, his muscles screaming as he tried to pin the stronger man down with just his body.

Megan's second strike landed harder and cleaner. Instantly, Blake went slack, his head rolling to the side.

Joseph rolled off him, his chest heaving, wrists raw from the ties as he sucked in ragged gulps of air.

'Bloody hell, are you alright?' Megan asked, crouching beside him.

'I'll live,' Joseph wheezed. 'But we've got to move. Call Chris, tell him to evacuate the debate before it's too late.'

But Megan was already holding up her phone, the darkened screen spiderwebbed with cracks. 'Not with this, I can't.'

'Then use the Volvo's radio. You'll need to drive because I'm in no fit state.'

'No problem, let's go.'

They headed together towards the unmarked police car. Megan snatched a multi-tool from the glove box and sliced through Joseph's restraints. The DI flexed his hands, his blood circulation prickling back into his fingers.

Then a shout cut through the night. A split second later, the air sang with bullets as bark splintered from a nearby tree.

'Go, go, go!' Joseph roared, throwing himself into the passenger seat as Megan floored it.

Their vehicle fishtailed, tyres screaming on the track, before they bit in and the Volvo surged forward. A bullet punched out the rear screen in an explosion of glass, shards stinging their necks. Joseph ducked low as Megan gunned the engine and they tore down the track.

'That was too fecking close,' Joseph muttered, heart hammering.

'Better call this in,' Megan said through gritted teeth, her eyes locked onto the darkening road ahead.

Joseph snatched up the radio, stabbing the transmit button. Then he froze as he took in the damage. The same bullet that smashed the rear window had travelled on to punch a perfect hole through the casing of the radio. The display was dead, but he pressed the buttons anyway, desperate for even a crackle. Nothing but silence.

'For feck's sake,' the DI muttered.

Megan's jaw tightened as she wrestled the wheel around a bend. 'We could try flagging down a motorist, borrow their phone—'

Headlights flared behind them. Joseph twisted in his seat to see a black Range Rover eating up the track behind them, its lights glaring in the gathering gloom.

'I don't think Blackwood's men are going to let that happen,'

Joseph said. 'Our best chance is to beat them back to Oxford. And if anyone can do it, it's you.'

Megan flashed him a look. 'So, that's an order?'

'Damn right it is.'

The DC grinned as she dropped a gear and stamped down on the accelerator. The Volvo snarled, spitting bits of stone from its tyres like gunfire as it clawed forward along the rough track. They punched through a sagging gate in an explosion of wood, the impact rattling through every aching bone in Joseph's body. Then the tyres screeched onto tarmac, as they skidded towards the drop of an embankment.

'Megan!' Joseph said, pressing himself back into the seat.

But the DC was already on it. With a brutal flick, she hauled the Volvo straight and slammed her foot to the floor. The engine roared, the bonnet trembling under the strain as they hurtled away along the road.

Behind them, the Range Rover powered through the wreckage of the gate, suspension bouncing, headlights locking again like a spotlight on their rear window.

Joseph shot his colleague a sideways look. 'Good thing I'm over my phobia of cars, hey?'

'You better be,' Megan replied, eyes fixed on the road, knuckles white. The blue strobes on the dash flared to life, washing the hedgerows in pulses of light. Their speed climbed, eighty, ninety, a hundred. 'Because I'm only just getting started.'

The Volvo hurtled into the night with the Range Rover glued to its tail, as both vehicles raced towards Oxford.

―――――

Twice already, Megan had dragged their vehicle back from the edge of disaster. The first time involved just missing an overhanging tree that had been brought down in the previous night's storm. The second near-death experience was on a blind bend, where she'd forced a tractor into the hedge with a blast of its horn. Each time Joseph thought they were done for, but somehow the DC had found a sliver of road to hang onto and get them past. The only problem was, they still had the Range Rover pursuing them.

Now, the city lights were finally getting closer, Oxford's spires glowing in the distance. With a flick of the wheel, Megan wrenched the car off the A34 and onto the slip road for Oxford, the Volvo's tyres howling. The Range Rover clung to them like a wolf hunting down its prey.

'They're still fecking on us,' Joseph said, his chest tight, as they sped through a roundabout without giving way. Thankfully, the blue lights did their job to clear their way onto Woodstock Road.

'Not for long,' Megan shot back.

A couple of turns later, they were tearing down a treelined road filled with tall houses, and then onto Walton Street. Late-night drinkers outside the Victoria watched them shoot past, slack-jawed at the police car being chased by the Range Rover, and not the other way around.

The houses gave way to shops as they raced through Jericho. Megan didn't flinch as the Range Rover finally began to pull alongside them. She jinked left at the last second, forcing the Volvo between a van and a steel bollard with millimetres to spare.

The pursuit vehicle ripped through the bollard and lifted off the tarmac, its momentum carrying it into a brutal roll. Joseph turned in his seat as the vehicle cartwheeled across the street in a storm of sparks, its windscreen shattering before coming to rest in a heap of twisted steel. Smoke and flame licked from its underside as onlookers rushed to help. The DI was certain no one was getting out of that wreck.

Still, Megan kept her foot to the floor. After Joseph had briefed her about what he knew, the DC was very clear about how every second counted.

'You did that on purpose,' Joseph said to his colleague.

'Damn right I did,' Megan snapped. 'Unfortunately, I don't think we're out of it yet. Before they crashed, they're bound to have let someone know we were on our way to the debate.'

His stomach clenched. 'You're fecking right. And I can guarantee Chief Kennan will already be calling us terrorists by now.'

'But why would Kennan do...?' The DC's eyes widened. 'You're not trying to say she's involved in all of this?'

'Damned right, I am.'

'Bloody, bloody hell.' She shot him a look, her knuckles white on the wheel. 'So what do we do?'

'They'll put up roadblocks to form a cordon around the political debate. We just need to get to one officer we know we can trust. Then they can raise an alert about the bomb placed beneath the college in the sewers.'

'Then let's just hope someone is prepared to listen rather than shoot first.' Then her brow smoothed out. 'Actually, I may have an idea about how to get past them.'

Joseph narrowed his eyes at her. 'I can already tell I'm not going to like it.'

'Maybe because you know me too well. Anyway, I'm going to drop you off here. Then, whilst I'm drawing all the attention, you do your best to slip past the barricade. That way, we won't be putting all our eggs in one basket.'

'And if they shoot you on sight?'

'Then that would have happened to both of us, so at least it will only be me. The only thing that matters is saving the lives of everyone in and around that venue. But we have to maximise our odds of stopping this massacre. Whether we get through this alive or dead is secondary to that. You know it's our best play here.'

Joseph stared at his colleague, his mind railing at her proposal—not at the sacrifice of his own life, but of hers. But deep down, he also knew it was their best plan of attack.

'You're far too fecking brave for your own good, Megan.'

'Just like you, so let's do this.'

'Okay, but can I borrow your baton and PAVA spray? I have a strong suspicion I'm going to need them if I'm going to get into the venue.'

The DC nodded, digging into her jacket pocket and passing both to him. 'See you on the other side of this.'

'I certainly hope so. I already owe you a drink for saving me.' He dipped his chin towards her as he got out of the Volvo.

The two officers shared one last lingering look. There was so much Joseph wanted to say, but the poet in him had deserted his mind temporarily. 'Good luck,' was all he could come up with.

'You too.' Then Megan floored the Volvo and shot away along Walton Street towards the Blavatnik School of Government just beyond the line of shops.

As Joseph set off at a jog behind her, he could already see the glow of blue lights pulsing up ahead coming from the line of police vehicles fanned across the road. The dark silhouettes of armed officers had their weapons raised as Megan and the Volvo sped towards them.

Don't leave it too late, Joseph thought as his heart rose into his mouth.

Overhead, the spotlight from a helicopter had locked onto the speeding vehicle.

Just as the DI became convinced his colleague had lost all sense and was going to actually try to ram the blockade, she brought the vehicle to a shuddering, standing on the brakes, stop. That was followed by shouts of a challenge from the barricade.

'Exit the vehicle with your hands up!' Sergeant Erol Kentli's amplified voice called out.

Joseph relaxed a fraction at hearing his familiar voice. If there was one man he knew he could trust right now, it was the TU sergeant.

But as Megan climbed out of the Volvo, her warrant card held in one hand as she raised her arms, he saw Chief Kennan heading over to Erol on the barricade line.

'She's got a pistol in her hand, shoot to kill!' she bellowed at the TU officer.

'Negative to that, I don't see a weapon,' Erol replied as Joseph crept closer, keeping firmly to the deepening shadows on his side of the street.

'Then you're fucking blind,' Kennan replied. She snatched a pistol from Erol's holster, raised it, and fired.

It all happened in shocking slow motion: the spurt of blood from Megan's chest; her strangled cry; the DC being spun by the bullet's impact as she tumbled to the ground.

Erol had already wrestled the pistol away from Kennan. 'Stand down!' he bellowed at the senior commanding officer.

Joseph felt tears stinging the back of his eyes as a line of armed officers moved forward with Erol, pistols pointed towards Megan's prone body, but some also aimed at the Volvo. Yes, someone had definitely radioed ahead, telling them to expect both of them.

For a moment, the DI's resolve faltered, desperately fighting the urge to rush to his colleague's aid. But he could already hear Megan's voice in his head. *Don't you bloody dare, Joseph.*

The DI nodded. *Aye, I know...* The priority, even if he hated it, was to stay the course and not let Megan's sacrifice be in vain. He just prayed that, despite her lack of movement, the

DC was still alive despite Kennan's best efforts to the contrary. But what if she wasn't? Then, he concluded he would have to grieve later. The lives of the many outweighed the life of even someone he respected and also loved.

Whilst everyone's attention was still on Megan, exactly as she'd intended him to do, unnoticed, the DI slipped past the side of the vehicles, heading towards the Blavatnik School of Government beyond their barricade.

CHAPTER TWENTY-EIGHT

THE STACKED cylinders of the Blavatnik School of Government rose like a modernist ziggurat, steel-banded tiers shining like some vast lantern in the darkness. And Joseph knew somewhere below the building in the sewers sat enough C4 to blast it and everyone inside to kingdom come.

His heart thumped in his ears as he took in the guarded cordon wrapped tight around the inner perimeter across the entrance. Floodlights illuminated the whole paved forecourt area. He also recognised none of the officers standing guard there, probably because they were all from the Counter Terrorism unit. That was underlined by the fact that every single one of them was carrying a weapon, their gazes constantly scanning for any potential threat.

Joseph's pulse drummed. Despite the storm of adrenaline tearing through his chest, he knew he was the only chance those people inside had. But how? Was he already too late? He glanced at his watch: ten minutes after nine. Twenty minutes until the time Holgate had said Blackwood would have to slip out to avoid the blast.

Two choices surged into his mind. He could run straight at

the cordon, scream his warning about the bomb, in the hope someone listened before they shot him. But with Kennan compromised and Blackwood pulling the strings, how many of those armed figures might be working for the Night Watchmen? How many would gun him down on the spot and bury the truth with his body?

The other option was riskier, but cleaner, to find where Blackwood intended to slip away. The front entrance was too obvious, crawling with uniforms and press inside the foyer. No politician with survival instincts would take that route. No, Blackwood would slither out the back, like the snake he was, leaving everyone else inside to die.

Joseph kept low, skirting wide around the perimeter, shadow to shadow, the seconds stretching onwards. Finally, he reached the rear of the circular building. And then he saw the open fire exit. No guards, no cameras, no one watching as there should have been. Of course not, not when Emma Lawson was the one coordinating the security arrangements with Kennan. Everything was in place for the massacre that the Night Watchmen and their cronies were about to unleash upon the nation.

The DI checked his watch again. Fourteen minutes to go. His breath felt like glass in his throat.

Then he caught movement coming from the rear exit. A figure stepped out, framed in the glow of the fire escape lights. It wasn't Marcus Blackwood but his deputy, Eddie McAllister.

Joseph glared at the man. So the little shite was in league with his leader. Of course he was.

The DI didn't have time to think, he just moved, sprinting the last few yards, baton in hand. He caught Eddie by the arm, forcing him up against the wall.

'Where's Blackwood?' Joseph demanded, his voice low and dangerous.

Eddie blinked at him, a smirk tugging at his mouth. 'Inside, in the middle of his precious debate.'

'He is?' Joseph stared. 'But that doesn't make sense. Not with the bomb—'

The words snagged in his throat. The smirk, the calmness, the lack of fear in the man before him, all snapped into place like tumblers in a lock.

'It's fecking you,' Joseph whispered, his grip tightening on the baton. His voice rose, steadier now, hard with fury. 'You're the fecking one I saw being anointed in that occult ceremony.'

A razor-thin smile filled McAllister's face. 'I wondered how long it would take you to work it out, Stone.'

'You're the Night Watchmen's leader?'

'I like to see it that way, although you may get a different answer from Alison, who helped me get there. Regardless, tonight is the night our plan all comes together. So, if you would please get out of my way, I really do have somewhere to be. Or have you forgotten we already have your girlfriend as leverage?'

'Feck you!' Joseph pulled his hand back, ready to pummel seven shades of shite out of the man.

McAllister just grinned at him as though this was all one big game. 'But that's not the only leverage we have on you, is it? It seems you're a wanted man, Stone. Oh, about that. You see, we put in motion a little insurance plan when we took you prisoner.'

Amy had mentioned something about that back at the dovecote.

'What sort of insurance policy?'

'This...' McAllister took his phone out of his pocket, pulled up a video, and turned it to show it to Joseph. The footage showed a man running away down the alley. It was the one next to the hydropower station where Sally Green had been murdered.

'Is that the footage from the dashcam Kate was negotiating to buy?' the DI asked, confused.

'It was. All part of a ruse to suck her into our little trap. And thanks to Ricky Holt, that video is everywhere.'

'But I don't get it. You're dropping one of your own people in it? Although I shouldn't be surprised after what you did to Sally Green.'

'Exactly, although she had no idea what she was caught up in.' McAllister's grin widened. 'Maybe if you look closer, you'll understand the answer that's staring you in the face.' The minister used his fingers to zoom in on the man's face as the video looped.

Joseph stared in horror at himself. 'What the actual feck? I was nowhere near there that night.'

'I know that, you know that, but right now the great British public doesn't. And Ricky Holt has spun quite the piece about this evidence proving that you've been working with Iron Dawn, and killed one of their own because you were worried that the waitress was going to talk. Of course, it's all based on what we've been feeding the little cockroach.'

Joseph stared at the man, his thoughts spinning. 'But how did you do this?'

'Good old AI, of course. We took out the real person who killed her and, with the modern-day magic of computers, super-imposed your face onto him. Thank you for being so cooperative with Gareth. That 3D photo he took of you really did the trick.'

Joseph's mind spun. 'But why do any of this?'

'As I said, it's an insurance policy, and we can release another doctored version of some poor scapegoat I'm happy to throw under the bus. I did rather enjoy watching the life being crushed out of that stupid woman. She barely had a brain cell in her head, and she was so gullible. Of course, she had no idea that it was poison she was sprinkling onto Martin Chambers's food. But Alison rather approved of how I dealt with it all and felt I had finally proved my worthiness to her.'

'You are one sick bastard.'

McAllister shrugged. 'Probably. Anyway, please be a good chap and step aside so I can pass because you're finished, even if you don't know it yet.'

'Over my fecking dead body.'

Before McAllister could reply, a spotlight suddenly locked onto him as a helicopter roared into a hover almost directly overhead.

'Back away from the minister with your arms up,' an amplified voice from a speaker mounted beneath it called out. 'A sniper has you in their sights. This will be your one and only warning.'

The minister smirked at him. 'It seems your wish is my command.'

The DI looked up at the hovering helicopter, his mind racing. But he only had one play here.

He grabbed hold of McAllister and, using him as a shield, pulled him back towards the fire escape door just as armed officers emerged from both sides of the building in a move to encircle him. Joseph spotted DCI Greg Charlton, another of the Night Watchmen stooges, armed with a pistol and wearing a bulletproof vest, among them. Without so much as a warning, the man fired. The bullet ricocheted off the wall a few centimetres from Joseph's head.

With a snarl, the DI heaved the deputy leader backwards through the door, slamming it shut just in time as a flurry of bullets hammered into it. Joseph quickly grabbed a nearby chair and hooked the legs through the handle so it would slow anyone trying to open it from the other side.

The DI spun back to see that any cockiness had completely disappeared from McAllister's face. 'Don't be stupid. We need to get out of here.' He glanced at his watch. 'We only have six minutes to get as far away as possible from the blast radius.'

'I don't think so. First, we're going to warn everyone inside about the fecking big pile of explosives planted beneath this building so they can all get the hell out of here. Then you're going to take me to wherever the feck it is you've hidden it, and you're going to bloody defuse it. That is, unless you want the remains of your body to be smeared over a very wide area.'

'Just try and make—' The rest of McAllister's sentence exploded out of his mouth in a puff of air as Joseph drove Megan's baton hard into the man's stomach.

'I wasn't fecking asking.' The DI grabbed the man by the shoulder and herded the minister ahead of him. They headed along a curving corridor towards the sound of a voice that sounded a lot like Blackwood's.

'So you wanted to murder the leader of your own party, along with all the others,' Joseph asked McAllister as they closed. 'But why?'

'Can you imagine the public's anger when their elected leaders are wiped out by Iron Dawn? They'll be releasing a statement shortly after the explosion, claiming responsibility. Then One Nation, led by my good self, of course, will swiftly be elected to parliament, having campaigned on a strong security and anti-terrorism stance.'

'Jesus, so that was your plan all along, to seize absolute power and use Blackwood as a scapegoat?'

'Yes, because only then can I elicit real change. If you haven't noticed, this country has gone to the dogs.'

'Not yet, it hasn't. No thanks to you and your Night Watchmen henchmen.'

'I'm afraid they're a means to an end. Sometimes real change has to be paid for with blood.'

'God give me strength,' Joseph said, pushing the man into the wide, round atrium of the college.

A ripple of heat from the lighting rig washed over them as he stepped into the open space. Circular tiers rose colosseum-like in an upward spiral, all filled with people looking down at a raised centre stage that had been erected. Spotlights blazed down on the debate currently underway, where Marcus Blackwood held court before the audience and cameras. He had his hands spread like some sort of modern-day preacher as the other four party leaders listened to him, two of whom were shaking their heads.

Joseph pushed McAllister forward behind a row of technical booths that offered partial cover.

'You try anything, and I'll drop you where you stand,' he hissed.

McAllister raised his hands. 'You're too late anyway, Stone.' He glanced at his watch again. 'Five minutes until boom.'

Joseph's blood ran cold. 'So where the hell is it?'

But the minister only gave a tight smile and shrugged.

A cry went up near the camera rig as one of the event crew spotted them. Joseph brandished his warrant card and shouted back. 'Detective Inspector Joseph Stone! Clear the building, now! There's a bomb—'

A gunshot cracked from the doorway.

The lighting rig above Joseph's head exploded in a shower of bright shrapnel as screams rippled through the audience.

He looked over to see DCI Greg Charlton aiming his pistol directly at him.

Joseph shoved McAllister behind a column as a second bullet punched into it. He heard Blackwood shouting something onstage—not panic, not confusion, but pure rage.

And then came the click of a microphone, audible as the

monitors that had just been filled with the One Nation leader's face went dark as someone decided to cut the live feed.

In all the confusion of shouts and screams that followed, McAllister decided to seize his moment. He twisted under Joseph's arm and landed an elbow to his ribs. Joseph staggered, just long enough for McAllister to break into a run, darting around the outer curve of the atrium towards a stairwell marked *Maintenance*.

'Dad!' Ellie's voice rang out.

He clambered back to his feet to see that DCI Charlton had grabbed hold of his daughter, who was desperately trying to get free.

Joseph stared at her in disbelief. He'd had no idea she'd be there tonight, but of course she would. This was her college.

'If you touch one hair on her head,' he bellowed at the man.

Ellie shot her dad a questioning look before her expression hardened, and she gave him the barest nod. 'You asked for it,' she muttered.

His daughter drove her foot backwards into Charlton's shin.

Charlton grunted as he loosened his grip on her.

Ellie reacted before Joseph could even take a step. She spun around and struck the DCI square in the chest with an open hand, but hard enough to drive the air from his lungs.

As the man was gasping for breath, Joseph dashed forward and struck him across the back with the baton, hard enough to make the man collapse to the ground.

'Get out of here now, Ellie,' Joseph shouted as armed officers surged through the lobby towards the debate area, the front doors thrown wide behind them.

'And you?' Ellie asked.

'Don't worry about me. I need to stop the fecker behind all of this shite show.'

'Please don't get yourself killed.'

'I'll do my best.' But even as Joseph turned to head after McAllister, his thoughts had already returned to Kate. What if, because of his actions, the Night Watchmen had already executed her?

He pushed the terrifying thought from his mind. He couldn't afford to go there. Not yet, at least. First, he had a job to do.

Joseph rushed towards the maintenance door and threw it open to reveal the emergency staircase. Not going down as he'd half expected, but up. He took them two at a time, heading for the roof. But why had McAllister headed up here, where he would be trapped when the building blew?

With just ten minutes left before the building came crashing down around his ears, the DI ran. He heard a door crash closed high above him. Yes, the man was making for the roof, but why?

He pushed himself harder, forcing his legs to move faster. The DI's lungs were burning by the time he reached the top and threw the door to the roof wide.

McAllister was standing on the edge, gesturing up at someone. No, not someone. Something. Specifically, the police helicopter that was turning towards him.

For feck's sake, just how many people have the Night Watchmen got their claws into? Joseph wondered.

He had taken only three steps towards the man when a bullet pinged off the roof right next to his feet. The DI dived for cover behind a venting duct. Another barrel flash came from the helicopter, and a second bullet hissed over his head as the helicopter started to come into land.

'Just tell me where the bloody explosives are,' the DI bellowed.

McAllister turned to smirk at him. 'And why would I do that when we can still blame Iron Dawn for all of this? You'll be dead anyway.'

'Blackwood and the other leaders will have already been escorted out of the building. You missed your chance.'

The minister shrugged. 'Have I?' He held up a little box in his hand.

'What the feck is that?'

The deputy leader smirked at him. 'Another insurance policy. It's a remote trigger for the explosives. I'll trigger the moment our helicopter gets clear. Hopefully, Blackwood and the other leaders are still close enough to be killed in the blast radius. If not, well, then I can always ask Alison to cook up one of her little potions to poison them, just like we did for Martin Chambers.'

'Alison is the alchemist?'

Just for a moment, McAllister seemed taken aback.

'How do you know that name?'

'Just a bit of research a good friend did on my behalf.'

'Well, I'm impressed. Professor Shaw, I presume? Don't worry, I'll have him killed along with everyone you hold dear, including your daughter if she makes it out of here alive. But you'll be the first one to die when this building explodes.' His finger hovered over the switch.

'You fecking monster!' Joseph roared, getting ready to throw himself at the madman. If he got shot in the process, so be it.

Suddenly, the door flew open, and Derrick Walker burst through it and out onto the roof. A bullet made him duck, and then, spotting Joseph, he darted towards him, taking cover behind the vent.

'What the feck are you doing?' Joseph asked.

'Finishing this, that's bloody what. But you should know, Kate's safe. I told Chris everything, including where the Night Watchmen were holding her. He's just messaged me to say that he, Ian, and Sue rescued her.

Joseph gawped at the man. 'You helped Chris?'

'Of course I did, you fucking numbskull. I would have rescued her myself, but I had something to sort out first.' He held up a timer unit with broken wires hanging from it. 'I needed to make sure the timer was neutralised first, worked with the bomb squad to have it disabled.'

'Sorry, you're saying you're actually one of the good guys?'

'Of course I bloody am. I just couldn't risk you or anyone else knowing about any of this until I knew exactly what McAllister and his Night Watchmen were really up to. And I only learnt that last night when you were captured at the Grange.'

The helicopter's thumping wings made it hard to hear as it hovered over the rooftop, getting ready to land.

'I need to finish this,' the DSU continued. 'Maybe you'll think better of me now, Joseph.'

Before the DI could stop him, Derrick jumped up and, head down, rushed towards McAllister. Another shot rang out, and Derrick staggered as he was hit squarely in the chest.

'Fucking bastards,' the DSU bellowed, spittle flying from his mouth. But he kept staggering forward, arms reaching out towards the minister, who'd backed away from him towards the edge of the roof.

Another shot ripped a bloodthirsty cut through Derrick's leg. But even as the DSU started to stumble, he clamped his hands around the minister's chest in a rugby-like tackle. McAllister's eyes widened as he was driven by the bigger man's momentum towards the edge of the roof.

Joseph was too far away to do anything as the two men toppled over the balustrade and plummeted out of view. In those last moments, Joseph caught the expression on the big man's face. No fear, no anger. If anything, the man Joseph had once called a friend back in a different life actually looked at peace with himself.

In stark contrast, McAllister's face had been twisted with utter terror. His scream was cut short by a sickening thud.

With a roar, the helicopter banked steeply, and raced away over the rooftops.

Joseph pulled himself to his feet and then headed towards the edge of the roof to look down. Derrick had landed a short distance away from the minister, pools of blood already seeping out from both of their battered bodies.

'Are you alright, Joseph?' Chris's voice said from behind him.

He turned to see his friend standing there.

He nodded. 'I've had better days.'

'So I hear. Where's McAllister?'

Joseph dipped his chin towards the edge.

The NCA agent crossed the roof to join him and looked down.

'Shit, not Derrick, too,' Chris muttered. 'And after everything he did.'

'I know that now, and I think we both probably have a lot to tell each other. But first, please tell me Megan's okay?'

'She took a bullet through the lung, and she's in an ambulance on her way to the hospital, but she'll live.'

'Oh, thank God. That woman's too reckless for her own good.'

'That reminds me of someone.'

'Aye, tell me about it. And the video that's circulating, claiming I'm the one who killed Sally Green—?'

Chris cut him off with a sharp shake of his head.

'You'll be pleased to know that Neil Tanner, our white-hat hacker, got straight in contact the moment that hit the social media feeds. He immediately suspected it wasn't the real deal, and ran some of his analysis tools on it, which quickly revealed it was fake. So relax, your name has already been cleared.

Anyway, if you'd like to follow me, Kate is waiting outside in a police vehicle. She's worried sick about you.'

A huge lump filled Joseph's throat. 'So I hear you, Sue, and Ian saved her?'

'Actually, it was mostly Derrick's doing. He told us exactly where to find her and what to expect. He also told me everything, including how he'd effectively been working undercover to work out exactly what the Night Watchmen were up to.'

'I had no fecking idea.'

Chris sighed. 'You weren't the only one.'

'And Emma's involvement?'

'Yes, he told me about her too.'

'And he paid the price for that with his life...' Joseph looked down at his senior officer's body. Then his throat tightened, eyes burning with tears. 'Fecking hell...'

'I know,' Chris said quietly. He laid a hand on Joseph's shoulder. For a moment, they stood together in silence. Then, without another word, they turned and walked away, the weight of what lay ahead pressing down on their shoulders.

CHAPTER TWENTY-NINE

CHRIS'S BRIEFING hadn't even begun yet, but it promised to be a major one with so many strands of the investigation finally drawn together for the first time.

As Joseph waited in the incident room of St Aldates the morning after the events at Blavatnik, he kept beating himself up, his mind continuously circling back to the events of the previous night. Not only had they lost a colleague with Derrick's death, but now everyone was fretting about Megan's recovery in hospital. If he was honest with himself, he knew exactly where he wanted to be, back at her side in the JR, now that she was out of surgery.

'Joseph, you look like you need this,' Ian said gently, like a man walking on eggshells.

The DI blinked, dragged out of his thoughts, and looked up from his hands clasped in front of him, which he'd been staring at.

Ian stood there with a cup of coffee, but not the usual instant swill he brewed like dishwater. This one carried the Roasted Bean logo.

'I know you like their coffee, so I thought you might appreciate it,' Ian said, offering the cup to him.

'I do, and thank you,' Joseph said, taking it and letting the warmth seep into fingers that felt chilled despite the warmth of the day.

Ian gave a small nod but didn't immediately head away. 'Look, I just wanted to say I'm really sorry about Derrick. I know he was a pain in all our arses sometimes, but you two used to be mates, didn't you?'

'Aye, we were back in the day. And maybe we found our way back there, right at the end. I certainly owe Derrick a lot for rescuing Kate, not to mention almost certainly saving my life, as well as all those other people.'

'He was certainly a hero when it came down to the line,' Ian said quietly.

Joseph dipped his chin towards Sue, who was sitting at the next booth. She wasn't doing the best job of pretending she wasn't listening. 'Thanks to you both for what you did there, too.'

Sue didn't waste any time and wheeled her chair closer. 'He really did lead from the front when it came to making sure we rescued her.'

Of course he did, Joseph thought.

Kate might have left Derrick, but the man had still been head over heels in love with her.

Sue's gaze softened on Joseph. 'Any update on Megan?'

'None yet, but the doctors seem confident. They said she should make a full recovery from her collapsed lung.'

Ian exhaled, shaking his head. 'To think Chief Kennan pulled the trigger. I still can't get my head round it.'

'None of us can,' Sue murmured. 'So, care to tell us exactly what's been going on? Word is you were mixed up in some sort of undercover mission.'

Joseph shook his head and flicked a glance towards Chris, who was standing at the front with a senior officer he didn't recognise. 'That's for those on a higher pay grade than me to explain.'

Joseph's phone buzzed in his pocket. He took it out, and his chest loosened when he saw it was an incoming video call from Megan. He answered it immediately.

The DC's face filled the screen. 'Hi there, missing me yet?' she asked with a smile.

Joseph's heart lifted at the sight. The last time he'd seen her, just out of surgery, she'd been pale as a ghost, barely able to string a sentence together.

'Not doing as well as I would if you were here to keep me in line,' he said.

'That goes without saying. Has the debriefing kicked off yet? I really don't want to miss it.'

'I was planning to come over straight after and talk through everything.'

'I'd rather hear it straight from the horse's mouth. Besides, my parents will be here by then, and I don't exactly want to talk shop in front of them.'

'Fair enough. But you should really be resting, you know.'

'I'll get plenty of that; I've been signed off for six weeks.'

'The things coppers do to wangle themselves an extended holiday,' Ian cut in, leaning over Joseph's shoulder to grin at the screen. He turned to the rest of the room. 'Megan's on the line!'

A loud cheer went up, followed by applause. Even Chris and the unfamiliar officer standing with him joined in.

Megan gave a dutiful wave and a grin as Joseph turned the screen so the DC could see everyone.

Chris came straight over. 'How are you doing, Megan?' he asked.

'I could have done without getting shot, but apart from that....'

'That's good to hear. I'm going to make sure we get a food hamper put together for you, including your body weight in Krispy Kreme doughnuts.'

'You're so my sort of man.'

Joseph caught the way Chris's eyes crinkled at hearing that, and he couldn't help but think, *Megan is very much your sort of woman too.*

'So, do you mind if I just listen in on the briefing?' she asked.

'Not a problem for me,' Chris said. 'But I'm sure the doctors won't be thrilled about you not resting when you should be.'

'I'm not about to get much sleep until I hear exactly what's happened.'

'In that case, pull up a virtual chair, because we're about to begin,' Chris replied. He gave Joseph a nod, then moved to the front of the room and clapped his hands for attention.

'Okay, everyone, let's get this debriefing underway,' the SIO began. 'First of all, I know we're all really feeling the loss of DSU Derrick Walker keenly. His dedication to duty right to the end was unquestionable. Many of you already know, Derrick was the one who tackled Eddie McAllister moments before they both fell from the roof. What you won't know is that Derrick had been working undercover with the NCA to expose police corruption linked to a major crime syndicate known as the Night Watchmen. Not only did he help bring their operation into the light, he also helped us to free Joseph's partner, Kate, who'd been taken prisoner by the crime syndicate in an attempt to use her as leverage.'

There were whistles, mutters, and a wave of shock across the room. Joseph caught Megan's voice from his phone: 'Bloody hell.'

'Aye, I know,' Joseph whispered back to her.

Chris pressed on. 'I'm sure you've also heard by now that Chief Superintendent Amanda Kennan was arrested last night after shooting DC Anderson. Kennan, along with a number of other senior officers, had been on the payroll of the Night Watchmen for some time. They're all in custody now.'

Murmurs of disbelief rippled through the room, some faces twisted with real anger, others in stunned silence.

'This has been the culmination of a year-long surveillance operation by the NCA, an operation that itself was compromised. Agent Emma Lawson, whom most of you have dealt with recently, was, in fact, feeding intelligence to the Night Watchmen. Because of her betrayal at the agency, DI Stone's life was put on the line more than once. Thankfully, I can now confirm she's also been taken into custody and is actually being very cooperative.'

'I just can't believe it,' Megan said.

'And now we get to another major revelation. DI Stone had been working with me to uncover the extent of the Night Watchmen's infiltration into Thames Valley Police.'

Every head turned towards Joseph. The silence was only broken by Megan's voice crackling out from the phone: 'What?'

Joseph turned the camera on himself and shrugged. 'It just needed doing, and I was in the right place, at the right time.'

'Talk about a dark horse,' Ian muttered, shaking his head.

The DI cast the man a smile. 'Well, you know me. I like to keep my light under a bushel. Wouldn't want to blind you all.'

A ripple of chuckles broke the tension, though more than a few faces still held looks of quiet respect towards Joseph.

'You and me are so going to have a talk,' Megan said.

'Looks like you're in trouble with the boss now,' Sue added, arching a brow.

Joseph gave a resigned shrug. 'Tell me about it.'

'Well, Megan, before you give your colleague too hard a

time over this, you should know I swore him to secrecy about the whole operation,' Chris said.

'Wait. So, you were working together? But with what authority?' the DC asked.

'I'm actually an NCA agent. I've been working undercover at St Aldates, helping to expose what's been going on.'

The room went deadly quiet. The silence stretched on, the collective disbelief hanging heavy in the air until Ian finally broke it.

'Blimey, is there anyone here not working for the NCA?'

'Actually, we all are, except you,' Sue replied.

Ian gave her a straight look. Then, at last, a grin cracked his face. 'Idiot,' he muttered, chuckling.

Chris let the laughter ripple through the room before speaking again. 'Anyway, I wanted to say this. Joseph has put his neck on the line time and again for this operation. That's why I'll be recommending him for immediate promotion to DCI. What do you say, Joseph?'

The DI blinked at him. 'Seriously?'

'From what I hear, you've more than earned it,' said the light brown-haired woman standing beside Chris.

Chris nodded toward her. 'This is the moment I should probably formally introduce your new DSU, Fiona Fraser, who'll be taking over from Derrick.'

The sharp-eyed woman in her early fifties, by Joseph's guess, let her gaze sweep across the room. 'I only wish I were joining you under happier circumstances. Regardless, I'm sure you'll all join me in congratulating DCI Stone on his well-earned promotion.'

The response was instant—applause, whistles, and even Megan clapping along at the other end of the video call.

Despite part of Joseph harbouring a desire to be promoted,

he'd be responsible for the detectives who'd be working under him. And with that came a certain sort of weight.

'Thank you, all of you. But you'd seriously trust me to be in charge of some of you?'

Ian clapped a hand on his shoulder. 'I think I speak for everyone, abso-bloody-lutely. And it'll be an honour. But tradition says you'll have to buy the first round at the Scholar's Retreat.'

Joseph snorted. 'Now you tell me.'

'Hang on, what about you, boss?' John called out from the back.

Chris's smile faded just a touch. 'Well, now that this operation's concluded, it's time for me to return to the NCA, hence the vacancy that Joseph will fill so well after I'm gone. But I want you all to know, it's been an absolute honour and a privilege working with each and every one of you.'

It was clear to Joseph, just from the looks on their faces, that Chris's words meant a lot to the team. But for him, it went deeper than that. This wasn't just a briefing, it was a farewell speech. He felt a swirl of emotion in his chest. It would mean that Chris wouldn't be living close by anymore. The man might have been his senior officer, but he'd become more than that. He was a friend in the truest sense, and Joseph knew he'd miss him at every level on a day-to-day basis.

'So, before you're finally shot of me...' Chris said, raising a ripple of chuckles, 'I'd better brief you on the case. First and foremost, Marcus Blackwood, the other leaders, and every person inside the Blavatnik School of Government were successfully evacuated thanks to Joseph's efforts. However, the man behind the plot to blow them all sky-high was Eddie McAllister, the deputy party leader. Blackwood was unaware of what he was up to. As an example of this, and the man's warped sense of humour, Joseph, would you want to talk for a moment about the lamp McAllister had given his leader?'

Joseph nodded. 'In Marcus Blackwood's home, there was a black lantern in a glass case. I now know it was a copy of the one in the Ashmolean Museum, which Guy Fawkes used when he tried to sneak beneath Parliament to blow them all up in the Gunpowder Plot.'

'Bloody hell, so McAllister giving Blackwood it was an in-joke? That he was going to actually target him and all the other leaders?' Ian muttered.

'Only among McAllister and his inner circle, and Blackwood was the butt of it,' Joseph said. 'I expect McAllister spun him a line about the lamp being a metaphor for what their new party would do to Parliament. But in reality, it was his calling card for the real plan. When we studied it, we even found Azrael's sigil on the back of a plaque attached to the lamp. Like McAllister had with his other victims, he'd marked Blackwood for death. If I'd made the connection sooner, maybe we could've stopped it before it even started.'

'Don't second-guess yourself,' Fiona said. 'Things like this only ever look obvious in hindsight.'

Ian frowned, scratching at his jaw. 'But why would McAllister want to blow up his own party leader? I can understand the rivals, but Blackwood?'

Chris gestured to Joseph. 'I think you're on a roll, so carry on.'

'Because he intended to step straight into the dead man's shoes,' Joseph said. 'Then, on a ticket of ramping up security and flooding the police with funding, the country—traumatised by what had happened—would probably have swept One Nation and its new leader into power. And once there, with the Night Watchmen's syndicate backing them, who knows what kind of things McAllister would have dragged the country into.

But there's another thread here too, and it has everything to do with Alison Blackwood. Have you managed to arrest her yet, Chris?'

He shook his head. 'No. She didn't attend the debate, claiming a headache at the time. Now, she seems to have disappeared off the face of the planet.'

Sue frowned. 'Sorry, you're saying Alison Blackwood was colluding with Eddie McAllister against her husband?'

'Yes. And it's a lot more than just collusion. She seems to have been actively involved in the plot, even drugging everyone at Ellensmere Grange before the Iron Dawn raid by targeting the water supply at their home.'

'But she was affected by the drugs too,' one of the other detectives said.

'That was the point,' Chris cut in. 'To make sure no suspicion fell on her. And now, thanks to two of Blackwood's security detail who've agreed to cooperate for a plea bargain, we know Iron Dawn was nothing more than a Night Watchmen creation. The plan, until Joseph got in the way of it, was to abduct Blackwood, hold him for ransom, then allow an anonymous tip-off to reach the police via their unwitting stool pigeon, the journalist Ricky Holt. The rescue would have generated a tidal wave of sympathy for the One Nation party. And the coup de grâce would have been Marcus Blackwood's death, along with the rest of the leaders at the debate.'

'Bloody hell, talk about a Machiavellian plan,' Sue muttered.

'Aye, tell me about it,' Joseph said. 'But that's not all. From what I've discovered, Alison was the one who actually helped McAllister climb to the top of the Night Watchmen, and through them, position him to run the country.'

Sue stared at him. 'You're seriously suggesting Alison Blackwood is the real mastermind behind all of this, and actually plotted to murder her own husband?'

'I'm sure McAllister had his own ambitions as well,' Joseph replied. 'But I believe that through him, Alison and her followers intended to run the country in his name.'

'Sorry, followers?' John asked, looking baffled.

Joseph's jaw tightened. 'I stumbled across Alison and a handful of others performing some kind of initiation on McAllister. He was masked, so I thought it was Marcus Blackwood at the time. But one of her followers branded the man's wrist with a circular sigil with a line through it. But it was clear as day, the man was being welcomed into the cult's inner circle. Apparently, they call themselves the Order of the Midnight Sun.'

'So who are these other members?' Sue asked.

'I wish I knew. Unfortunately, they were all wearing hoods. The only person I could clearly identify was Alison.'

'Well, the autopsy has confirmed the presence of the brand mark on McAllister's wrist.' Chris said. 'And in case you were wondering, no, Blackwood certainly doesn't have any such marking. That seems to confirm that it must have been McAllister you saw during this occult ceremony, Joseph.'

'We have no idea where Alison and the other members of this cult have disappeared to?' Sue asked.

'Unfortunately, that seems to be the case. We even had a technical team from the NSA check cellular connections to the nearest masts, but on the night of that ceremony, no unknown mobiles pinged it. That probably means they were all careful to turn off their phones for that initiation ceremony.'

'So just how dangerous are these people?' John asked.

'Based on what they almost pulled off, very,' Chris said. 'It's a rare breed that can seize control of a syndicate as ruthless as the Night Watchmen and get their man to the top of it. What the cult's agenda is remains to be seen. At least this particular threat has passed for now. But talking of people going missing, I feel duty-bound to inform you about another individual who was working with the Night Watchmen—our very own SOCO, Amy Fischer.'

Joseph watched the blank looks ripple around the room, replaced gradually by dawning realisation.

It was Sue who voiced what the room was starting to get to. 'You're saying she was in on this, too?'

'Aye, I'm afraid so,' Joseph said. 'She was on the Night Watchmen's payroll from the start. She made sure key evidence went missing from crime scenes whenever it threatened to expose them.'

'So, she betrayed us?' a uniformed officer asked.

'She did, but she was arrested at a ferry terminal this morning as she tried to flee the country,' Chris answered.

'Thank God for small mercies,' Joseph said, who was looking forward to testifying against the woman.

Chris nodded. 'The extent of her meddling has come to light. Apart from many previous indiscretions, she deliberately suppressed an image from the charity ball at Christ Church College. One of the attendees' photos caught something in the background—Sir Reginald Harrington, who was seated next to Chambers, dusting powder over the minister's food while he was distracted. It seemed he used one of Alison Blackwood's poisons to kill a man who had a genuine shot at being our next PM. Sally Green seems to have simply delivered the sigil and nothing more. The Night Watchmen set her up as scapegoat in case the use of poison ever came to light. All this cleared the way for One Nation, the party Harrington was bankrolling. It also turns out he was the one who stole Martin Chambers's smartwatch from the crime scene. Apparently, the plan was to use it to frame Blackwood for Chambers's murder so Eddie McAllister could step into his role. The TFT has already found the data showing heartbeat disruption patterns, which would have helped identify the fact he'd been poisoned far more quickly.'

'And Harrington has been arrested as well?' John asked.

'Actually, no. His wife found him dead in his bedroom this morning. From the looks of it, he realised it was only a matter of time before we connected him to Chambers's murder. The irony is, he seems to have poisoned himself.'

'Or someone framed it to look that way,' Joseph added.

'Is there a reason to think that might have happened?' Sue asked.

'Yes,' Chris said. 'Sir Harrington bore the same brand on his wrist as McAllister, proof he was one of Alison's inner circle. For all we know, he could've been down in that ceremony the night McAllister was initiated.'

Ian shook his head. 'A conspiracy within a conspiracy.'

Chris nodded. 'Talking of which, we need to get to the murder of Sally Green, the waitress and alleged Iron Dawn member. You'll all have seen the dashcam footage that went viral, showing Joseph fleeing the murder scene. Well, thanks to Neil Tanner, we now know the footage was AI. The original showed McAllister fleeing the scene. This was confirmed by Gareth Holgate, Blackwood's head of security, who's also in custody. He confessed that one of his own security team recovered the file from a car that had been deliberately positioned there to capture the footage, so it could be doctored and used as an insurance policy. They then used that same footage to lure Kate, Joseph's partner, into a trap where she was taken hostage. They released the doctored video, once again via their stooge, Ricky Holt, to make it look like Joseph was complicit in Green's murder and actually working for Iron Dawn.'

'None of us really suspected you for a second,' Ian said.

'It didn't exactly feel that way for a while there,' Joseph replied. 'I owe you, Megan. If it hadn't been for you following

Derrick's tip-off and dragging me out of the Blackwood estate, I wouldn't be standing here now.'

There was no response.

Joseph frowned, but then saw why when he glanced at the phone. Megan's head had lolled to the side, eyes closed, mouth slightly open as she breathed deeply.

He lifted the phone for everyone to see before ending the call. 'Best let her get her beauty sleep, especially after what she's been through.'

Chris gave him a wry look. 'I thought she was unusually quiet. Anyway, that's all we have for you for the time being.'

'Megan won't be happy she missed the end of this debriefing,' Sue said. 'As these things go, it's been a corker.'

'Don't worry, I'm going to swing by later and bring her up to speed,' Chris said.

Joseph suppressed a smile because he had a fair idea of what that meant. Now that Chris was no longer undercover and, more importantly for him, no longer Megan's senior officer, there was nothing to stand in the way of them getting together. When Chris caught his eye and gave him the briefest of smiles, it all but confirmed it. And Joseph wished them the very best from the bottom of his heart. That was at least one good thing to come out of it all.

'So, that's where we stand,' Chris said, raising his voice again. 'We all have a few i's to dot and t's to cross, but as of now, we've no further intel on the Order of the Midnight Sun cult. But rest assured, the NCA will throw considerable resources into uncovering who they are.'

'And I'm certainly going to make it my personal mission to track them down,' Joseph said.

'I thought you might.' Chris gave a nod. 'My door's always open at the NCA if you hear anything.'

'And vice versa,' Joseph said.

The two men held each other's gaze for a moment, then nodded.

'On that note...' Chris said, turning to Fiona. 'If it's all right with you, I suggest we end things here and continue the conversation at the Scholar's Retreat.'

'I can already hear my wallet groaning,' Joseph muttered, earning a ripple of laughter as everyone began to gather their things.

But as the room slowly emptied, Joseph lingered by the window, watching sunlight glint on Tom Tower of Christ Church College next door. For all the talk of closure, a weight still sat in his chest. Alison and her people were still out there somewhere, and until he brought them to justice, he knew this wasn't an ending at all, but really just a pause before the next battle.

CHAPTER THIRTY

Rows of grey lichen-covered headstones stretched away behind the group of people around a grave at the edge of Wolvercote Cemetery. The morning sunlight seemed at odds with the mood of those gathered to say goodbye to a senior officer of Thames Valley Police.

Kate had Joseph's hand clasped in hers, his anchor as a storm of emotions swirled through him.

'How are you doing?' she whispered.

'About as bad as I expected. But more to the point, how about you?'

Her mouth pinched as she gazed at Derrick's coffin that Joseph had helped carry from the church to the grave it now sat in. 'A little bit broken, if I'm honest. I can't help wondering if I hadn't left him, would he still be alive today?'

'You know you can't second-guess yourself like that. The past is the past, and that's where it should stay.'

'Even so...' Kate gave a small shrug.

'Aye, I know. Part of me feels the same way. But at least I know Derrick never truly lost his way.'

Kate turned to look at him as the other mourners from the

church began to gather around. 'I just wish you'd shared with me what was really going on with the Night Watchmen.'

'Chris insisted, because it was all part of the ongoing NCA investigation.'

'Yes, and speaking of dark horses.' She nudged him gently and gestured with her chin towards Chris, standing on the opposite side of the grave with Megan. They were so close their elbows were touching. 'Am I reading the signs right there?'

He gave her a small smile. 'You are indeed. They've started seeing each other, but Megan wants to keep it low-key for now. She's worried about what people will think, though she really shouldn't be. Everyone'll be as happy for them as I am. Besides, thanks to that, I'm not about to lose my mate.'

Kate nodded. 'Yes, I heard about Chris transferring from the London NCA office to the South East Regional Organised Crime Unit over in Kidlington.'

Joseph nodded. 'Aye, being based down the road there means he won't need to sell up and can stay in Cumnor. Handy for the job... and, if we're honest, for Megan too.'

'Which sounds like a win on all sides to me. That will be handy for when they move in together.'

'Whoa, slow down there,' Joseph said. 'They've only just got together and you're already planning their wedding?'

'It's the sort of place my mind goes at funerals. Sorry.' She cast him a sideways look before gazing at the casket again. 'I really can't believe he's gone.'

'None of us can.' He gestured towards Fiona, who'd chosen to attend the funeral as a mark of respect even though she hadn't personally known Derrick. 'She's certainly got some big shoes to fill, but the early signs are promising. She's certainly less volatile than Derrick, but maybe more no-nonsense. But to be sure, Derrick's left a hole behind all the same. He could be a royal pain in the arse to deal with at times, but you know...' Joseph looked down at the coffin.

Kate blinked several times. 'Oh, Derrick...'

At that moment, Megan materialised by Joseph's side.

He raised his brows. 'I'm surprised to see you here. Shouldn't you still be tucked up in a nice hospital bed?'

'They let me out a day early for good behaviour. Besides, Chris said he'd look after me, as you can see. He's even invited me to stay at his cottage while I recuperate.'

'Did he now,' Joseph said, a wide smile breaking across his face.

Megan scowled. 'Wipe that look off before everyone notices.'

'I wouldn't worry,' Kate said. 'Just get on and be a couple. To hell with what anyone else thinks.'

'So Joseph's obviously told you about us.'

'I did,' Joseph said. 'And Kate here's already planning your wedding.'

Megan gaped at her. 'You are?'

'Not literally,' Kate said, 'though it's lovely to see a little happiness in the middle of all this sadness.'

The DC nodded. 'I know. And what about Joseph here being promoted to DCI? Very well earned and long overdue, in my opinion.'

Kate smiled at her. 'For most officers that would normally mean less time in the field, but we both know what he's like.'

Megan grinned at him. 'Oh, we do.'

'Ladies, I am standing here, you know.'

'Well, it's more fun than gossiping behind your back,' Kate replied. 'Megan, I just want to grab this opportunity to thank you for rescuing Joseph. But please, in future, try not to get shot.'

She grimaced. 'Don't worry, I've already had the talk from

Chris. I'll do my best, but who knows with Joseph as the boss now?'

'Hey, a man could take that personally,' he said.

Megan winked at him as she went to rejoin Chris as the vicar opened his prayer book.

A hush fell over the mourners as the first words of the service drifted on the still summer air. Behind them, the trees stirred faintly in a gentle breeze, and in the distance, the midday bells of Oxford tolled. In Joseph's mind, they weren't just marking the hour, but also the end of a life.

Joseph shifted his weight, his eyes fixed on the polished oak of the coffin. Across the grave, Chris moved a little closer to Megan, his hand brushing her arm. For a moment, Joseph caught his gaze—an acknowledgement of how much they'd gone through together. Two colleagues who were now firm friends.

As the vicar spoke of Derrick's service, his family, his sacrifice, Joseph's thoughts drifted. If Derrick hadn't appeared when he had that night at Blavatnik, there was every chance it would've been Joseph, not his boss, who lay in that coffin.

Kate sniffed quietly, brushing away tears. Joseph wrapped his arm around her and pulled her close as the vicar's words rang out across Wolvercote Cemetery and the bells faded into silence.

For a long moment, he let the stillness settle inside him. In his mind, Derrick's voice was still there—gruff, impatient, but solid as bedrock. A man he hadn't always agreed with, but who'd stood firm when it counted.

Joseph lowered his gaze to the coffin, its polished oak glowing in the sunlight, and gave the smallest nod to himself. Yes, the world might go on, but he would not forget this man.

EPILOGUE

The Sheldonian Theatre rang with music. Strings swelled in Handel's *Water Music*, the bright sound filling the venue all the way up to the ornate domed ceiling overhead. When the final notes faded, the predominant background sound became a shuffle of gowns like leaves in a breeze, and the low murmur of proud parents punctuating all of it. Then the organist shifted into the old university anthem, *Gaudeamus Igitur*, its solemn chords lifting into the dome as if the very walls were breathing with the centuries of ceremony the building had witnessed.

Joseph sat with Kate on one of the wooden benches polished smooth by generations, the carved heads along the gallery peering down, all silent witnesses to another rite of passage.

He leaned in closer to his partner, keeping his voice low. 'Feels wrong, doesn't it? John and the others waiting outside while we get the good seats.'

Kate's eyes stayed on Ellie, poised among the robed students, the scarlet and grey of her hood glowing against the black gown like a coal among ashes. 'That's the way of it, unfortunately. Two guest tickets, and no more. We're lucky John insisted that we should get them.'

'Technically, but I can't help feeling he deserves to be here more than me.'

Kate brushed her hand across his. 'Nonsense. Besides, he'll have his moment. When she heads down those steps, he'll be the first she runs to. Just this once, I think we're allowed this indulgence as her proud parents.'

'Aye, maybe you're right.'

When he thought about it, there'd been so many steps to get to this moment. After Eoin's death, all their grief and love had been poured into their daughter. Certainly, every ounce of their hope had been bent towards helping Ellie thrive and find her voice in a world that was increasingly difficult to navigate. But here she was now, the astonishing woman their daughter had become, blazing with the brightness of it.

Joseph's throat tightened as he looked at her, pride surging with a force that startled even him, fiercer than the medal or commendation he'd just received.

The Vice-Chancellor rose and began calling out the names of the graduates one after another to applause, all part of a rhythm Oxford had followed for centuries.

And then Ellie's name came.

Joseph's breath snagged in his chest as she stepped forward, head held high, eyes alight, her confidence rippling outward like sunlight. She crossed the stage and received her degree with both hands. And in that heartbeat, her gaze lifted, finding him and Kate in the gallery. The glance was fleeting, but it carried a world of gratitude, of love, of a silent, *I did it!*

Joseph clapped until his palms stung, a sting he welcomed to try and stop the tears flowing.

When the ceremony finally ended, the graduates spilled out into the blaze of summer light to the thunderous applause echoing off the Sheldonian's stones and timber.

Outside, the bells of St Mary's tolled, their peals spilling across Broad Street, folding into the chatter of families and the click of tourists' cameras. The golden stone gleamed with sunshine, and for once, it felt like the whole city had joined in the celebrations.

On the cobbles, Joseph spotted John craning for a view, his grin broad and wide. Near him, Megan shaded her eyes, laughing at something Chris had said. His hand brushed her cheek, hesitant, tender, and her gaze softened. Further back, Dylan and Iris stood together, radiant with smiles, the professor's jacket slung over his arm.

Ellie headed away from the gaggle of students she'd been hugging. Robes swirling, degree clutched to her chest, she half-ran down the steps. As Kate had predicted, she made straight for John. Their daughter flung her arms around his neck and kissed him, before turning to her parents.

'Congratulations, love,' Joseph managed as she hugged him, his voice tight and, the big softy he really was, right on the edge of tears again.

Before Ellie could reply, Dylan and Iris arrived. She hugged them both as well, kissing Dylan's cheek. 'Thank you for all your help with my dissertation. I wouldn't have got here without you.'

'Nonsense,' Dylan said, though his eyes betrayed his pride. 'This was all you.'

Although the professor waved a dismissive hand at Ellie, Joseph recognised the same fierce swell of pride he'd felt inside the theatre in his friend.

Chris and Megan pushed through the throng just in time for Ellie to fold them into her embrace. Joseph realised then that his daughter, and Kate for that matter, already counted Chris as family. He looked startled at first, but then warmed to it, as though realising it for the first time himself.

Dylan drew Joseph aside. 'I've been making slow progress on that tattoo you sent me. The Order of the Midnight Sun and the circle with the line through it keeps surfacing. I've traced it through manuscripts in the Bodleian, scraps of Gnostic text, alchemical diagrams, even old maps. Right now it feels just out of reach, but I'll get there with Iris's help, eventually.'

'So you're still digging?' Joseph asked.

'You know me,' he said with a faint smile. 'The Order of the Midnight Sun might be a knot of shadows, but we'll unravel their secrets eventually.'

Joseph glanced back at Ellie, radiant in the sunlight, laughing with John and Kate, Megan and Chris close beside her. 'But maybe not today, hey,' he said softly. 'Today belongs to her.'

'Absolutely right,' Dylan said, smiling broadly now.

A call came out from among the graduates. Then Ellie and her classmates slipped on their mortarboards. Another shout rose, and then in one joyous burst, their black squares flew skyward, silhouettes against the blue sky. The hats tumbled back amid cheers and applause, like dark confetti showering the cobbles. Ellie caught hers with both hands, her face flushed with joy.

As cameras clicked and the cheers rang out, Joseph felt something inside him loosen a fraction. A weight lifting.

Yes, today really did belong to his daughter.

Joseph breathed in the warm air, sunlight glowing on Oxford's stone, and allowed himself stillness. Whatever darkness still lingered out there to do with Alison Blackwood's cult, there would be time enough to face that in the future.

For now, as far as he was concerned, there was only joy. And Joseph intended to make the most of it. He walked back with Dylan and Iris to rejoin his family. Afterwards, they were all going to celebrate at Chris's, who apparently had a brand new

Green Egg barbecue he was getting ready to fire up in honour of Ellie's achievement.

Behind them, the bells of St Mary's tolled again, rolling across the city like a blessing, marking not just an ending, but maybe a beginning too. But even as the last bell faded, Joseph knew shadows never vanished—they only waited for their hour to come, and come they would again.

THE DARKNESS IS ONLY THE BEGINNING...

A new series is coming—where murder, myth, and science collide, and the pursuit of truth turns deadly. Join J.R. Sinclair's newsletter for early news, cover reveals, and exclusive previews. Use this link to start your journey. https://subscribepage.io/n4zom8

Printed in Dunstable, United Kingdom